The shooting started shortly  radio watch; Hamilton and were sleeping. Hamilton urgent, purposeful rattle of small arms and machine-gun fire, followed by the very loud *whump-whump-whump* of incoming mortar rounds. For a fraction of a second he lay still, thinking, "Oh, hell, here we go again," then jumped out of his cot, into his shower shoes (which, for just such occasions as this, were always placed where his feet would come down when he popped out of the cot), and, since for the moment there were no more incoming mortar rounds, stepped into the radio room. Parelli was lying on his stomach on the floor by the radio table talking into the microphone.

"Sleepy Onion Alfa"—this was Tuy Cau's call sign— "this is Sleep Onion Echo. Sleepy Onion Echo, over."

Hamilton recognized Sergeant Osbert's voice when Tuy Cau replied, "Echo, this is Alfa. Over."

"This is Echo; we got contact."

VALLEY OF PERIL

SOLDIER of FORTUNE
MAGAZINE PRESENTS:

VALLEY OF PERIL

ALEX McCOLL

TOR

A TOM DOHERTY ASSOCIATES BOOK

VALLEY OF PERIL

Copyright © 1987 by Alexander M.S. McColl

First printing: June 1987

A TOR BOOK

Published by Tom Doherty Associates, Inc.
49 West 24 Street
New York, N.Y. 10010

ISBN: 0-812-51213-8
CAN. ED.: 0-812-51214-6

PRINTED IN THE UNITED STATES OF AMERICA

0 9 8 7 6 5 4 3 2 1

DEDICATION

To the Regional Force and the Popular Force, and their advisers; they received little recognition and no glory, but they stood their ground and died as bravely as any.

INTRODUCTION
By
MAJOR GENERAL JOHN K. SINGLAUB,
U.S.A. (Retired)

When I was asked to write an introduction to Alex McColl's *Valley of Peril*, my first reaction was to say no; this is a book on the District Senior Advisers who were working with the grass-roots level of the Vietnamese civil-military effort. My own experience on the ground in Vietnam was in other and entirely different areas of this extremely complicated war. It would therefore be difficult for me to write something assuring the reader that this is an authentic portrayal, based on my personal experience and observation, of the kinds of things that happened in that part of the war. *MACCAT*, McColl's other book on Vietnam, is based on the activities of MACV SOG. As I was Chief, SOG, during the period of the adventures portrayed in that book, I felt comfortable in writing that introduction.

On the other hand, there is nothing carved in stone to the effect that the introduction to a book has to be a "certificate of authenticity" and nothing else. As I said in my introduction to *MACCAT*, that is certainly an authentic portrayal, within the limits of telling the story in the form of a novel, of the ground reconnaissance activities of SOG, and some other things. McColl is a trustworthy character (well, at least we gave him a Top Secret clearance at SOG), and I found nothing in *Valley of Peril* that did not ring true.

From the professional and, if I may say so, literary or historical viewpoint, one of the most interesting aspects of the Vietnam War was the incredible variety and complexity of activities all going on at the same time in what was really a not very large war in a rather small country. Each of us who was there generally knew a good bit about his own specific piece of the puzzle, had some general notion about what was going on in adjacent parts, and knew very little about everything else. It was a stock saying and a truism that the more time you had in-country, the less you were able to come up with sweeping generalities about the whole business. As Chief, SOG, I had little official contact with the whole complex structure of Regional and Popular Force troops, police, civil administration, public health, what the South Vietnamese called "political warfare" and so on, that was fighting the small-scale, anti-guerrilla war in the hamlets and rice paddies. It has since come to my attention that, with the exception of the not very large number of American Officers and NCOs who were in that business, extremely few other Americans who served in Vietnam, to say nothing of the general public, have any idea at all of what was involved in the subsector business. Simple things like the fact that the Republic of Vietnam was divided into 44 Provinces, which were also military sectors, and further into about 250 districts, which were also military subsectors, much less what really went on.

Some day, no doubt, there will be a thorough, detailed and statistically analytical history of the whole "civil-military operation," based on official records and MACV's computerized statistics. Meanwhile, if you're interested in what went on in a remote, insecure, backcountry district, where most of the troops on our side didn't have steel helmets or M-79 grenade launchers—not only the battles, but the internal politics and clashes of personality, the love affairs, the odd things that did happen, and . . . well, read McColl's book. It's also one of the better adventure stories since Ian Fleming.

AUTHOR'S PREFACE

Valley of Peril is the story of what happened to and around me as a District/Subsector Senior Adviser in Vietnam in 1967 and 1968. I will not certify that each of these episodes actually happened to me personally, or exactly in the form stated, but they all happened, if not to me, to people whom I know. In some cases parts of several similar episodes have been consolidated to make a better story. There seems to be no way to portray the boredom and repetitiousness of our lives without being boring and repetitious. Names of people, places, and military units have been changed to protect the innocent—and also the rest of us.

The war as seen by politicians, reporters, historians and bureaucrats in Washington and Saigon was not quite the same war as seen at the working level. Even within the Army, with the exception of those directly involved, what went on with the Districts and Subsectors, and the Regional Force and the Popular Force, was very little understood. Likewise, the working-level advisers with Vietnamese units and entities went their way unnoticed and unrecorded. No doubt one of these years some careful and hardworking researcher will write a detailed and factual history of the whole civil-military advisory effort, based on the mass of facts and statistics which were reported, collated, adjusted and filed at the various levels of command. Meanwhile, this is a collection of snapshots of what was really going on, at least in one corner of the war. I have tried to avoid getting into the larger political issues, except in the sense of reporting what the Americans on the ground were saying and thinking about these matters. There is also a descriptive glossary attached to avoid explaining technical terms in the text or leaving the non-technical reader thoroughly baffled.

atavistic exhilaration at having met and beaten the enemy. After all, it had not been the first time, nor had the night's activities really been so remarkable.

They had had warnings, of course, but then they always did—usually of things that didn't happen. Hamilton's counterpart, Captain Lan, spent quite a lot of money on informants, and probably to good effect, but it seemed as though at least every two weeks there was a report that within the next fifteen days either the 299th NVA Regiment or the 58th VC Provincial Force Battalion, or both, were going to attack the district headquarters (it was not sufficiently important to be a headquarters with a capital "D" and "H") or the Special Forces camp at the other end of the valley. The last really serious attempt to overrun either place was about four months back, shortly after Captain Hamilton's arrival. On reflection it seemed like four years. Sometimes he suspected that Charlie deliberately spread the word that he was going to attack, as a cover for any leaks as to his real intentions; there was also the thought that Captain Lan's informants were not above inventing stories when they didn't have any real information to pass on. Considering the grisly things that happened to people Charlie suspected of ratting on him, and to their families, and the not very large sums of money paid out, the amount of good information they actually got this way was probably remarkable.

Hamilton finished shaving, rinsed out his razor in the basin (the compound's jury-rigged running-water system was one of the night's casualties), dipped a corner of his towel, wrung it out, wiped the excess shaving soap off his face, and reflected that there was no more futile endeavor than trying to guess what Charlie was going to do or why. Perhaps the indefinite "they" at Higher Headquarters could do so, but if they did, the results of their deliberations never filtered down to the subsectors in any very useful form. One didn't have to be told that Charlie liked to stir things up to celebrate Ho Chi Minh's birthday, or to disrupt a national election.

Outside, with the exception of a crew of about eight Popular Force soldiers repairing one of the bunkers, the compound wore its usual air of sunlit midafternoon somnolence. Lan had apparently gone into his quarters, the usual four or five daytime sentries were at their posts, and the rest of the hundred or so Regional Force and Popular Force troops (Captain Hamilton refused to call them RF/PF or "rough puffs"; he had stood beside them too often in battle) in the compound were out of sight. Some of them, with the truck, were burying the fifteen dead NVA whose bodies had been recovered, and the rest were resting up from the night's exertions and for whatever might come tonight. It was not unknown for Charlie to come back the next night, especially when the morning after his first try had not elicited a vigorous pursuit and ground sweep. But you do not go hunting an NVA battalion, even one that has been hacked over the night before, with an understrength Regional Force Company and two PF Platoons—at least not more than once. And the Koreans, not having scheduled and planned the operation a month in advance, had claimed other commitments.

The Korean battalion commander had come out during the morning, inspected the dead NVA, the two prisoners (both wounded—Hamilton had had quite a hassle with Lan about getting them on a medevac chopper; Lan had wanted to keep them there for interrogation but ended up sending his intell sergeant along to interrogate them en route and, if possible, at the hospital), and the captured weapons (among other things four AK-47s, which would make superb "trade goods" at Phan Hoa air base), and had made complimentary remarks. But Hamilton had not been able to persuade him to go in after the bad guys when they had a hot trail. Of course, it may have been that the Koreans couldn't move anything over a platoon without prior consent of their Division Headquarters, and didn't want to cost anybody "face" or risk a rebuff by requesting permission to do something not directed from on high. On the occasions when they did get cranked up, the Koreans were very impressive: brave, tough, patient, methodical, and relentless. But those last three characteristics also applied to their staff work, which did not lead to short reaction times and flexibility.

Walking across the compound, Hamilton felt the warm sun through his shirt and the tiredness in his shoulders. Good old sun; as long as it's out, everything is usually quiet; but the night still belongs to Charlie, even though we do have a lot of ambushes out every night, and so do the CIDG down the road, mostly hammock ambushes. Several times Hamilton had persuaded Captain Lan to sit up all night with him on an ambush; so far none of these had produced any action. Once, since he had been there, a PF squad on an ambush had killed two VC and captured a carbine, and occasionally one of the ambushes laid by the CIDG would catch something, but . . .

With an effort, Hamilton brought his mind back to the present. All necessary after-action actions had been taken: resupply of ammunition (and even, by some curious miracle, a resupply of sandbags and concertina wire; must remember to do something for Captain Clark, the supply officer at province; maybe give him one of the AK-47s), evacuation of the wounded, repairs to the perimeter wire and bunkers, filing of a spot report and follow-ups with the score (MACV and their beloved goddamn statistics). The written after-action report (commonly known as the afterbirth report) could jolly well wait.

The bodies of the two PF soldiers who had been killed were in a small building across the street that ran in front of the compound; their womenfolk were wailing over them in a high-pitched, grief-stricken, thoroughly traditional, and rather unnerving manner. War is awfully tough on the families. The fifteen dead NVA had been displayed, along with the captured weapons, in the main square of the village for most of the morning so the people would know who had won, and were now being buried in Captain Lan's boot hill down by the river. Probably their families would never know what became of them nor be able to visit their graves. Hamilton reminded himself that morbid thoughts lead to madness, especially in the subsector business, which is not good for mental health, in any event.

The weapons had been turned in by Captain Lan and had gone out on one of the choppers, except the four AK-47s that Hamilton had scarfed up and a very attractive ChiCom pistol that Lan had acquired, probably to donate to one of his political connections at province. "Trade goods," same-same as the AK-47s, but in the Vietnamese channels.

Hamilton stepped out of the sunlight and into the large, perpetually semidark room that served his little team as living room, dining room, and radio room. The radio was on a plain wooden table; in front of it, taped down under a sheet of clear acetate, was a 1:50,000 map of the district. Except for the fact that the big tile roof of the building didn't give much protection, this was a convenient setup, and it always seemed that available cement and other materials were needed for projects more urgent than building a proper team bunker. Harley, the radio operator, was sitting at the table, shirtless, reading a paperback Western and half listening to the steady hiss of the radio. In addition to several grease pencils and other prescribed items, an open beer can sat on the table. Hamilton decided to ignore both the lack of shirt and the beer, but some comment seemed to be required.

"Anything going on?"

"No, sir. Tuy Cau had a medevac—some woman with problems in childbirth." Tuy Cau was the subsector between them and the coast; it was also the relay between Hamilton and the radio at the Sector Headquarters (barely high enough to be entitled to capitals) in Phan Hoa city.

"Did they pick her up?"

"Yessir. I heard Tuy Cau talking to the chopper."

"Then things must be pretty quiet all over."

"Let's hope they stay that way."

"Harley, I thought you liked excitement."

"Sir, I do, but last night'll hold me for quite a while."

"I know what you mean, and they may be back tonight. . . . Let's see, you're off radio watch at four, and then it's Doc's turn, isn't it?"

As soon as it had been daylight and the shooting over with, Hamilton had had Harley turn in to get some sleep, while he and the other members of the team accomplished the various after-action actions, which wound up about noon, at which time they had had lunch. After lunch, Doc and the other two NCOs had turned in; Hamilton would have done likewise, but Colonel Nhieu, the province chief, and Hamilton's immediate boss, Lieutenant Colonel Dace, the sector senior adviser, had turned up and, of course, had to be briefed on the action. Fortunately, they had had the grace not to stay very long or to notice Hamilton's evident lack of shave or less than perfectly polished briefing.

"No, sir. We decided that Doc had had a pretty rough night, and Sergeant Parelli asked to take Doc's place."

"Okay. . . . Would you ask him to wake me up about 1800?"

"Okay, sir."

Before he turned in, Hamilton double-checked to make sure that his weapon, an M-2 carbine with a folding stock, had a full magazine in it and that each of the two pouches on his pistol belt had four more clips, each fully loaded (i.e., with twenty-eight rounds; if you load a "banana clip" for a carbine with thirty rounds and leave it that way for any great length of time, it sets the spring and greatly increases the chance of a malfunction), made sure his map and grease pencil were in their appointed pockets, and slowly, wearily, but not without pleasure, began taking off his boots. He had put them on fairly late in the action, during a lull; most of the night he had worn shower shoes. When things started happening, one was ill-advised to waste time with boot laces. His bunk was a standard GI iron cot with pillow, mattress, poncho liner, and a makeshift assemblage of iron rods holding up a mosquito net—a much better place to sleep than many he could remember. Oh, well. . . . He was asleep at once.

The shooting started shortly after midnight. Parelli was on radio watch; Hamilton and the other members of the team were sleeping. Hamilton was awakened by the sudden, urgent, purposeful rattle of small-arms and machine-gun fire, followed by the very loud *whump-whump-whump* of incoming mortar rounds. For a fraction of a second he lay still, thinking, "Oh, hell, here we go again," then jumped out of his cot, into his shower shoes (which, for just such occasions as this, were always placed where his feet would come down when he popped out of the cot), and, since for the moment there were no more incoming mortar rounds, stepped into the radio room.

Parelli was lying on his stomach on the floor by the radio table talking into the microphone.

"Sleepy Onion Alfa"—this was Tuy Cau's call sign—"this is Sleepy Onion Echo. Sleepy Onion Echo, over."

Hamilton recognized Sergeant Osbert's voice when Tuy Cau replied, "Echo, this is Alfa. Over."

"This is Echo; we got contact. So far about five rounds of incoming mortar and some small-arms fire. Request you advise Zulu." Zulu was the net control station at Phan Hoa. "We may need the Spooky. I'll call you back after I move this thing into the bunker. Over."

"This is Alfa, will relay to Zulu. Roger, out."

By that time the other members of the team had appeared: Sergeant Chambers, the senior NCO, lean, gray-haired, a veteran of World War II; Sergeant Tinsley, "Doc," the team medic, a dark, small, slender man with a dapper mustache; and Harley, the radio operator, fair, powerfully built, from a farm somewhere in the South. All were in rumpled jungle fatigues (which doubled as pajamas), but bareheaded and in shower shoes; they were rapidly putting on their battle harness, each with a full load of ammunition and grenades. For the moment, there was no firing in the compound with small arms; the four mortars within the compound were steadily thumping away, and from the high hill about a thousand meters west came a steady crackle of small-arms and automatic-weapons fire, punctuated by thumps that could have been hand grenades, satchel charges, or mortar shells. Parelli and Harley were disconnecting the radio from its antenna cable, preparatory to moving it to the bunker.

Hamilton nodded to Sergeant Chambers and said, "Let's go find the district chief and find out what's going on. The rest of you get into the bunker with both radios and one of these things"—indicating the four small, police-type "handy-talkie" radios they had acquired from somewhere—"and reestablish contact with Alfa or preferably direct with Zulu. Use the other radio to call the Special Forces and let them know what's going on."

It was almost an unnecessary order; this was not the first time they had gone through the drill. The only real question was who got to go with Captain Hamilton to see what was going on, rather than being cooped up in Captain Lan's cramped and smelly radio bunker with a lot of excited Vietnamese. This time it was Sergeant Chambers's turn. Chambers had picked up one of the handy-talkies, turned it on, and was blowing into the mike to make sure it was working; it was. The others were quickly and smoothly getting radios and other gear into the bunker, which was just outside the door of the team's radio room. Hamilton said, "Let's go," and they moved out into the compound.

Judging from the volume of fire on the big hill—small arms, automatic weapons, and heavier explosions—the 309th Regional Force Company was under pretty serious attack. Just as Hamilton turned to stick his head into the bunker to tell Doc (the senior man in the bunker) to get hold of Alfa or Zulu and tell them to send the Spooky, all hell broke loose within the compound itself: two very large explosions on the other side followed by small-arms fire and hand grenades. Hamilton and Chambers both hit the dirt. A few small shards from whatever was blown up landed near them, but the attack was on the other side of the compound. Hamilton got over to the bunker, told Doc to get the Spooky, then he and Chambers began working their way toward the shooting.

The mortars were still firing illumination, so the area was lit up by the wavering, bright white glow of flares. At a corner of the building they found three PF soldiers huddled up, one of whom would occasionally peer around the corner, then quickly draw back. They were the first Vietnamese troops Hamilton had encountered since things had begun; they were obviously shaken. Hamilton and Chambers moved up to them, and Hamilton tried his limited Vietnamese: "*Dai-uy o dau?*" (Where is the captain?) All he got in reply was "*Nguy hiem, nguy hiem! Beaucoup VC, beaucoup VC!*" (Very dangerous. Many VC.)

The battle was around the corner, judging from the sound and the occasional spurt of dirt as bullets struck the ground. But at night, without knowing which side was where, caution was indicated. Taking advantage of a shadow cast by the overhanging roof as a flare descended, Hamilton looked around the corner. The roof of one of the corner bunkers sagged down; from sounds and muzzle flashes Hamilton guessed that a few VC had gotten into the bunker and the adjacent section of trench, and the rest, possibly a platoon, were outside of, or in the outer edge of, the wire. Both 4.2″ mortars and one of the 81s were still firing in support of the 309 Company. A machine gun behind a little parapet on top of a bunker which looked down on the corner bunker was firing long bursts into that bunker and along the edge of the wire, and there was considerable other firing by BARs, carbines, and AK-47s. From previous experience, Hamilton was fairly sure that Lan was the man firing the machine gun. The only problem was that the intervening space was being raked by fire from both sides.

Chambers tapped him on the leg. "Doc says that the Spooky's on its way. Be here in about two zero."

"Thank God for that. I bet that's the district chief with the machine gun."

Chambers, who was carrying the handy-talkie, took a quick look around the corner and nodded. "Yeah, it sounds like the Dai-uy . . . but goddamn, that's open space between here and there."

"I know, that's what we get paid for. Gimme some covering fire. When I get there, I'll try to get the Dai-uy to pin 'em down with the machine gun."

They both checked their carbines to make double sure each had a round in the chamber, was on full automatic, and had the safety off. Sergeant Chambers wormed himself into a low prone firing position. Hamilton was crouching beside him. He said to himself, "If John Wayne can do it, Charlie Hamilton can do it, even in shower shoes." Aloud, but quietly: "Here we go."

He sprinted the fifty yards or so to the bunker,

firing a couple of bursts with his carbine in the general direction of the enemy as he went, then dropped down behind the bunker, shook the gravel out of his shower shoes, and crawled up on top. It was the Dai-uy. He was wearing striped white and light blue pajamas and shower shoes. He was firing long bursts into the collapsed bunker and the two sections of trench on each side of it. Three PF soldiers were bringing him boxes of ammunition. Hamilton reflected on the wondrous durability of Browning machine guns and crawled up alongside him. After one look at the Dai-uy's congested face and squinched-up eyes, he thanked God the bastard wasn't gunning for him.

Lan glanced at him and fired another burst of about fifteen rounds. He said, "Maybe ten VC down there."

"Let's go in after 'em."

"No have troops."

"Okay, just you and me and my sergeant."

"Where your sergeant?"

"Over there. You give some covering fire and he come now."

Sergeant Chambers was crouching in the shadow of the corner of the building, ready to make a dash for it.

"Okay, we go kill beaucoup VC." This last with a very lethal grin. "Good God, I think he really likes to kill people," Hamilton thought. He had spotted a couple of muzzle flashes in the corner bunker, and, when Lan nudged him, cut loose on them with a long burst with his carbine. At the same time Lan fired another long burst with his machine gun, and Chambers popped up and dashed across the open space, firing on the run, and dropped down behind the bunker. Hamilton distinctly remembered seeing several spurts of dirt near his feet and heard the nasty whine of a bullet that had hit a rock and ricocheted off. No damage, though. And all of it as smoothly done as if they all spoke the same language and had been practicing it all week.

One of the Regional Force sergeants had appeared beside Lan, who spoke to the sergeant briefly in Vietnamese and handed the machine gun over to him, then turned to Hamilton and said, "We go now?"

"Wait," Hamilton said, and pointed. Someone was crouching by the corner of the building, waiting to cross over. Lan spoke to the sergeant, who fired a long burst, and the man by the corner of the building made his dash for it, drawing fire, but made it without getting hit. It was Harley, carrying his M-14 rifle and one of the PRC-25 radios.

"Sir, I thought you might want to talk to the Spooky when he gets here."

"Yeah, and you don't like staying cooped up in that bunker when there's something going on. Who's on the radio?"

"Doc and Sergeant Parelli, sir." Military courtesy always seemed to improve when people were doing something contrary to orders.

"Well, before the Spooky gets here, we've got some other work for you. Is that rifle loaded?"

"Yes, sir. Twenty rounds, one and one tracer and ball."

"Okay, here's the deal: Thuong-si here, with the machine gun, pins down the bastards outside the wire. You and I and Chambers and the Dai-uy go in and clean out the bastards in the corner bunker and the trenches each side of it. You two slip into the trench and work along it—and for God's sake try not to kill any PFs while you're at it. The Dai-uy and I will rush the bunker. Okay?"

Everyone nodded, Lan spoke briefly to Thuong-si, whose English was less than perfect, Harley pulled out a bayonet and stuck it on the end of his rifle, Hamilton suppressed the urge to suggest that this was being a bit melodramatic, and they all moved off.

Chambers and Harley dropped into the trench and were momentarily out of sight, and Thuong-si cut loose with a long burst into the wire. Hamilton and the Dai-uy, each with his carbine in one hand and a grenade with the pin out in the other, rushed across the open space toward the corner bunker, firing on the run, rolled their grenades in, and hit the dirt. Fortunately, both grenades went off inside the bunker. They both rolled into the trench (not the one that Harley and Chambers were cleaning out), coming down back-to-back, with the Dai-uy facing the bunker. There were scrabbling and moaning sounds in the bunker, so the Dai-uy stepped up to it and fired four short bursts with his carbine in the door. Hamilton saw no movement in the trench in front of him, only four bodies, but whether they were alive or dead, VC or friendly, he couldn't tell, so he held his fire. Lan turned around and clapped Hamilton on the shoulder. He was grinning, not a pleasant grin.

"Many VC, all dead."

Hamilton began wondering what had happened to Chambers and Harley; all he could do at the moment was wait and listen. The firing at the 309 Company's position on the big hill seemed to have fallen off a little; at least they hadn't been overrun. Then, very close at hand, in the other trench, he heard two shots, obviously Harley's M-14, and a few moments later a loud thump and a strangled cry. Then he heard Chambers's voice:

"Sir, is the bunker clear?"

"I think so."

The compound was quiet. Even the mortars had ceased firing for a moment. And Hamilton heard a lovely sound: the deep-throated, almost lazy roar of the engines on a goony bird.

"Gentlemen, the Spooky is here. I guess I better get on the horn and talk to them. Harley, where's the radio?"

"Up by the other bunker, sir."

"By the way, what happened in your trench?"

"One of them was trying to pull the pin on a hand grenade, so I shot him, and one of them tried to pull a knife on me, so I hit him with my rifle butt. Sergeant Chambers is guarding him now."

"Still alive?"

"I'm afraid so, sir."

"Maybe the Dai-uy can get him to talk."

They were walking up to the bunker where Harley had put down the PRC-25 radio. Two squads of PF soldiers had reoccupied the trench and corner bunker and were policing up the dead and wounded and weapons of both sides. Already four enemy dead wearing NVA uniforms and a couple of SKS rifles had been recovered, so it was clear that the visitors had not been the local talent. The NVA outside the wire had faded back—how far was anyone's guess. Hamilton picked up the mike on the radio and called the Spooky: "Spooky, this is Sleepy Onion Echo. Over."

"Roger, Sleepy Onion Echo, this is Spook Three Two. I hear you've had a little trouble and may we be of assistance? Over." Somewhere between courtly and cocky, and definitely spoiling for some action. A Spooky is a C-47 (military version of the venerable DC-3 transport) with three 7.62mm electrically driven Gatling guns, commonly called miniguns, each with a maximum cyclic rate of fire of about 3,000 rounds per minute, firing broadside out of the left side of the aircraft; it also carries flares. Except in really foggy or cloudy weather, it is the sovereign remedy and equalizer when Charlie or Clyde, his big brother from up north, comes calling at night. On the big hill it appeared that the enemy had also heard the sound of the engines, for the firing had suddenly fallen off. Clyde, or Charlie, or whoever it was, was at least bright enough not to stand up to the Spooky. Hamilton was on the radio again.

"Roger, Three Two, this is Echo. We're on the little hill in the middle of the valley, about two klicks north of the river with the big iron bridge. The trouble right now is on the big hill one klick west of my location. Friendlies on top of that hill and the bad guys trying to push them off. Over."

"This is Three Two. Roger, I have the little hill in the middle of the valley and the big hill to your west. I see tracers coming out of the top of the big hill. Where shall I fire and where do you want your flares? Over."

By now Hamilton could hear the engines of the Spooky quite clearly overhead; Lan had called off the mortars and it was dark, although a clear night with a sliver of rising moon.

"This is Echo. Please to put out a flare right over the big hill, and hose out the area north and west of the big hill. Over."

"Roger. . . . First flare's out now."

After several seconds, the first flare popped. It was too far north.

"Three Two, this is Echo. Please put the next one out about five zero zero meters farther south. Over."

"Roger, five zero zero farther south. Over."

Spooky was circling to put out the next flare. Sergeant Chambers came up. He was breathing hard.

"It's tough work for an old man like me, sir."

While Hamilton was trying to think up an appropriate reply, Spooky saved him the trouble by announcing, "This is Three Two, flare out."

It was close to where Hamilton wanted it, and the wind would carry it across the top of the big hill, so he replied, "Roger, Three Two, that's just right. Keep illuminating there, and can you give us a little fire north and west of the big hill? Over."

"Wilco, that's what I'm here for. Over."

Hamilton sighed; he, too, was beginning to feel more than a little weary from the night's proceedings, now that the immediate excitement was over. It was clear that the rest of the night would consist of staying on the radio, adjusting flares, and relatively minor sniping back and forth to prevent the bad guys from recovering bodies and weapons out of the wire, especially on the hill.

"Sergeant Chambers, would you please try to get Alfa or Zulu up on the alternate push and give them a spot report on what's happened so far . . . also that we'll undoubtedly need an ammunition resupply in the morning, especially 81mm illuminating. God knows how many rounds they fired off before the Spooky got here. Also ask Doc to take his little bag of tricks and look in at the dispensary; I expect they have some casualties who will need looking at. And thanks for the covering fire . . . and everything."

"No problem, sir. Like you say, it's what we get paid for."

And he headed for the commo bunker. Hamilton reflected that there isn't enough money anywhere to hire people to do what combat soldiers are expected to do every day and that, by a supreme paradox, this is most perfectly illustrated by the exploits of such mercenary corps as the Gurkhas and the French Foreign Legion. And what are we going to do when splendid old soldiers like Chambers die or retire? Harley and Parelli are both getting out—no chance of changing their minds—and Tinsley's a medic, even if he is also a damn fine combat soldier and NCO.

"Echo, this is Three Two. I commence firing in about one zero. Over."

"This is Echo. Roger, will adjust. Over." And to

Lan: "Dai-uy, Spooky shoot now. You tell me if he shoot right place." Lan nodded. The Spooky fired; first came a stream of pink tracers, like a solid ray of light, then, perceptibly later, came the sound, utterly unlike the rattle of a normal machine gun, more like the growl of a foghorn. Lan talked on his radio, apparently with the people of 309 Company, and grinned again. The grin was a bit less lethal this time.

"He say they shoot number one, maybe kill many VC. Maybe shoot all 'round north and west of hill."

The rest of the night, as expected, consisted mainly of adjusting flares and the occasional bursts of fire by the Spooky. After daybreak and breakfast, Hamilton and Parelli, with the district chief and a platoon of PF, had walked up the big hill to inventory captured weapons and check the body count. Lan took the opportunity to make complimentary remarks to the 309 Company for their resolute stand under attack by most of an NVA battalion.

II.

A MEETING
NEAR THE BEACH

There were five of them sitting on the porch of the
Tuy Cau Subsector team house: Captain Hamilton
and Sergeant Chambers from the Dong Hai Subsector;
Captain Lund, the Tuy Cau Subsector senior adviser,
handsome, affable, and very professional (on a previous tour he had been senior adviser to a Ranger
battalion); George Hargrove, Lund's civilian deputy,
a big man with a long face and merry eyes, one of
the very few civilians in-country whom the army
officers regarded as "one of us, not one of them,"
and deservedly so; and Sergeant Osbert, Lund's senior NCO. Osbert was very much an infantryman.
He had been wounded and later decorated for bravery
in the Pork Chop Hill battle in Korea and had spent
most of the intervening years training recruits. His
family had been very poor, his education and gram-
mar informal, and, probably even more so than it

was for Lund, the army was his life. He was very lean, with an unobtrusive and ageless toughness, and, from the army's point of view quite incidentally, he was black. Lund was speaking.

"That was a pretty good show you had the other night." Hamilton and Chambers had stopped off at Tuy Cau en route to the more or less monthly meeting of all subsector advisers with the province/sector staff at Phan Hoa. Except for the fact that this was a chance to get away from the loneliness of the subsectors and talk with the other subsector people at the bar afterward, everyone loathed these meetings.

"Well, it was mostly the 309 Company's show, plus the mortar platoon and the Spooky, and the Dai-uy with his machine gun."

By immemorial tradition, Hamilton was careful to avoid anything that sounded like glory hunting.

"I understand he's something of a bastard," said Lund, "and that Colonel Nhieu sent him up there to get rid of him."

"There's no question that Dai-uy Lan is a certified, triple-distilled, gold-plated, grand-slam-redoubled bastard. He is almost entirely resistant to advice, at least from me, and he takes the old mandarin attitude toward the peasants that the proper relation between superior and subordinate is one of overt contempt on the one side and cringing submission on the other, and several other things, but"—Hamilton paused for emphasis—"he's a thoroughgoing Vietnamese patriot or nationalist, I'm not quite sure which, he's militarily competent, *and* he's a fighter. Which is most important. The one thing I can do without,

especially in a subsector like that, out in front of the
Koreans and with a whole goddamn regiment of
NVA looking down my neck, is one of your smiling
yes-men who disappear into a funk-hole somewhere
when the first shot goes off and can't be found, and
there's no one around to lead the troops or tell yours
truly what's going on. He's the only Vietnamese up
there who speaks usable English, and my Vietnamese
really isn't good enough for crises. Which is why I
haven't tried to get him fired.''

"People at sector don't like him, and that can hurt
you.''

"I know, and if I could get someone as good as
your Lieutenant Dao''—the Tuy Cau District chief,
generally and deservedly regarded as the best in the
business—"I'd dump Lan in a minute and start working on a reputation as a wonder-worker; but I'd rather
be unpopular at sector, and even with my rating
officer, than have a model pacification program, on
paper anyway, and some night get the place overrun
and some holes in my T-shirt. You don't know how
lucky you are in your selection of a counterpart.''

"You're damn right I do," Lund countered. "I'm
not that stupid. I'm glad I don't have your job. But
look, this guy can ruin your career. Colonel Dace is a
pretty good head, even if he is obnoxious, but there
are all sorts of people and influences around him who
detest Lan, and probably for good reason after what
you said, and it's bound to rub off on you and affect
your efficiency report, to use a dirty word.''

"And it only takes one so-so efficiency report to
put the Indian sign on your career forever. I know.

But damn it all, we're here to do a job, to fight a war, and, so far as I'm concerned, what Dace sees fit to put in my efficiency report is his problem.''

"But it's your file it goes into, not his," Lund said.

"Well," Hamilton said, "I just hope that this never gets to be a case of having to choose between doing the job right and keeping the boss happy. Back in the States it's not so hard to say, 'The boss may not always be right, but he's always the boss,' but out here it's a real live war and theoretically at least we're supposed to be professionals.''

"You're very lucky. You're a bachelor and I bet there's a well-paid spot in the family business waiting for you if you ever get out, so you can say things like that and maybe even act on them." Lund did not add that his own father had been a small-town schoolteacher, that he had a wife and three children and no income other than his army salary, that he was thankful to have a Regular commission, and, even though he had not been to the Military Academy, hoped to make full colonel someday. He also was thankful to have Lieutenant Dao for a counterpart.

Hamilton was staring at the top of his beer can. He was reflecting on how much pleasanter life would be if he had a counterpart like Dao. A couple of even more morose thoughts were lurking around the edges, but he suppressed them. No point in upsetting yourself over what can't be prevented. Chambers and Osbert had drifted away into some private, NCO-level discussion. Hamilton changed the subject.

"You've got a very nice setup here." It was the

truth. Tuy Cau Subsector was on top of a small hill, well away from the village (unlike Dong Hai, which was surrounded on three sides by the hamlet of Dong Hai), with a lovely view to the east of the South China Sea and to the west of the foothills of the Chaine Annamitique. The nearest of these, locally called pagoda hills, rose to fairly impressive heights beginning just on the other side of Highway 1, which ran across the front of the compound. It was a "key terrain feature," and two Korean companies had dug in strongpoints at opposite ends of that general ridge line. Since they were several miles apart, however, the VC had, on occasion, come over the center of the ridge and shot up the Tuy Cau Subsector. The compound included two ARVN 155mm howitzers, which guaranteed fairly impressive counterfire. The Americans at Tuy Cau at least had their own team house, a long, low building made of angle irons and gypsum board, and a massively revetted sunken porch tucked in between the front of the team house and their bunker. Both the porch and bunker had been built with scrounged materials.

Lund's reply was true to the custom of self-deprecation. "It's all right, except it rattles and shakes like hell when the wind blows."

"Isn't that what happened to the previous version of this porch?" asked Hamilton.

"That's why we built this thing," Lund replied. Then: "Have another beer."

"No, thanks. I think we better push along. You're going to this meeting, aren't you?"

"You mean I had a choice?"

"I was thinking if we both go together, there's a little more firepower if something happens on the road."

"Okay, I'll crank up my people and we'll all go together. Dao and his crew will be going, too; he has some business with Colonel Nhieu."

"That's even better. That goddamn bodyguard of his is lethal as hell."

Lund grinned; he was remembering several fairly drastic incidents involving Dao and his bodyguard. "I wouldn't care to have him gunning for me."

"I've heard that little thug's a Nung."

"He's an ethnic Vietnamese. In fact, I think he's some sort of cousin of Dao's. The Nungs have a reputation, so they get credit for lots of things they don't do. What does Lan do for a bodyguard?"

"He has a PF corporal whose wife and son were murdered by the VC. He's a quiet little guy, but he's the best soldier in the county."

So they took off in three jeeps, Dao's, Lund's, and Hamilton's. Dao was driving his own jeep, with a "liberated" M-16 across his knees (this was before M-16s had been issued to any but a very few Vietnamese troops, so possession of one was a real status symbol); the bodyguard rode beside him. He had Dao's M-2 carbine, which had a folding stock, like Hamilton's. In the back rode another PF soldier with an M-79 grenade launcher. Two more PF soldiers, variously armed, rode in the back seats of Lund's and Hamilton's jeeps. As this stretch of Highway 1 was comparatively secure, they were quite formidably armed, everything considered. The three extra PF soldiers had private business or relatives to visit in Phan Hoa city and were there for the ride and to save bus fare.

They arrived in Phan Hoa city without incident, the extra PF soldiers got off at the market square, Dao with his jeep and bodyguard headed for the Vietnamese Province compound, and the Americans drove on to the MACV compound by the beach.

Phan Hoa city, capital of the province of that name, lies mainly in the northeast quadrant of the intersection of Highway 1 and the railroad (which run north and south, close together, about four miles in from the coast) and the Phan Cao River, a lazy, shallow stream draining the Phan Cao Valley, a rice-growing deltalike plain, which supports a little over half the population of the province. The city was laid out by the French, with wide streets on a rectangular plan, and a traffic circle and covered market at the main intersection. It was pretty thoroughly smashed up in the fighting between the Vietminh and the French, and has since been rebuilt, mostly with boxy pseudo-modern buildings of cement blocks, plastered over with more cement and painted in various pastel colors. Most of these are the typical East Asian two-story affairs, with an open-front shop of some kind (bars, tailor shops, and bicycle-repair shops predominating) and rooms for the family upstairs. Hamilton had heard that in some of the bars the rooms upstairs were used for other purposes. He had little taste for whoring and even less for interfering with what his NCOs did on their own time, provided they didn't get gathered in by the MPs; the town was

theoretically off-limits to all U.S. personnel, and
there was a curfew. He saw no reason to look into
the entertainments, whatever they might be, of downtown Phan Hoa.

Between the city and the shoreline was about a
mile of salt marsh, then some low sand dunes
and the beach. A causeway led from the city to a
road along the beach; here were located the Provincial
PF training compound, the MACV compound, the
headquarters of the Vietnamese 38th Regiment, various province and sector compounds, and, in considerable luxury, the compound for the various U.S.
civil servants assigned to the combined civil-military
province/sector advisory team. The MACV compound,
where the military lived, was a collection of low-
lying buildings of mixed construction, mainly wood,
angle iron, gypsum board, and much sand, with a
considerable defensive berm around it, right on the
beach. It was a fine beach. Hamilton always brought
his swim trunks when he came to Phan Hoa, and
about every third time he got a chance to go for a
swim. By the time he and Chambers had checked in
and gotten themselves bunks (Hamilton in the upper
bunk in Captain Clark's room, and Chambers somewhere in the NCO billets), it was too late to go
swimming or to the sector compound (where the
offices were), and too early to hit the bar or eat, so
after what little unpacking was necessary, Hamilton
went to the mess hall, got a cup of coffee, and sat
down to write a letter.

Sergeant Chambers had disappeared. Hamilton knew
that Chambers's program for the night would include

getting laid and then thoroughly drunk with some of the other NCOs; also that he would have a perfectly clear head and be as competent as ever by the time they were ready to take off for Dong Hai the next day. Sergeant Chambers never had more than two beers at Dong Hai, which had no more effect on him than so much soda pop, and from Dong Hai the closest place for getting laid was a scruffy-looking shack about ten miles away down a not too secure road, which catered mainly to the Koreans. It was not surprising that the enlisted members of the team were always willing to make trips into Phan Hoa city.

The letter never got written. Captain Clark had walked into the mess hall, got a cup of coffee, and sat down opposite Hamilton. A heavyset young man with close-cut dark hair and a deceptively mild, slightly jowly, cherubic expression, he was the adviser to the Vietnamese Sector Administration and Logistics Company (commonly known as A&L), which supposedly took care of all the support for the RF and PF units in the province.

"I understand you killed some VC the other night."

"They were really NVA, and the credit goes mostly to the 309 Company on the hill and Dai-uy Lan's little palace guard inside the compound. My counterpart is quite an artist with a Browning machine gun."

"He burns up a lot of bolts and barrels, too."

"Now you're making a noise like a supply officer. I admit I don't like fifty-round bursts, either, but he does kill VC. By the way, many thanks for all the concertina wire and sandbags the other morning."

"Well, you're my source of crossbows." Dong Hai District included the only Montagnard settlement in the province where crossbows could be had, so Hamilton and the Special Forces had a monopoly of them in the area. Hamilton bought quite a few of them with his own money and shamelessly traded them for necessary items not otherwise available, sometimes through Clark. He was also good friends with the Air Police at Phan Hoa Air Force Base.

"I've got something even better for you this time."

Clark's normally flaccid, slightly sleepy expression brightened considerably. "I thought all the captured weapons had been turned in," he said. "Colonel Nhieu's people have latched on to them and I haven't got the first one for trading."

"Come with me." Hamilton realized that this mysteriousness was childish, but both of them were enjoying it. He led the way to the room he was sharing with Clark and, with as much of an air as he could manage, presented him with one of the captured AK-47s. Clark whistled softly, hefted it, and said in an almost rapt voice, "Beautiful. What do you need?"

"Mostly a bigger radio. Even with a 292 antenna, those PRC-25s don't really have the power to talk to this place reliably, and all the time. It is twenty-five miles, you know."

"Don't you relay through Tuy Cau?"

"They go off the air at 2100. Theoretically, if something pops at my place, the Vietnamese there call the Vietnamese at Tuy Cau, who are supposed to wake up Captain Lund's people and get them up in the net. What I need is a VRC-46 and some truck batteries.''

"Do you have a generator?"

"Lan has one he uses to recharge the batteries for the perimeter lights. And if push comes to shove, we can recharge them with the jeep."

"Batteries, really no problem, but that kind of radio is hard to come by. What else do you need and what other trade goods do you have?"

"In addition to a few crossbows, I have some NVA uniforms, rucksacks, web equipment, and stuff like that, but I didn't bring any of it with me." He omitted mention of the other AK-47s. No point in letting everything show at once. "Aside from a radio, the main thing I need is enough cement and other building materials to build a decent bunker for my people."

"There's always a good demand for those NVA brass belt buckles, especially the ones with the five-pointed stars cut in them."

"I'll take a closer look at those old uniforms and stuff."

To himself he added, "The first one of those buckles with the star engraved on it I keep for me."

"Thanks a lot for the AK-47. I'll see what I can do about a radio for you. Isn't it about time for supper?"

It was, and they went in and ate. The subject of radios, cement, and trade goods was not mentioned again that evening. It wasn't necessary. Hamilton had had dealings with Captain Clark before and been given reason to trust him—up to a point.

At the bar, after dinner, there was a lot of talk, especially by the Infantry officers stuck in staff jobs at sector telling war stories. Since most of them were airborne as well, jump stories got mixed in. About the third time everyone got through singing "The Ballad of Roger Young," Hamilton, who was a tanker and not a jumper, felt moved to point out that Roger Young was a "leg" (i.e., not airborne) in the 41st Division, a National Guard outfit from a very unfashionable state.

Having unburdened himself of this unpopular truth, he decided that he had had enough to drink and quite enough of the company of all these airborne grunts, bade them good night, and left. Outside, the night air was mild and fragrant, and over the hubbub of voices from the Officers and NCO club bars (which were side by side in the same building) he could hear the waves sighing softly on the beach.

"Poor bastards," he reflected. "Most of them joined the army after the Korean War, and here they are, stuck in staff jobs while a tanker like me ends up getting the dismounted combat experience they need and I don't. And all their brave little war stories about peacetime training exploits with or without jumping out of airplanes . . . I wonder if they get this drunk every night, or only when the subsector people are in town to remind them that there really is a war out there."

He further reflected that feeling superior to your fellow creature is a pretty cheap thrill, and went off to bed.

Captain Clark was already in bed, peacefully sleep-

ing. At least he's bright enough not to get his head
smoked up every night . . . but then he's a Quarter-
master Corps officer and probably has no more taste
for all this Infantry bragging than I. Then an old
voice from somewhere reminded him that, *quand
même*, the Infantry, the poor dumb bastards who
fight on foot, take 80 percent of the casualties. Rest
in peace, Roger Young . . . and involuntarily he
remembered the faces of the dead NVA he had seen
while checking the body count on the big hill. The
goddamn body count, another neat numerical statistic
for the computers at MACV Headquarters, only it's
not dollars, but living, breathing human beings who
are now dead forever, even if they are the enemy.
More victims of the Hanoi megalomania. He firmly
decided that he had had very close to too much to
drink, reminded himself that morbid thoughts lead to
madness, and eventually got to sleep.

The next morning it took two more cups of coffee
than usual to clear Hamilton's head; it wasn't very
good coffee, and the prospect of the monthly meeting
didn't brighten his mood at all.

The meetings followed a set pattern. They took
place in a large, airy hall (which the province chief
also used for his meetings and briefings); it was
painted a buff-brown color, decorated with the insignia of the various ARVN units in the province. The
assembly consisted of the heads of the various civilian and military staff sections at province/sector and
the subsector senior advisers. Occasionally some high-
ranking Koreans or some colonel from the air force

base or the army hospital next to it would attend. Except for the province chief, who would sometimes be on hand to make welcoming remarks, the Vietnamese were not invited to these sessions. When all were in readiness, Colonel Dace would announce, "Gentlemen, the senior adviser," and everyone would pop to attention for the grand entry of Mr. Jack Leary, the province senior adviser. Hamilton and most of the other officers were starchy enough to regard it as thoroughly degrading and repellent that this essentially military sign of respect should be accorded to a "goddamn civilian," especially since it was accurately symbolic of their subordination to an essentially civilian chain of command.

Leary looked about thirty, a little over average height, very well muscled, with close-cut, curly, dark reddish hair and the open countenance and frank, informal manner of a really expert con man or politician. After letting everyone, including Colonel Dace, who was ten years his senior, stand at attention about two seconds longer than was necessary or courteous, Leary said, in a frank, gracious, well-modulated voice, "Please be seated, gentlemen."

Dace was the first speaker. He was a very handsome black, with bony features that suggested ancestors who had been chieftains of warrior tribes, "flashing" eyes, and a courtly, slightly swaggering manner. Blacks do not get to be lieutenant colonels of artillery without having quite a lot more than average on the ball. Dace knew it and showed it. No one envied him his job as Leary's deputy. Dace was abrasive, sarcastic, and demanding, and for that reason was commonly referred to as "the head nigger," even by people like Hamilton who had no particular feelings about blacks in general. His speech, as always, was short and crisp, consisting of a summary of the military and political situation in the province, followed by concise directives on what was desired to be accomplished during the next month, and concluding with his usual pitch on "professionalism," his favorite subject for discourse. Hamilton took notes on all of it but the last part.

Dace was followed by presentations by the heads of the staff sections, mostly elaborating on Dace's summary of the past month's activities with the civilian sections—refugees, public health, education, police, and whatnot—consisting mostly of recitations of the quantities of bags of cement or school kits or whatever had been handed out that month. Very little of this ever got up to Dong Hai, so Hamilton ignored it, except for a few items in the S2 and S3 briefings which seemed worth writing down.

After a short break, the subsector advisers each gave their "presentations," summarizing their activities since the last meeting. First was Major Yamata, a stocky, moonfaced Hawaiian-Japanese, a senior Air Defense Artillery major who had Phu Xuong District, the area of the Phan Cao Valley south of the river, including the air force base. He had once been mistaken for Vietnamese by a visiting congressman who had told him what wonderful progress "you people are making," had accepted the compliment with his best imitation of an inscrutable smile, and laughed like hell over it afterward. To the even semieducated eye, he bore no resemblance at all to a Vietnamese. His briefing was short and prosaic, but Hamilton noted with slight alarm that Yamata was using an elaborate set of briefing cards and a map board with acetate overlaps. The last thing he needed was to get involved in the "I can put on a fancier briefing than you" game, especially in a war, and especially since Dong Hai was remote from the sources of raw materials for making all this showy eyewash.

Phan Cao District, the part of the valley north of the river, including Phan Hoa city, came next, in the person of Major Harry MacCabe, also Air Defense Artillery, stocky, grizzled, an ex-NCO of many years experience. His briefing also had a rather elaborate set of visual aids.

Captain Lund, the first to represent one of the "up-country" districts, had only a map board, but he had a good deal of progress to report, and his delivery was excellent.

Captain Hamilton, who followed, also had only a map board and made his briefing short and to the point. The action the other night involving his subsector headquarters and 309 Company had been the most significant contact made by sector forces during the month, contributing fifteen of a total body count of twenty-eight for the period, but Major Scammell, the S3 adviser, had already mentioned it and given the score, so all that Hamilton felt like saying was: "The action on the night of the fifteenth to sixteenth at Dong Hai has already been discussed. I would like, however, to commend the exemplary performance in that action of the 309 Company, the 68th PF Platoon"

—Lan's "palace guard" platoon—"the RF mortar platoon at subsector, and the district chief, who personally led the counterattack that destroyed the enemy who had penetrated the compound."

He noticed several people, mostly civilians, but including the intelligence and psychological warfare officers (who had had no combat experience and rarely ventured up-country), wince and slightly shake their heads at anyone saying anything good about Captain Lan. He went on: "We are also very grateful for the Spooky, and for the excellent support from Sector and the Tuy Cau Subsector in getting us the Spooky that night, as well as the medevacs and the ammunition resupply the next morning."

The recipients of this gratitude would, of course, aver that it was only what they were hired to do. That was traditional, but it never hurt to make courteous and grateful noises. He did not mention the resupply of concertina wire and sandbags; that was a private matter between him and Captain Clark.

The rest of his briefing was short and uninteresting: a couple of rather minor contacts involving subsector forces, one successful ambush by Camp Strike Force (CSF, formerly Civilian Irregular Defense Force, or CIDG) troops from the Special Forces camp, and nothing remarkable in the "pacification" effort, except the negative but significant comfort that no hamlets or other places held by friendly forces had been overrun that month.

The last two subsectors were represented by Captain Marchant, stocky, dark-haired, really an outsider, as he was concurrently team commander of the Special Forces camp as well as district adviser of the Cung Hoa District, the upper valley of the Phan Cao River, hilly and sparsely inhabited; and Major Charlie Race, florid, pink-haired, slender, handsome, and debonair, who had the Song Nao District, a spectacularly scenic strip of coast in the northeast part of the province.

Mr. Leary spoke last. The style was undoubtedly that which he imagined would be used by a habitually victorious general in addressing troops needing to be inspired to achieve still another victory. The themes, as always, were, first, the wondrous things that CORDS (Civic Operations/Revolutionary Development Support, the official title of the civil-military advisory chain of command) was doing and going to do for the Vietnamese people; second, Mr. Leary's contacts with and brilliant success in selling Phan Hoa Province's achievements to the even more wonderful and exalted bureaucrats at Nha Trang; and last, "Emphasize the Positive," which meant, in effect, make everything in official reports look as good as possible without actually lying, and whatever else, make sure that pacification progress in Phan Hoa Province looks better than in the adjacent provinces. Not, of course, stated in quite such bald language. Modern officialese has all sorts of exquisite euphemisms for saying these things.

He also announced that there would be beer, steak, and lobster (Song Nao District was famous for lobster) at the civilian compound after the meeting, which terminated on this note. Mandatory attendance did not have to be stated.

Hamilton was chatting with Charlie Race; both of them were working away at the beer and lobster; in a minute they would switch to steak. The buildings at the civilian compound next to the sector compound were prefab trailer-type metal structures, sleek, air-conditioned, and very comfortable. The difference in standard of living of civilians and military, even at sector, was not lost on anyone, but they had long since ceased to let it bother them.

"Who paid for the lobster?" Hamilton asked.

"I brought them down," Race answered. "The mess fund paid for them. Why do you ask?"

"I thought that might be how you kept them off your back."

"I wish it were that easy."

"How do you keep them off your back?"

"Come up sometime and I'll tell you. Song Nao is the Riviera of the Orient. I don't think you've ever paid me the honor of a visit."

"I will next time I can, but I don't know when. The farthest I usually get in that direction is the Korean Regimental CP."

"Next time you get that far, sneak up to my place. We have a lovely spot by the bay."

"I've seen it from the air. I'll bring some crossbows."

"That will be much appreciated."

Hamilton reflected that, while the scenery in Song Nao was at least up to the Riviera, the hotels weren't. In a sane, peacetime world, there would be a Song Nao Hilton, and Charlie Race has just the right style to be the manager.

It was uncomfortably close to nightfall when Hamilton and Chambers finally drove into the Dong Hai Subsector compound. They had been sniped at once on the way, which was fairly common, but otherwise had had no incidents. Every time Hamilton returned to Dong Hai, he felt the weight of loneliness, responsibility, and danger almost as a physical burden. Nevertheless, he was heartily glad that the meeting was over and that he was not assigned at sector.

III.

A JOURNEY
TO SAIGON

About two months earlier, Hamilton had been sent to Saigon for a four-day course on the pacification effort. This was a requirement for all subsector advisers, among others, even those who, like Hamilton, had attended the Military Assistance Training Adviser (MATA) course at Fort Bragg before coming out. Apparently it was felt that the MATA course (which was taught by the Special Forces) did not fully present the in-country MACV-CORDS viewpoint and latest concepts. Hamilton regarded it mainly as an opportunity to get away from Dong Hai for a week and to see what had changed in Saigon since his previous tour, when he had been based there. There was another, more specific reason for looking forward to the trip. He had recently had a letter from an old college friend and political associate, Caroline Atkins, to the effect that a girl named Liz Parnell, an old friend of Caroline's, had a job with United Broadcasting Company in Saigon, and would he please look her up?

Caroline was extremely intelligent (also fairly sensible), witty, well read, and an excellent letter writer; she was also homely. Once or twice, after a long, well-oiled evening, Hamilton had made a pass at her, but without success and without provoking any seriously hurt feelings. Both had been fairly active, on the same side, in campus politics, and had remained good friends and pen pals ever since. He had never met or heard of Liz Parnell before, but decided that any friend of C. Atkins would probably be reasonably bright, if not beautiful, and might even not be infected with the enragingly negative attitude on the war and the army which seemed to be almost universal in the media. It had also been an awfully long time since Hamilton had sat at a small table with drinks and conversation with a real live female girl. The various Red Cross girls, nurses, and the like that he saw occasionally at Phan Hoa had struck him as generally underintelligent, overweight, and already committed; and the only available Vietnamese girls were the overt whores. For a variety of reasons, not least the offense to his vanity involved in paying to get laid, Hamilton abstained from that form of recreation.

So, on the appointed day, Hamilton put himself and his bag on the supply chopper, rode to the sector compound at Phan Hoa, reported to and chatted briefly with Colonel Dace, who seemed to be in one of his affable, nonabrasive moods, and went to lunch with Captain Clark.

"You're lucky to get away from this place for a while," Clark said.

"It's only a week, really less, counting the travel time."

"They say that Saigon is the Paris of the Orient."

"That's right: extremely high prices, a great many whores, and all the bars are clip joints. Also very handsome parks and boulevards and a lot of first-class architecture."

"I've heard there are good restaurants there, too."

"There used to be, but that was before the big buildup," Hamilton said. "What there is now, I don't know, but I intend to find out. Do you ever get down there?"

"Not yet, but I'm working on it."

They had finished their coffee.

"Do you need a ride out to the air base?" Clark asked.

"Of course, and thank you very much."

It was about eight miles to the air base, through downtown Phan Hoa city, across a long iron-girder bridge over the Phan Cao River, and past some unexciting suburbs on the Phu Xuong side. The passenger terminal was a large, undistinguished shed, with a ticket counter along one side and benches for waiting or hopeful passengers. Hamilton was fortunate to be able to book himself on a C-130 flight that left in about an hour, said good-bye to Clark, and sat down to wait.

Possibly twenty other waiting passengers were scattered about the building: miscellaneous U.S. soldiers and airmen, mostly in green jungle fatigues, but a few in khakis (apparently going either to or from R&R); some Korean soldiers wearing their habitual air of muscle-bound indifference; and assorted Vietnamese: a tired-looking ARVN captain with his family, several soldiers, three or four civilians (from their white shirts and light green waterproof porkpie hats, lower-level civil officials of some kind), and a number of women in black trousers and white or colored ''Chinese pajama'' jackets, with children, evidently ARVN dependents. All had the look of having waited, and of being prepared to wait indefinitely for their flights.

When Hamilton's flight was called, and the Phan Hoa passengers assembled at the gate to go out to the plane, he noticed with satisfaction that he was the only U.S. officer, so he boarded by the crew door, introduced himself to the pilots, an air force captain and major, and settled himself comfortably on the padded seat across the back of the flight compartment. This is a much more comfortable way to travel in a C-130 than on the web-strap troop seats along the sides of the cargo compartment; one also gets to see out. Loading did not take long, the airplane taxied and then took off.

After a brief glimpse of the shore, then parts of the Phan Cao Valley and the mountains behind it, they were up through a low layer of fair-weather cumulus, on course and climbing to cruising altitude for Saigon. Hamilton admired the skill of the pilots in accomplishing the precisely timed manipulations and adjustments required to do all this. He had his private pilot's ticket, and some acquaintance with flying light aircraft, but the mass of instruments and controls in this aircraft was far beyond anything he had attempted. Since he was, in effect, occupying his present comfortable seat only at the good pleasure of the pilot, he admired in silence and did not inquire.

It took about an hour to get to Saigon. There was a short view of the flat gray-green land and meandering rivers of the Saigon area, the varicolored buildings of the suburbs, mainly russet tile roofs and white walls, the rush and thump of landing, and they were taxiing to the ramp. Hamilton thanked the pilots, unloaded himself and his bag, and walked to the bus stop for the ride into town. Except for more and newer jet fighters and some new construction, apparently barracks for the air force, Tan Son Nhut Airport had hardly changed at all: the same jumble of miscellaneous buildings, rank plant growth, and mixture of Vietnamese and Americans of all categories, some full of purposeful bustle and others numbly waiting.

Neither had the city greatly changed. There was still the contrast between the lush, serene grace of the old French parks, boulevards, palaces, and villas and the rushing din and clatter of traffic and people. The muggy heat and various smells were the same. He saw lots of new construction, mostly apartment houses and office buildings; the bicycles and pedal cyclos of his last trip had been largely replaced by noisy motorbikes and motorcycles, and there were many fewer Americans than he had expected. Apparently the command had made it a point to keep them away from

Saigon as much as possible. Probably a very good idea.

It was getting toward evening by the time he had gotten in town, learned that government quarters would not be available, signed into a little hotel on Tu Do Street, unpacked, and cleaned up. The bar on the ground floor of the hotel was the usual Tu Do Street clip joint, amply garnished with girls of the "I ruv you too much, you buy me drink" variety and a loud jukebox, but the hotel part of the establishment was new and clean, and the plumbing worked. It was also not disastrously expensive. The next order of business was to try to get in touch with Liz Parnell. After some difficulty and with assistance from the desk clerk, he got through to the UBC offices. A male voice, American, answered. He sounded bored.

"UBC Saigon. Jenkins."

"This is Captain Hamilton speaking. May I speak to Miss Parnell?"

"I don't think she's in; just a minute."

Hamilton waited. Thirty seconds passed. The next voice was female, New England, and alert.

"This is Liz Parnell."

"This is Charlie Hamilton speaking. Caroline Atkins said I should look you up when I came to Saigon."

"Oh, yes. She told me about you."

"Nothing scandalous, I hope."

"That depends on your taste in scandal."

Hamilton couldn't think of a comeback, so he changed the subject. "When can we get together? Would this evening be all right?"

"Lemme see . . . I just came back from Tay Ninh

and I have a story to file, but that won't take forever. What time is it now?''

''About five-thirty.''

There was a pause. Hamilton could almost hear the gears turning. On the phone she sounded very much like C. Atkins.

''Would sevenish at the Continental Palace be okay? That's where I live.''

''Outstanding. I admire your taste. I'll be in the sidewalk café. The curfew's at ten, isn't it?''

''Yes. See you at seven.''

''Wonderful.''

Hamilton spent the intervening time wandering around downtown Saigon, savoring the teeming, vibrant atmosphere and refreshing his memory of the street plan. He had early learned the habit of making a thorough reconnaissance, even when he wasn't expecting trouble. Caruso's and the Mayflower were still in business, and the view down the river from the foot of Tu Do Street at sunset was as lovely as ever. Street vendors, shoeshine boys, furtive money changers, and occasional beggars peopled the area as before, but the old techniques of fending them off still worked. It was dark when Hamilton reached the Continental Palace hotel.

The Continental Palace is an old and massive building looking out over an open square. It shares the view with the National Assembly building (built as an opera house under the French) and the Caravelle Hotel (very modern, very French, extremely expensive, and inhabited mainly by visiting firemen and the more affluent members of the press corps). Most of the ground floor of the Continental is taken up by a great, high-ceilinged room with broad arcades on two sides looking out over Tu Do Street and the square in front of the National Assembly. Here there are small round tables and chairs and plump, inscrutable, middle-aged Chinese waiters in high-collared white jackets, who will bring you whatever you want to drink. Hamilton had heard that they would also carry messages, arrange liaisons, and accomplish other tasks of like nature. Through war, revolution, and inflation the Continental had preserved almost untouched the old colonial atmosphere. For this and other reasons, Hamilton liked it and was genuinely pleased that Liz Parnell had picked it for their meeting place, even if she did live there.

It was almost seven when he sat down at a small table in the arcaded sidewalk café, one row in from the side toward the Caravelle; it had an excellent view but, unlike the first row, was inaccessible to street vendors passing by on the sidewalk. Past experience had taught him that "sevenish" could mean anytime between now and nine; also that liquor works much faster in the tropics, so he ordered a lemon soda and settled back to observe his fellowman and enjoy the atmosphere. Perhaps two thirds of the little round tables were empty. At the others were mostly Americans or other non-Vietnamese, some of the men with Vietnamese or Chinese girlfriends. From their clothing, haircuts (or lack thereof), and general style, Hamilton concluded that most of the men were either employees of the various construction contractors in Saigon or reporters, along with a smattering of civil servants. Hamilton was wearing the only military uniform there.

In a corner two Chinese girls in Vietnamese attire were sitting quietly, but not invisibly. Hamilton suspected that it would not be difficult to make their acquaintance or, for a price, to play games with them. He had allowed his eye to rest on them a little too long, and one of them returned his glance with a quick, but very bold, come-on stare. He shook his head slightly and looked away. All very discreet and tidy, and very much better form than what prevailed elsewhere on Tu Do Street. Moments later it started raining, a typical short, violent rainy-season rain shower.

"You must be Captain Hamilton."

She had come up on the oblique behind Hamilton's right shoulder and was standing about three feet from him. He rose and turned.

At a guess she was twenty-six, about five feet four, slender to the point of being flat-chested, tanned, but not too much, regular features in an oval face, large, bright, dark intelligent eyes, short-cut, tousled dark brown hair. She had on a white sleeveless sheath, rather short in the skirt but high in the neck, minute jade earrings and green leather sandals, and no stockings.

"How did you guess? You must be Miss Parnell. Please sit down." He indicated the other chair at their table.

"Please call me Liz."

She sat and crossed one knee over the other. It had

been a long time since Hamilton had seen such well-turned knees.

"Only if you call me Charlie. What will you have to drink?"

She had a lemon soda, and Hamilton ordered a refill.

"Now, what sort of scandal did C. Atkins tell you about me?"

Her eyes were alert and amused, and not uninterested. She shook out a cigarette, offered one to Hamilton, who declined but lit hers, then held up the match for her to blow out.

"You know I'm not supposed to pass on scandal."

"I thought that's what reporting was all about."

"That's business, but talking with you isn't, and C. Atkins is a very old friend. I assume you know she hates to be called 'C. Atkins'?"

"Of course. We almost grew up together. At least we went to college together. I only do it to tease her."

"She said you were a tease."

"Is that part of the scandal?"

"But only part. She also said you were handsome and lecherous, but always a gentleman, which I find rather inscrutable, and intelligent and other things that indicate to me that she has a crush on you."

"C. Atkins and I are very old friends, but let's talk about you. Like whatever moved you to become a war correspondent?"

"I've never wanted to be anything else. Must be some hereditary corruption of the blood."

"Good grief. Anyone in your family in the fourth estate?"

"Not that I know of. Probably a recessive gene."

"Well, now that you're here, how do you like it?"

"Until today, everything was great, traveling around the country, meeting and seeing important people, being right there where the action was, and all that. For the first time in my life I felt like I was really living."

"And then what happened?"

Her eyes were grim and suddenly very frightened. She reached out and took his hand for a moment; her touch was warm and dry and firm. Hamilton surmised that today, for the first time, she had witnessed the grim facts of death in battle. He repressed a shudder.

"Charlie, let's not. Let's talk about you. What brings you to Saigon?"

"Officially, a four-day course, beginning tomorrow, on the how and why of the pacification effort. Actually, my main purpose was to see you."

"What did Caroline tell you about me?"

"Not much, but I have vanity enough to respect her taste in friends. And, frankly, what I find is infinitely more enticing than I had allowed myself to hope."

"Careful now, flattery will get you everywhere."

Hamilton glanced at his watch. "It's a quarter to eight. I suppose if we're going to go somewhere to eat and get back before curfew, we'd better be going."

"I was hoping you'd ask me out to dinner. Where are we going?"

She had finished her drink and was putting her cigarettes into a small green leather purse that matched her sandals and earrings.

"The Mayflower used to be very good, but that was three years ago . . ."

"I'm told it still is, but hard to get into without a reservation. I'll pretend I'm your secretary and call them; I know the desk clerk here."

They stood up.

"Also I have to powder my nose, as it were. See you in a minute." She left.

On his way back from the men's room, Hamilton decided that it was going to be a very pleasant evening, even if nothing happened. He couldn't remember when he had seen better knees, and admitted to a weakness for dark, merry eyes. She also reminded him, hauntingly, of a girl he had known, and been very fond of, in France, years before . . .

Since it was only a couple of blocks and the rain had stopped, they walked to the Mayflower. Already the streets were clearing of people, and the lamplight glistened on the wet, empty sidewalks. They walked briskly, without haste, in the tepid evening air; each breath seemed to bring in a different smell, sometimes strong and pungent, sometimes faint and fragrant. The tropic night, even in places far away from battle, always seemed to Hamilton to be full of the implication of stealthy violence, so they walked in silence, Hamilton sensing the night with the feral alertness that had become a valued habit, and Liz apparently reflecting on some private train of thought.

The Mayflower was warm and bright, with cream-colored walls and very closely spaced tables. Thanks to Liz's phone call, they had only a little wait before being seated. The food was a passable imitation of French cuisine, the Beaujolais was genuine, and all the traditional trappings were at hand. It came out that Liz and C. Atkins had both grown up in the same, mainly Irish and Italian suburb of Boston, and had been classmates in the same parochial high school. Each was an only child. Though they had gone to different colleges, they had been close for a very long time. Hamilton gathered that Liz shared C. Atkins's lack of sympathy for their respective parents' unquestioning submissiveness to the clergy, without loss of a more intellectual loyalty to the Catholic Church as a historic and social institution.

Liz had been working for UBC about two years, mostly in New York, and had been in-country a little over a month. Hamilton was very glad to find out that she would be covering activities in the Saigon area for the next several days.

The cheese was real, the bread as good as any in France, and they both went very well with the last of the Beaujolais. Liz was knowledgeably appreciative without parading erudition, and the bill, although high, was less than Hamilton had been dreading.

"I suggest we toddle back to the Continental for an after-dinner drink. We have time for at least one before curfew."

"Good thought."

They strolled back, hand in hand, through the wet, empty streets; the wine and warm, spicy food had done their magic—even Hamilton was almost relaxed. But there was still no desire to make conversation in the tropic darkness. When they got to the Continental, Hamilton was heading for their old table when Liz laid a hand on his arm. He stopped and turned. Her eyes were solemn and very bright.

"I have some Cognac up in my room. That way we won't have to worry about the curfew."

"Wonderful."

"Let's walk up. I don't like the elevator."

Liz lived on the fourth floor. The stairs were broad and not steep; on each floor the rooms were connected by an open arcade overlooking a back garden, rather than by a corridor. They mounted the stairs in silence. Her room was old-fashioned in the tradition of European hotels: large, high-ceilinged, with a ceiling fan and a small balcony looking out over the roof of the National Assembly. She poured Cognac for both of them; they drifted to the little balcony and stood side-by-side, close together, looking out over the rooftops. The hum of the city seemed far away. Somewhere, on the other side of the river, a flare winked on, and then two more. Liz looked up at him.

"Are they under attack?"

"I doubt it. Probably just nervous. For the moment, at least, it's not our problem."

"I know, it just seems so strange. Here we are in the middle of a war, and out there, where we can almost actually see it, men are fighting and probably dying, and you and I calmly have a drink together and go out to dinner . . ."

"Just like real people in the real world." He took up her thought. "But why not? Our being grim and dreadful here won't make things any less grim and dreadful out there. It will only make each of us less able to survive and do our jobs."

"But it's so horrible." Suddenly she was clinging to him, sobbing. He held her for a moment until she calmed down a little, then looked into very bright, tear-filled eyes.

"What is it, Liz?"

"They killed those men at Tay Ninh today. . . . Here I am, supposed to be a hard-bitten war correspondent and news hen, blubbering like a baby, but I can't help it, and . . . and I don't want to be alone tonight."

"Pray God you never get that tough."

He kissed her long and hard and slow. She stopped shaking and was clinging to him with amazing strength. He turned and gently guided her back into the room. With his free hand he moved the brandy glasses inside and closed the shutters. Then, holding her slightly away from him, he looked her squarely in the face.

"Liz, you've had a horrible experience, and you're very vulnerable tonight, and . . . and I can still get back to my hotel before the curfew."

It was the first time he had been close to a girl since leaving the States. As a male animal, he wanted her desperately and sensed that she knew this and wanted him, but, after all, we have our code. Even so, it struck him as horribly old-fashioned and corny as he said it. She was looking at him steadily with bright, frightened eyes.

"Stay with me tonight."

That settled it. He took her in his arms, kissed her again slowly, and gently unzipped her dress down the back. Her hands were inside his shirt making it very clear that she wanted him as strongly as he wanted her. They separated for a moment while she finished taking off her dress and bra. The white sheath had not been a fake: her proportions were lithe and slender and strong, if, Hamilton noted without regret, a little flat-chested. In the immemorial gesture, he picked her up in his arms and set her down on the bed, then started turning off the lights. She stopped him.

"Charlie, leave one of them on. I want to see you. That baggy uniform isn't the real you. I know it."

So he did, and she did. It was a big, square, French hotel bed with a brass frame and a very deep mattress. Hamilton reflected that, whatever else, the French do know certain things about certain things, like designing beds. . . . The first time, everything happened too fast, but that wasn't the bed's fault, rather that it had been so long since the last time Hamilton had made love. The second time, about an hour later, he had much better control over his reactions, so Liz had a climax also.

Afterward, they were lying close, her head on his shoulder, relaxed, happy and sleepy.

"Charlie, you must think I'm a dreadfully loose character, hopping into bed with you like this on our very first date."

The reply was equally traditional, if, in this case, also quite true: "Liz, I think you're wonderful."

"Now I know what C. Atkins meant when she said you were lecherous but always a gentleman."

"I don't know how she could have known. We were never lovers."

"She's a bright girl and can figure out all sorts of things without having tried them."

"Do you think she knows what she's missing?"

"Of course not, and I'm not going to tell her. At least not about you."

"Now you're getting adhesive."

"Every woman needs a man to cling to."

"And every man needs a woman who needs him."

"And you make me very happy." She wriggled contentedly.

"I guess we better try to get some sleep."

The next day, Hamilton moved out of his hotel and into Liz's room at the Continental. He was even on time for the first class of the course on the pacification effort.

The week went very fast, and for some reason Hamilton remembered very little of the content of the pacification course. Liz came out to see him off on his flight back to Phan Hoa; in fact, she drove him out in one of UBC's jeeps. He thought she looked very brave and jaunty in boots, camouflage fatigues, and a floppy jungle hat. He had much less of a liking for the fact that she, too, was going back up-country very soon, but in a different direction and to places of danger, and that they would not be again together for far too long a time. She was trying to be matter-of-fact about the whole thing, but the act was not a success; she only cried a little when he kissed her good-bye, and quite a lot more when she got back to her jeep.

"Well, how was Saigon?"

It was Clark, with his jeep, who had come out to pick up Hamilton at the air base.

"It's the Paris of the Orient."

IV.

SHOP TALK
AT THE REX BAR

For the return trip to Phan Hoa, Hamilton had ridden a C-123. This aircraft, which looks a little like a scaled-down, two-engined C-130, has no extra room at all in the flight compartment, so Hamilton made himself as comfortable as possible in one of the web-strap troop seats. The five nights with Liz had been magnificent: passionate, tender, and very frank; he could still feel the warmth of her against him and her hungry desire for his body. He felt pleasantly drained and doubted whether he could have kept up the pace the sixth night. No doubt he was going to have plenty of time up-country to allow his virile powers to recuperate. She had promised to try to get an assignment that would justify a trip to his part of the country, but had not sounded optimistic; they had also discussed going to Hong Kong or Bangkok together on R&R, but that would have to be at least four months away . . .

Except for a brief encounter after a late party at college, which had left her hurt, bleeding, and full of terrified remorse, this was Liz's second affair. Hamilton had gathered from her somewhat oblique references to it that the first had been shortly after she got out of college and had lasted only a few months; she had thought she was desperately in love, but had found that the man, an older reporter, was lying to her, regarded her merely as a convenient piece of tail, and was concurrently sleeping with at least two other women. Their breakup had left scars, and since then she had kept men at a distance and avoided physical or emotional involvements. Hamilton deferred the decision on what to do when and if she started talking about getting married.

Wednesday evening, she had to attend a "command performance" cocktail party for the press corps given by the GVN Ministry of Information, to which Hamilton had not, of course, been invited. For lack of anything better, he decided to go over to the Rex BOQ for dinner and maybe a drink before or afterward. The Rex is a large, eight-story converted hotel; it dominates the corner of Nguyen Hue and Le Loi, a major intersection with a traffic circle, circular grass plot, and fountain. The residents are mostly colonels, but lower-ranking officers are admitted to the Officers Open Mess upstairs, with its restaurant and terrace bar. Security in front of the building was considerably more elaborate than the last time, and the elevator, fortunately, was working.

The cocktail area occupies an open expanse of flat roof adjoining the corner toward the traffic circle; it is covered by a permanent awning made of corrugated, translucent plastic sheets held up by metal frames. At the outer corner of this area is a small stage or bandstand, and the bar is at the diagonally opposite corner. Since the plastic awning is about sixteen feet up, the view over the roofs of the city and across the flat country on the other side of the river is superb, even from the bar. It was about sunset when Hamilton arrived, and he was treated to the lovely splendor of towering slate-blue cumulus against orange-pink and lemon yellow. He stood for a moment by the parapet admiring the view and the sunset, thinking what a horrid waste it was that he couldn't share it with Liz, then strolled to the bar for a drink.

It was a general belief if you remain long enough at the bar of the Rex BOQ, you will eventually see everyone (at least everyone even remotely connected with the Officer Corps or the war effort) whom you have ever known. So Hamilton ordered a Bourbon on the rocks from the Chinese bartender, perched on a stool, and took a look around. The area between the bar and the bandstand was taken up with rows and rows of little tables and chairs, possibly half of them occupied. It seemed to Hamilton that there were a lot more civil servants, contractors' employees, and other civilians here, and fewer military, than had been the case during his previous tour; he did not regard them, generally, as the type of people who should be included in any great quantity in an officers' club such as the Rex. Many had not taken the trouble to wash up and change, and quite a few had brought along Chinese or Vietnamese dates, some of them obvious whores. There was also a lot more gross language than Hamilton, who admitted to being starchy on this point, thought proper for the inside of an officers' club. Apparently the military, at least the kind he was likely to have been acquainted with, were elsewhere, probably up-country trying to get on with the war.

He had about decided to get supper, go back to the Continental, and write letters or read a paperback until Liz returned from the cocktail party when a hoarse, resonant, baritone voice greeted him from behind: "Well, I never expected to see Charlie Hamilton in a low dive like this."

Hamilton turned and stood up off the barstool to greet his old boss, Colonel Harlan Sprague.

"Good evening, sir. It's a real pleasure to see you again. You're looking well."

They shook hands. Sprague was a great bear of a man with close-cut sandy-red hair turning gray, strong, almost heavy features, a permanently burned-in reddish suntan on what had been a florid complexion to begin with, and small, perpetually alert, amused blue-gray eyes. He was wearing short-sleeved khakis (at that time the normal duty uniform at MACV Headquarters), with General Staff collar brass, no ribbons (he had pungent views on "fruit salad") or decorations other than U.S. and French Army jump wings.

With the Spragues, father and son, the dividing

line between fact and legend was hard to discern. Harlan's father, Major General John Carlisle Sprague, had been a very successful large-scale wheat farmer and entrepreneur in the Midwest, and was one of the very few National Guard generals who had not been relieved at the start of World War II. The reason for this exception was said to be that no one, including General Marshall, then Chief of Staff of the Army, had the nerve to confront old Sprague when he was really angry. Instead, a few Leavenworth-trained staff officers were assigned to make sure that reports, operations orders, and the like were in proper format, and old Sprague's division carried its full share and then some in three years of tough jungle fighting in New Guinea, New Britain, and the Philippines. What old Sprague called his "cold-roast professionals" were appalled by his gruff, breezy informality with everyone from General MacArthur down to the last Pfc, his prolonged absences from the Division Command Post (he was usually up with one of the front-line rifle companies), and total disregard for established procedures and the "school solution" to tactical problems. They were also rather awed by old Sprague's immense energy and stamina in the muggy heat of the jungle, complete disregard for his own comfort and safety, and uncanny knack of knowing when, where and what the enemy was going to do and of being there ahead of them and in force. Old Sprague was a driver, who expected everyone in sight to share his own boundless stamina and enthusiasm, fiercely loyal to his people, even the cold-roast professionals, on whom he relied completely to see that the technical side of things got done. Needless to say, he was not promoted or offered a higher command during the war, and the postwar army had no need for tribal warrior chiefs.

Harlan took after his father, and an Infantry Division had been deemed too small a place for two such characters to coexist in harmony. He had walked out of Northern Burma with Stilwell and back in with Merrill's marauders; he had also been involved in training the Chinese at Ramgarh. Hamilton had heard that the younger Sprague had had to leave the army in 1949 over an obscure matter in which he had made an issue out of putting loyalty to one of his sergeants above compliance with the express desires of his battalion commander.

It was also alleged that Harlan Sprague had served at least one five-year enlistment in the Foreign Legion, had earned his jump wings the hard way by parachuting, without prior training, into Dien Bien Phu, had escaped the Vietminh and walked out through Laos with two other Legionnaires, a big black Senegalese rifleman, and the Eurasian mistress of one of the French colonels. He spoke impressively colloquial French and Vietnamese and could make himself understood in Burmese and several Chinese dialects. He had returned to the American army in 1957, mostly as a result of the efforts of a very senior general who had served in New Guinea under old Sprague, and decided that the army needed him. He was now, oddly, a full colonel, and no more popular with the cold-roast professionals than his father had been.

Colonel Sprague had ordered a beer (he never drank anything stronger) and a refill for Hamilton, and insisted on paying for both. They had taken their drinks to one of the tables next to the parapet, some distance from the bandstand, where a combo from Manila was setting up to provide what Hamilton feared would be noisy background music for the evening.

"Well, Charlie, what the hell are you doing in Saigon?"

"It's the four-day pacification course, sir. I have a subsector in Phan Hoa Province."

"Sounds like a good excuse to come to the big city. What's it like in the subsector?"

"Pretty interesting so far, sir; I've only been there two months. The scenery is spectacular, and the land isn't all rice paddies and marsh like the Delta. What do they have you doing, sir?"

"I have an outfit called MACV Concept Analysis Team, MACCAT for short. Our stated mission is to analyze operational and tactical concepts and prepare in-depth studies for the MACV staff."

Hamilton recognized the hooded, conspiratorial look in the little gray-blue eyes. It was very unlikely that Sprague would let himself get trapped shuffling papers and analyzing other people's battles when there was a war to fight, especially this kind of war. So he asked, "And what do you really do, sir, if I may ask?"

Sprague took a long sip of beer, looked hard at Hamilton for a moment, and said, "You know the answer to that has to be classified. Let's go in to dinner.''

At dinner they talked of other things, and Hamilton wondered just what sort of ''spook outfit'' went under the name Concept Analysis Team. Whatever it was, it was probably a lot more interesting than the subsector, especially if Colonel Sprague was running it. It seemed to Hamilton that Sprague's reply to his question was not only discreet and very cagey but might also be the beginnings of a come-on.

''Sir, is it really true that you were at Dien Bien Phu with the Legion and escaped the Vietminh?''

Hamilton had been wanting to ask that question for years.

''So you've heard that particular bit of gossip?''

''Well, the gist of it, sir, and some rather bizarre elaborations.''

''It was a very bizarre and tragic business. The night it was all over with, I and three other Legionnaires, two Germans who claimed they were Swiss, and a Spaniard, made it out of the west side of what had been the perimeter; we had seen too much of what the Viets did to their prisoners. Well, one of the Germans got strayed, and we never saw him again— probably the Viets got him or he died in the jungle— and as you've probably heard, we picked up two more people. One of them was a big black buck from the Senegal named Ibrahim; he could hear and see and smell and, I think, feel things better than any of us. Without him we would almost certainly have been gathered in at least four different times. Also a lot of the Meos, who had never seen a black man before, took him for something supernatural and were careful to be good to us, which helped. The other was a Eurasian girl named Thérèse, who was no use in the jungle, but would certainly have had her throat cut if the Viets had caught her, so we had to take her along. Some French colonel, who should have had better sense, had had her smuggled out there; he later got killed in the fighting, I don't know how. By the way it's not true that I had a child by this girl. She was already two months pregnant when we found her; she had a miscarriage on the trail and damn near died. She was very brave, as well as a very good-looking woman if your taste runs to Eurasians. Last I heard she was running a café in Phnom Penh."

Sprague didn't add that he had borrowed money from his father to set her up in this business, and that he had had a very enjoyable affair with her while he was on leave from the Legion. He went on:

"I was a *caporal-chef*, which made me the ranking man and therefore in charge; I also knew something about the hill tribes in Laos, who really aren't much different from the people in Northern Burma. So we got along more or less and finally walked into a French outpost at an obscure little place called Ban Peng. As the crow flies it was only about sixty miles, but it took three weeks. I don't like to think about what probably happened to those brave, loyal Meos for helping us escape the Viets."

They had finished dessert and coffee, and Hamilton sensed that the usually closemouthed Sprague had more to say.

"How about an after-dinner drink, sir? It's my turn."

The band was quite loud, their old table was empty, and a little Chinese waitress was there to take their orders: another beer for Sprague and Cognac for Hamilton, who insisted on paying. They sat for a moment in reflective silence, then Sprague began speaking again, very quietly:

"Look, Charlie, the trouble with this war is that nearly everybody is out here for the wrong reason. About 80 percent are here because they have to be, and are just counting off the time and rocking along until they can go home. At least another 15 percent are here because they think it will be good for their careers, so they go around trying to make themselves look good and hoping for a Legion of Merit and a promotion on the 10 percent list. Most of them have no more real aptitude or inclination for the kind of war you have to fight to get the job done than I have for designing stained-glass windows. The other 5 percent—if there are even that many—come under two headings with no clear dividing line: first, the idealists or romantics who really believe that stopping these bastards is a cause worthy of a personal commitment, or regard war as the Great Adventure, or have to prove to themselves their own manliness again and again, or whatever, and, second, the real fighters, who are glad to go anywhere, and do anything and make a good clean well-run operation out of it, mostly for the satisfaction of knowing that they're doing a damn tough and dangerous job in a first-class manner and causing some real damage to

the enemy by doing it. And they don't give a damn
for medals or generals or pompous MACV staffniks,
and they can be very difficult subordinates.

"Of this 5 percent, there are quite a few in the
Special Forces and the aviation outfits, especially the
gunship and medevac pilots, and damned few anywhere else, except my outfit, which doesn't have
anything else, at least where it counts."

"Sir, I hope you don't have these people writing
staff studies all day long."

"Of course not. You have to collect the information before you write it up. Mostly in the back hills
along the border with Laos and Cambodia. In some
places where the PRU can't or won't operate, we
also go in after the infrastructure."

He paused, apparently decided that no one was
within earshot and that the band was loud enough to
neutralize any possible listening device, and went on:
"We have what we call Combined Reconnaissance
Units, or CRU, alias Coordination and Research
Units, about one-third U.S., mostly people with Spe-
cial Forces or Ranger experience, and the rest mostly
Montagnards of various tribes, Cambodians and
Nungs—very few ethnic Vietnamese—all of them
very well-paid mercenaries, but they earn it."

"In-country, or . . . ?"

"Strictly in-country, unfortunately. The rest belongs in fee simple absolute to Big Brother. I couldn't
even go in to say hello to my friends up there without
causing a major scandal. But there's plenty to do in-
country, and it's interesting work."

"It sounds a lot better than what you said before dinner, sir."

"If I were really doing what my cover story says I'm doing, I'd take to drink or little Chinese girls in Cholon."

He sipped his beer and put down the glass with deliberation.

"I could definitely use you in this outfit."

"But, sir, I'm not even airborne, much less Ranger or Special Forces qualified."

"Spare me the list of things you say you can't do. I know what you can do. I know a lot more than you probably think I do about what went on between you and Victor Renaudin and the Wirets, and others, in Bordeaux, and I respect your discretion in not burdening your boss by telling me about it directly. Look, I can get all the brave, tough, unanalytical paratroopers I need, but officers with your abilities are hard to come by. We operate a couple of very good little training schools up-country."

"And the Vietnamese, sir?"

"Theoretically we're part of the ARVN Airborne Command, and there's a couple of ARVN officers at each of our base camps, mostly for liaison with the local officials and so that the GVN isn't completely left out of the picture. The indig on the teams are almost entirely not ethnic Vietnamese. We pay better than the CIDG, so we get the pick of the crop, and really train and lead them. They may not be as good as the Gurkhas, but they're up in that class."

Hamilton realized that every good commander thinks that his outfit is the best going, and that this was a recruiting pitch. He was also wondering about how much Sprague really did know about his relationships with Victor Renaudin and the various members of the Wiret family. The last time he had worked for Colonel Sprague, they had stubbornly battered their way to a relationship of very solid mutual trust and respect. He was also not a little flattered that Sprague wanted him.

"I'm for it, sir, but how do I get pried loose from my present job?"

"Let me have a try at that. I should know what the form looks like by noontime Friday. Can you meet me here for lunch?"

"Delighted to, sir. And thank you very much."

"Don't thank me until I deliver the goods. It isn't going to be too easy; CORDS is adhesive as hell, and the J-1 people are not always cooperative."

"Sir, I never knew you to let yourself get scared by a bunch of bureaucrats, in or out of uniform."

"It gets worse every year. Those people, especially the civilians, have kinds of power you just can't work against. You play by their rules or you don't do business with them; and their first rule is that they always win. And they're a lot more interested in preserving and building their little empires and in their next promotion than in fighting the goddamn war."

"You had the TASCOM bureaucracy pretty well lined up."

"Yeah, that took a long time and a lot of very tricky maneuvering, *and* they were military, so you could talk to them, even the ring knockers. Also,

I've only been here three months, and fairly busy with other things. . . . Anyway, Charlie, I'll give it a try, but don't get too hopeful.''

Lunch on Friday was not a festive occasion. The MACV-CORDS position had been that, in the interest of continuity on the job, advisory personnel should spend their whole tours where first assigned, and they had flatly refused to release Hamilton until he had spent at least nine months in Phan Hoa Province. Even this was a concession, extracted by means of considerable pressure and cajolement. They had started out insisting that he stay in place the full year.

"And that," Colonel Sprague wound up, "is really no concession at all, since they jolly well know that there's no profit at all in assigning you to CAT for only three months."

"What if I extend for six months?"

"You'd better think that one over. How long have you been in country?"

"About two months, sir."

"Well, you've plenty of time to decide. Not that I don't need you now, or seven months from now, but . . ."

"I know what you mean, sir. . . . I assume that you knew I was very fond of Michèle Wiret."

Her resemblance to Liz had refreshed Hamilton's memory of their relationship, including the way it had ended.

"I had noticed. Don't tell me you feel you still have a debt to pay on that behalf?"

"Something like that, sir, and I do like the idea of working with your 5 percent."

"Okay, when and if you do put in your papers, be sure to state that they're conditioned on your being assigned to CAT, and send me a copy, by mail and not through channels, so I can work on it from this end. I wouldn't put it past those bastards to extend you six months and let you rot at Dong Hai."

"Dong Hai really isn't that bad, sir."

"You're not planning to extend for the privilege of spending another six months at Dong Hai?"

"That would be carrying devotion to the idea of continuity a bit far."

They finished lunch and it was time for Hamilton to go back to class.

"Look, Charlie, next time you're in town, do look me up . . . if you're not too busy corrupting the press corps."

"Sir! What gave you such an idea?"

"I've been in the business for a long time. She seems like a nice girl, but . . . well, have fun."

He had been delicate enough not to mention her resemblance to Michèle Wiret, or the fact that an officer assigned to an operation like CAT would be extremely well advised not to have any close contact with the fourth estate. Hamilton told him he would always be welcome at Dong Hai if he ever came that way, and they shook hands and parted.

And there was no question at all in Hamilton's mind that he would extend, and take the job with Colonel Sprague. Of course he never mentioned either Colonel Sprague or Liz to anyone in Phan Hoa

Province, and in his next letter to C. Atkins, he
limited himself to stating that he had looked her up
and found her to be a very pleasant person; he also
thanked C. Atkins for having such good taste in
friends and for the introduction.

Hamilton and Chambers each had a beer and were sitting in silence, not the tense silence of strangers or adversaries, but one composed partly of a natural courtesy and reticence, reinforced by the fact that in a "normal" military context, officers and NCOs do not mix socially, and partly of the fact that they had really long since talked themselves out and realized that life at such very close quarters can be made tolerable only by exceptional forbearance all around. So each meditated on his own thoughts and listened to the small, unexciting sounds that, if anything, made more acute the great rural silence. The sky was heavily overcast and fast draining of light since the sun had set. It was going to be a very dark night.

In the three months since they had parted, he and Liz had exchanged friendly letters. It had not been possible for Liz to promote a trip to Phan Hoa, nor for Hamilton to get to Saigon. Hamilton had requested R&R in Bangkok in about two months and sent her the dates; she would very probably be able to join him there. He had also put in his papers for an extension and transfer to CAT, hoping that Colonel Sprague would be able to enforce the promise by CORDS to release him after nine months.

Within the district, nothing much had happened since the last monthly meeting. The 309 Company had been replaced on the hill by another outfit, the 608 Company, of whom Hamilton had mixed reports. A new Revolutionary Development (RD) Team had been assigned to the district a few days before and were now located in Thanh Lanh hamlet with the mission of providing security and the beginnings of a better life for the inhabitants. The hamlet was located south of the big hill and on the other side of a railroad embankment that ran along the west side of Dong Hai town. Since everything west of this hamlet for about forty miles was strictly "Marlboro country," one platoon of the 608 Company was in the hamlet for additional protection. Except for two sniping incidents and the discovery of a mine in the road between Dong Hai and Phuoc Tre (which Hamilton and Chambers had blown in place), the enemy had not been heard from since the attack on 309 Company and the subsector compound about a month before. Charlie was probably busy moving his more vulnerable installations out of the range fan of the eight-inch battery at Phuoc Tre.

"Sir, I don't like those clouds. If something happens tonight, we won't be able to use the Spooky."

"That's why we have the mortars . . . but I know what you mean."

Things had been quiet too long, and neither the 608 Company nor the RD Team had been tested in this district. The VC were quite aware that if the RD effort were a success, their own hold on the country people, the very basis of their power and hopes for eventual victory, would be lost. The RD Teams were armed and had had some military training, and their members were generally younger and fitter than the run of Regional Force and especially Popular Force troops, but. . . . Captain Lan, accompanied by Hamilton, had spent most of the preceding afternoon with the RF platoon and RD team in Thanh Lanh, apparently making sure that they had a good, coordinated defense plan, and Hamilton had made a visit for similar purposes to the artillery at Phuoc Tre.

The overcast made the tepid night air seem stuffy and oppressive. Hamilton had finished his beer.

"Who's on the radio tonight?"

"Parelli's on now, sir, Harley has the midnight-to-three shift, and I have the last shift," Chambers said.

"Well, I think I'll turn in. If something happens, it's nice to get a little sleep."

"Very good, sir. I'll be turning in in a little while."

Lan had not come out on the porch this evening, as he sometimes did. After his supper, he had toured the compound, then gone into his quarters. Hamilton checked his weapons and equipment, said good night to Parelli, took off his boots, and lay down. Usually, when it had seemed clear that any particular night would be a likely time for Charlie to do something, he didn't. Hamilton couldn't think of any reasonable additional precautions to take, reflected that there was no profit in worrying, and eventually got to sleep.

He woke up with a start shortly before midnight. Since he could not identify what had wakened him, he lay there and listened, wide awake and uneasy. After a moment, there were three or four more shots, a short burst from an automatic weapon, what might have been a hand grenade, all quite some distance away.

Parelli came in and said, "Sir, I think they've got contact down in Thanh Lanh. The Dai-uy's up."

Parelli was twenty-two, slender, with a boyish, Latin handsomeness. Hamilton got up, collected his battle harness and weapon, and went outside; Parelli had already gone to waken the other members of the team. Chambers was at the radio.

"Sleepy Onion Zulu, this is Sleepy Onion Echo. Over."

"Echo, this is Zulu. Over."

Hamilton didn't recognize the voice, but was thankful that tonight, at least, they had communications all the way through to Phan Hoa.

"This is Echo, we got contact at Thanh Lanh. I spell—Tango Hotel Alfa November Hotel, break, Lima Alfa November Hotel—hamlet. Coordinates Golf Zulu"—he paused to glance at the map on the radio table—"eight niner niner eight zero one. No other details at this time. Over."

"This is Zulu, Roger. Do you need assistance? Over."

"This is Echo. Negative at this time. Will report further details when I have them. Over."

"Roger, will be standing by, out."

Captain Lan was standing beside Hamilton, in uniform, including boots, but bareheaded, with carbine. He looked impatient.

"What's up, Dai-uy?"

"I don't know! Maybe many VC in Thanh Lanh. Get rice from people. I think RD Team not stay in hamlet."

Abruptly he turned away and stepped over to the radio bunker, squatted by the entrance, and conversed briefly in Vietnamese with someone inside, then came back to Hamilton.

"I go find out. You come?"

"Sure, let's go."

Chambers was coming out of the radio room, in fatigues and shower shoes, with battle harness and carbine. Hamilton sent him back to get one of the handy-talkie radios and make sure that Parelli, at the radio, had another one that worked. So they set out: Lan; his bodyguard, a wiry, middle-aged PF corporal; one of Lan's RF sergeants; Hamilton; and Sergeant Chambers, five in all. It took quite a lot of zigzagging and careful stepping to get past the movable barbed-wire barriers across the entrance to the compound; then they turned left and headed down the silent and apparently deserted street leading toward where the trouble was. Their movement was silent and fairly cautious, Lan's bodyguard leading, then Lan, then Hamilton and Chambers, with the RF sergeant as rear point. If Lan knew how far the VC had penetrated the town, he had not advised Hamilton. They passed the market square and finally got to an intersection at the foot of the street where it passed out under a gate and became the road leading to Tuy Cau, Phan Hoa, and the rest of the outside world. There was also a street to the west there, running along the south side of Dong Hai town, across the railway embankment and through Thanh Lanh.

In the shadows under a great tree at this intersection Lan found and talked several minutes with several Vietnamese, apparently members of the Popular Force Platoon securing this side of Dong Hai. Lan came back to where Hamilton was standing.

"Well, Dai-uy, what's up?"

"NVA, maybe one company, maybe one platoon,

in Thanh Lanh. RF Platoon over there." He indicated the general area where the railway embankment stretched across some open rice fields between Dong Hai and the river. "RD Team—I don't know. NVA get rice from people."

"Hell, Dai-uy, if it's only a platoon, let's get out your 68th Platoon and run 'em off."

It is an ancient cavalry maxim: When in doubt, attack. More often than not, it works. Lan stood silent for a moment, then grinned.

"We go get PF Platoon and run 'em off."

Lan spoke briefly to the Vietnamese under the tree, and they headed back up the street.

Back at the compound, they found out that a hamlet about two miles northeast of Dong Hai was also under attack, reportedly by an enemy platoon. They were not, however, in serious danger of being overrun and, except for fire support by the mortars, which was already going on, there wasn't much that could be done for them. While Lan was issuing a string of orders and generally getting his palace guard platoon rounded up, Hamilton and Chambers went inside to get their boots on and advise the others of what was going on. Hamilton decided not to broadcast an additional status report at this stage, as Charlie might be listening, and Doc had already sent out a preliminary report on the problem in the northeast corner of the valley. Eventually, after some argument (all of them wanted to go along), Hamilton decided that he, Chambers, and Harley should go, and Doc and Parelli remain at the compound. He had selected Chambers because of his prior experience in this type of operation, and Harley mainly because he was the only one who could hold down an M-14 rifle on full automatic, and had one; he was also to carry one of the radios. Hamilton had Doc and Parelli move the other radio into Lan's radio bunker just in case.

It was close to one o'clock when they moved out from the compound, the PF troops spaced out in two files, one each side of the street, with Lan's little command group and the Americans in the middle. It was as overcast as ever, but the moon had risen and a little light filtered through the clouds. They moved quickly but cautiously and without haste, and made very little noise, turned the corner by the big tree and the gate, and headed toward Thanh Lanh.

Since he had heard no shots for nearly an hour, Hamilton was beginning to wonder if the enemy hadn't just quietly faded back. But when the lead element rounded a slight bend into sight of the railway embankment, there were two quick shots—from the sounds very clearly not friendly—followed by a long burst with an RPD machine gun and a lot of other small-arms fire. The lead squad was apparently pinned down, and, of course, the rest of the column had stopped, faded off the road, and gotten down. Lan was by a tree down a little bank on the south side of the road with his radio operator, talking on the radio. Hamilton and Harley, who had faded into the shelter of a low wall in front of a house on the north side of the road, sprinted across and flopped down beside Lan, drawing several shots and a short burst from the RPD en route. Neither was hit, but it was clear that whoever was on top of the railway embankment had no intention at all of fading back. Hamilton looked around for Chambers and saw that he was behind the tree next west of the one sheltering Lan and Hamilton.

After several minutes on the radio, Lan stopped abruptly and turned to Hamilton with a smile (Hamilton could sense the smile in the darkness) and said, "Two minutes."

"Dai-uy, you need some eight-inch west side of Thanh Lanh when VC pull back?"

"Not now. Later."

Hamilton got on his radio, not a little relieved at being able to do more than just come along for the ride. He called Doc: "Sleepy Onion Echo, this is Echo Six. Over."

"Echo Six, this is Echo. Over."

"This is Six, call Jerky Possum and have them stand by to fire concentrations Echo One through Echo Four. Over."

A new voice broke into the net.

"Echo Six, this is Jerky Possum Six. I monitored your last transmission and will be ready to fire in zero two. Over."

"This is Echo Six. That's great. Roger, out."

Thank God for that. Captain Rodman and the eight-inch were up in Hamilton's net and apparently had already laid their ponderous cannon in the general direction.

At this moment several things happened in quick sequence: The enemy, possibly sensing that his position was not quite as secure as it seemed, started intermittently raking the street with fire. It was noisy, including some nasty-sounding ricochets, and showy with muzzle flashes and the occasional blue tracer, but not particularly dangerous, as everyone was down, and it permitted Hamilton and several others to pinpoint the location of the RPD. They were behind the stump of what had been some sort of railway fixture, just at the north of where the road went over the embankment. Next, an illuminating round from one of the 81mm mortars at subsector popped almost directly over the crossing and the RF Platoon out in the rice field astride the embankment opened fire and began working forward. Simultaneously, someone got busy with a machine gun from the south end of the 608 Company's position on the big hill and began raking the top and west side of the embankment. Hamilton judged that they were loaded about one and four tracer and ball, and firing rather longer bursts than are considered good for a Browning machine gun. The enemy's fire began to slacken; things did seem to be getting hot on the embankment.

Lan said, "Fourth flare, we go."

"Okay, Dai-uy." Harley had heard, and no doubt Chambers would go along when they stood up and charged.

At the fourth flare, the machine gun on the hill fell silent, and Lan stood up and charged the RPD firing his carbine full-automatic. The rest of the first wave of the assault consisted of Hamilton, Chambers, Harley (firing the M-14 from the hip on full automatic), and Lan's bodyguard. A moment later the rest of the platoon were also up joining in the assault, but not firing for fear of hitting the five in front. It was perhaps sixty yards to the embankment, which they covered at a dead run, firing long bursts all the way, then pitched grenades over the embankment, crouched while they exploded and went over the top. There were several dead bodies and a few weapons here and there on the far side, but the rest had apparently lost their nerve and departed north along the embankment, probably heading across the brushy lower slopes of the big hill for a safer place. They fired a few shots after fleeing shadows, then Lan sent two squads of the PF Platoon to pursue them a little way up the tracks. Hamilton did not feel inclined to advise a pell-mell pursuit, at night, of an enemy platoon which could well have been sent as bait.

The Regional Force, meanwhile, had formed a skirmish line south of Thanh Lanh and were cautiously clearing the hamlet. In this they were joined by part of the RD Team, several of whose members reappeared. Hamilton conferred hurriedly with Lan, agreed on possible enemy routes of withdrawal, and called some eight-inch on them. Lan's mortars were doing the same.

"Sir, I think they got me."

It was Chambers, who had come up beside Hamilton and was now standing, his carbine slung, holding his left shoulder with his right hand.

"Let me put a dressing on that."

Hamilton tied on two Carlisle dressings, one over each hole (the bullet had apparently gone clean through), and noted that in the rush he had no recollection of seeing Chambers get hit or drop out. Then he got on the radio to the compound:

"Echo, this is Echo Six. Over."

"Echo Six, this is Echo. Over."

"This is Six. They got Echo Five, so we'll need a dustoff, possibly more than one. Over."

"This is Echo. Wilco, out."

Lan and his bodyguard and two others were making a thorough search of the brush along the west side of the embankment north of the road crossing. They found and killed two NVA who had been hiding, apparently waiting for a better moment for their departure. The RPD had disappeared; its former location was marked by a pile of empty cartridge cases and the distinctive black metal link-belts used in that weapon. The other PF troops were giving first aid to their several wounded, collecting weapons dropped by casualties on both sides, and locating and checking dead bodies.

Harley handed Hamilton the radio headset. "It's for you, sir."

His rifle, still with bayonet fixed, if unbloodied, seemed to grow out of the end of his right arm. He seemed very calm. The voice on the radio was Parelli's.

"Echo Six, this is Echo. Meat wagon on the way. Over."

"This is Six, Roger, out."

Hamilton went over to Chambers, who was sitting beside the road where it sloped up the embankment. He noticed that the old soldier had picked a spot where he would not be silhouetted against the sky. Hamilton and Harley squatted next to him almost as if, by their closeness, they could infuse some new strength into the wounded man. The mortars had ceased firing illumination, and in the dark it was hard to see Chambers's face. He spoke to Harley; the voice was calm, quiet, and sounded very tired.

"Would you light me up a cigarette, please?"

Harley lit up one of his own, took a puff on it, and put it between Chambers's lips. The sergeant, who was still holding his wounded shoulder, took a long draw on it and exhaled through his nose. On Harley's radio, Hamilton could hear Parelli calling in for the medevac. He felt a wave of guilt at thus exposing this old soldier, who had surely had his fair share of being shot at, this one more time. Nothing could be done about it now, though.

"How're you feeling now?" Hamilton inquired.

"Not so bad. It's mostly quit bleeding, I think."

"Good. The ambulance is on its way, so you won't have to walk back to the compound, and they've called in a medevac."

By now they could hear the engine and occasionally see the headlights of the subsector jeep ambulance coming up the road.

"I'd better walk. Several of these PFs have leg wounds and can't, and one of them got hit in the gut. He's in pretty bad shape; he might not make it."

Wearily, and with Harley's help, he got to his feet. Lan and his crew were coming back down the embankment. He seemed pleased with his night's work, chatted briefly with the PF Platoon leader, and advised Hamilton, "I think we go back now."

"Okay, we call medevac for wounded."

Lan and his command group headed on up the

street toward the compound. The subsector medic jeep arrived; behind it was Hamilton's jeep driven by Doc Tinsley, alone. It was a very well-settled MACV rule that, up-country at least, Americans always operated at least in pairs. Hamilton had no qualms about saying nothing, then or later, to Tinsley about his violation of that rule. Under the headlights of the two jeeps, Doc and the two RF medics did what they could for the wounded: Chambers, one PF with a bad gut wound (Doc got on the radio and told Parelli to call Phan Hoa and make it an emergency medevac), two with leg wounds, one of whom was bleeding badly, one RF soldier with a superficial wound in his forearm, and an old woman with a scalp wound. She was old and brown and gnarled, with gray hair and rusty black pajamas. She was unconscious and bleeding. Two other Vietnamese, apparently relatives, had carried her up, somewhat hesitantly, as if fearful of being out and about at night where the shooting was going on, and uncertain as to whether they could get any help for her from the military.

Tinsley and Hamilton had greeted each other briefly; both adhered to the rule of work first, then talk. Between the two jeeps, they could carry all the wounded except the RF with the arm wound. The vehicles had been turned around and loaded.

Tinsley looked up at the sky and spoke to Hamilton: "Sir, it's going to be a bitch getting a chopper in here with that goddamn overcast."

"I know. We may have to stay up all night with these people."

He glanced at his watch. It was a little after two.

"That PF with the gut wound might not make it. There's a limit to what I can do for him here."

"Well, do what you can for them and hope that the chopper pilot can get in here—and out again."

"I guess so. See you at the compound, sir."

The two vehicles departed with the wounded. Hamilton and Harley unslung their weapons, each making sure he had a full magazine and a round in the chamber, and started cautiously up the very dark and apparently empty street back toward the compound. The RF with the arm wound and the two civilians who had brought the old woman trailed along uninvited but not unwelcome. Doc's carbine was the only effective weapon with the vehicles, but it was only a short way, and in town, so Hamilton felt no real need for concern for their arrival; his own precautions before walking back were more a matter of habit and training than anything else.

The wounded had been laid out on stretchers in a small building inside the compound that ordinarily served as the office for the military side of the operation; the subsector dispensary was outside the perimeter and too far from the helipad. By the time Hamilton and those with him had arrived, Doc and the RF medics had changed the bandages on several of them, administered cautious doses of painkiller where necessary, and rigged up IVs for Chambers and the others who had lost blood or were still bleeding. Parelli reported that the medevac chopper was on the way up the coast but the pilot was not at all sure he could get in through the overcast.

In addition to the six wounded at Thanh Lanh, one

RF and one PF had been killed, and several members of the RD Team, with weapons, and two RF were missing; they would probably turn up in the morning. Six NVA had been killed and four weapons recovered: two AK-47s, one SKS, and a carbine, plus grenades, ammunition, and assorted minor equipment. The amount of rice, if any, collected by the enemy in Thanh Lanh had not been reported. The hamlet at the northeast corner of the valley had reported one RF killed and one wounded, but not seriously, and had recovered one dead VC and one carbine. After getting all this from Captain Lan and congratulating him on the night's action, Hamilton put it all together in the prescribed format and gave it to Parelli to send to Phan Hoa.

Parelli, who had been on the radio all night, reported, "They've also had some pretty heavy contact in Tuy Cau tonight, sir."

"Oh? What happened?"

"It's kind of hard to tell, sir, but it sounded like they had a Regional Force company overrun. I marked the coordinates on the map."

Hamilton looked. He was acquainted with the location; it was a little hill overlooking Route 1 in fairly open country. It had only recently been occupied by a newly formed RF company.

"Sleepy Onion Echo, this is Dustoff Four One. Over."

It was the pilot of the medevac chopper.

Hamilton replied, "Dustoff Four One, this is Echo. Over."

"This is Four One. I'm entering the valley now,

en route your location. Be there in about one zero, if I can get in. How is your LZ marked?"

"This is Echo. Roger. We have three smudge pots in a triangle and can have jeep lights if you wish. Are you familiar with this LZ? Over."

"This is Four One. That's affirmative. I won't need the jeep lights unless there's a wind problem. Over."

"This is Echo. Roger. No wind here, just a very low ceiling. There is also a big radio mast just west of the compound. Recommend you make your approach from the east. Over."

"This is Four One. Roger, understand. Over."

The smudge pots consisted of metal ammunition boxes sunk in the ground, filled with dry sand and gasoline. Harley got a gas can from the jeep, made sure they were filled, and prepared to light them. Tinsley was leaning against the door post of the subsector office building, smoking his usual cigarette. Hamilton passed on to him that the chopper was trying to get in and might be there in ten minutes.

"I hope he can do it. The one with the gut wound's in shock."

"Well, we'll know shortly."

They could hear the chopper coming up the valley. Harley had the second radio set up in front of the subsector office where they could observe the pad.

Hamilton got on the horn again: "Four One, this is Echo. I can hear you now. Over."

"This is Four One, Roger. It looks like a thin deck of stratus sitting right on the valley floor. I can't see

your place at all. Can you light up the smudge pots
and send up a hand flare? Over.''

Harley had heard and was moving out to light the
smudge pots, then jogged into the team house and
got a hand flare.

"Four One, this is Echo. I'm sending up a hand
flare now.''

Harley popped off the flare, which went up into
the murk.

"This is Four One. I have a green flare. Is that
your location? Over.''

Hamilton, who had not checked the color of the
flare, glanced inquiringly at Harley, who nodded.

"This is Echo. That's us. Over.''

"This is Four One. I'm going to let down through
this stuff and come in from the east. How much
ceiling have you?''

"This is Echo. Maybe a hundred feet. Over.''

The distinctive *thump-thump-thump* of the chopper
was getting nearer, and suddenly there it was, perhaps a quarter mile northeast of the compound. Once
through the overcast, the pilot spotted the compound
and the smudge pots, came in low and slow, bril-
liantly illuminating the pad and the compound with
his landing lights, and, just before setting down,
swung the tail of the chopper around so the nose was
pointing east. This way he could get out, even with a
heavy load, without risk from the radio mast on the
police station. The pounding noise, flying dust, and
drastic lights and shadows from the chopper's landing lights, flaming smudge pots, and scurrying figures loading the wounded on the chopper, all struck

Hamilton as almost absurdly melodramatic. He wondered why Charlie didn't see fit to attack such a lucrative, vulnerable, and well-marked target.

There had been an argument, Chambers insisting that he would be all right in a little while and that all the wounded PFs should go first, and Doc insisting that Chambers really should go to the hospital and that there was room for everyone on the chopper. Doc had won. Lan did not put the RF with the arm wound on the chopper, and had to be quite firm about keeping off the two Vietnamese with the old woman. If the chopper had been going to the Vietnamese province hospital, it would have been necessary for them to go along to provide food and other nonmedical care for the old lady, and it had taken quite some explaining to make them understand that she was going to the American army hospital at Phan Hoa air base, which provided everything, including food.

Hamilton, Doc, and Harley had escorted Chambers to the chopper. He had insisted on walking, and rode sitting up in one of the seats at the side of the chopper. He seemed weak and very tired, and said nothing. Hamilton could think of nothing appropriate that wasn't trite, and Doc seemed worn out by his argument with Chambers and his efforts with the casualties.

When Chambers was settled in his seat and the chopper about to move out, Harley shouted to Chambers over the din: "Just think, if you'd been shot by a jealous husband, you wouldn't be getting a Purple Heart."

Chambers smiled, very much a "That's just what I need" smile, the chopper lifted off and almost immediately doused its landing lights, and disappeared into the overcast.

"Harley," Hamilton said, "remind me to get that pilot's name and unit so I can write him a letter of appreciation through channels. Let's try to get these smudge pots put out. Doc, I guess you're the first sergeant now, in addition to everything else."

"At least for the time being, sir."

"How bad is Sergeant Chambers's wound?"

"Well, he lost a lot of blood, but it's really a flesh wound. He should be all right in a couple of months."

"And the others?"

"If the one with the gut wound makes it to the hospital, I'll be surprised. Some of the others lost some blood, but otherwise nothing to worry about."

Hamilton reflected that they were all very fortunate that antibiotics had almost entirely eliminated the danger of infection in these wounds, and that the chopper pilot had had the skill, courage, and luck to get in through the murk and get out again.

"Well, Doc, I guess we all earned our pay tonight."

"I think we did, sir."

Next morning, after breakfast, Hamilton walked up the little slope to the subsector office to get the results, if possible, on missing people, weapons, and rice. Three people were standing at rigid attention in the middle of the room: the commander of 608 Company, the RF Platoon leader who had been in Thanh Lanh, and the leader of the RD Team. Captain Lan was slowly pacing up and down in front of them. His steps were jerky and stiff, his face congested. It did not take much knowledge of Vietnamese to perceive that he was letting the responsible leaders know his extreme displeasure at their respective units' performance the night before. Occasionally he would pause and give one of them three or four violent slaps in the face. The three were silent; Hamilton noticed tears running down the RD Team leader's face. Several members of the subsector staff were sitting at their desks, very still, obviously wishing they were somewhere else. Hamilton decided that details on the final score could wait, and quietly departed. Such methods could not be used in the American army, he reflected, but maybe they will persuade these men to stand their ground next time.

VI.

THE MONTAGNARDS
AT PLAY

The Phuoc Tre Valley is about a mile wide and seven miles long, oriented generally southwest to northeast. A lazy stream meanders down the valley between thickets of bamboo brush. The rest of the valley floor is mainly rice fields with occasional hamlets of mud-wall houses with thatched roofs. A passable dirt road runs along the east side of the valley; at the southwest end of this road were the Phuoc Tre Special Forces Camp, an airstrip, two sizable hamlets (one of which was the only substantial settlement in the district not having in it a PF platoon or other government force), and the only significant Montagnard settlement in Phan Hoa Province. The northeast end of this road joins the road from Dong Hai to Tuy Cau just south of a bridge over the small river draining this part of northern Phan Hoa Province. The several hamlets along this road were more or less under government control, but the mountains west and south of the valley, including the western slopes of the valley itself, definitely were not.

It was a bright, clear day, not too warm. Captain Lan had advised Hamilton that the Montagnards at Phuoc Tre were having a ceremony today and that they were invited. Hamilton decided that this would be an appropriate time for the team to hold a short review on the Montagnards and other minority groups in Vietnam. Since he had agreed with Lan on a two o'clock departure time, the lecture was delivered immediately after lunch.

"Gentlemen, as you know, the ethnic Vietnamese Mahayana Buddhists, who are also somewhat Confucianist and spirit-worshipers, constitute possibly 75 to 80 percent of the population of the country, and they are subdivided into three distinct groups: Northern, Central, and Southern, with distinct differences in accent and outlook. The division equates approximately to the old French colonial division into Tonkin, Annam, and Cochin China. A good many Northerners emigrated to the South after the settlement in 1954, but have kept their distinct identity.

"The other 20 to 25 percent can be conveniently divided for discussion under four headings: the religious minorities, the ethnic Chinese, the Montagnards, and what I shall call 'others.' The religious minorities are, in effect, ethnic Vietnamese but with a significant difference in religious outlook; there are three major groups here: Catholics, Hoa Hao, and Cao Dai. Vietnam has the largest concentration of Catholics on mainland Asia. Under the French and the Diem regime, they were a favored group, and their generally better education and economic position have given them a degree of influence all out of proportion to their numbers. Many Catholics came south after the 1954 settlement; there has not always been perfect harmony between the Northern Catholic refugees and the Southern Catholics.

"The Hoa Hao is essentially a reforming, purist Buddhist sect founded about thirty years ago; their strength is mainly in the Delta southwest of Saigon. The Cao Dai is a curious mixture of Buddhism, Confucianism, Catholicism, and I don't know what all; their main center is at Tay Ninh, northwest of Saigon. Both are political as well as religious organizations. At one time, during the latter part of the French regime and the early part of the Diem government, they both had substantial military and paragovernmental structures, which were eventually brought under a degree of government control.

"The ethnic Chinese are mainly located in the Saigon-Cholon area and other large towns, and are primarily businessmen and artisans; their economic power is substantial. They are acquisitive, clannish, apolitical, and resolutely loyal to their Chinese cultural heritage, for all of which they have been persecuted from time to time. There are very few of them in the Vietnamese Armed Forces.

"I shall discuss the 'others' next, saving the Montagnards for last. This heading includes three major groups: Cambodians, Chams, and Nungs. The ethnic Cambodians, or Khmer, are, of course, similar in religion, language, and appearance to the inhabitants of Cambodia. They are generally darker and more heavily boned than the ethnic Vietnamese, their language is written in a variant of the Sanskrit alphabet, unlike Vietnamese, which used to be written in Chinese characters and now uses the Latin alphabet, and their form of Buddhism is distinct from that practiced by the ethnic Vietnamese. Cambodians cremate, rather than bury their dead. They are mostly found in the Delta, which was at one time Cambodian territory.

"I know relatively little about the Chams. At one time they had a considerable kingdom along the coast here, based mainly on trade and seafaring, rather than settling and farming the land. They were eventually conquered by the Vietnamese and reduced to a few small settlements around Phan Rang and Phan Thiet. Here and there along the coast you can still see ruins of old Cham towers and temples, including a very handsome specimen on top of the hill behind 22nd Division headquarters at Ba Gi, a few miles from Qui Nhon. It's worth looking at if you get up that way.

"The Nungs are a Chinese or semi-Chinese group who have been primarily bandits and mercenary soldiers. Originally they come from the northeast part of North Vietnam, along the Chinese border. The in-country Nungs are therefore mainly refugees and most of them are in the CIDG. They are supposed to be very good fighters. Generally, members of all these linguistic minorities are not employed by the regular Vietnamese forces. I suspect that one of the reasons for creating the CIDG is to provide a means of employing these folk (other than the Chinese) without having to include them in the regular force.

"*Montagnard* is a French term meaning 'hill man' or 'highlander.' The Vietnamese word is *Moi*, which means 'savage.' The Special Forces call them 'Yards.' It is believed that they were the original inhabitants of the whole country until they were pushed back into the hills by the Chams and the Vietnamese. They are divided into numerous tribes and subtribes, with a wide variety of languages, customs, and religious beliefs. In a very general way it may be said that they all have these features in common: Their worship of spirits and ancestors does not have the overlay of Buddhism and Confucianism seen in the ethnic Vietnamese. Their farming consists of clearing a strip of jungle, raising a few crops on it until the fertility of the soil gives out, then moving on to a new place. They build wood and thatch houses, always rectangular but of different shapes, raised off the ground on posts, and their womenfolk wear mainly turbans and wraparound skirts.

"The Montagnards in Southwest China, North Vietnam, and northern Laos consist primarily of tribes speaking variants of Thai, who come under the generic term 'Hill Thai,' and the Meos, who, among other things, grow a lot of opium and provide the best soldiers on the friendly side in Laos. Generally, they speak languages akin to Chinese and Thai, and racially resemble the Chinese.

"The Montagnards in South Vietnam and the adjacent parts of Laos and Cambodia, including our friends down the road who make crossbows, are, as you have seen, darker and heavier-boned than the ethnic Vietnamese. I understand that their languages fall into two groups: Mon-Khmer, akin to Cambodian, and Malayo-Polynesian, akin to Malay. They are further subdivided into numerous dialects, many of which are not written. The most important tribes include the Jarai, Brou, and Katou in western I Corps and northern II Corps, and the Rhade and Bahnar in southern II Corps. The Yards down the road are Haru, which I understand are some sort of branch of the Bahnars.

"In the Indochina War, the Montagnards north and south sided generally with the French. Under French rule, they were protected and taken care of, and there has never been much love lost between the ethnic Vietnamese and the hill people. The ethnic Vietnamese regard them as primitive savages occupying very large areas of good land which could be put to better use under settlement and cultivation by the excess population of the Delta; the main obstacle to this scheme in its various forms is that the flatland Vietnamese don't care to live in the hills. And the Yards generally regard the flatlanders as grabby outsiders and a threat to their tribal lands and customs. The South Vietnamese government has been very wise in not being excessively visible in the hills and letting the U.S. Special Forces, whom the Yards identify as having the same benevolent attitude as the French, represent them in the highlands; the Montagnards oppose the VC and NVA mainly because they are seen as ethnic Vietnamese.

"Well, this is a subject on which scholars can

write doctoral and other learned dissertations—and have—so I hope you're not too thoroughly confused. Are there any questions?''

"Sir, did they invent the crossbow?'' It was Doc Tinsley.

"Chinese invented the crossbow. I suspect that before firearms came in, it was a pretty generally used weapon by everyone in this part of the world.''

"Sir, do those Montagnards at Phuoc Tre belong to the Special Forces Camp?'' It was Harley.

"No. The settlement chief down there is responsible to Dai-uy Lan. The troops in the Montagnard settlement are what's called a Truong San team, which is about the same as an RD Team, but composed of Montagnards and specially trained for work with them. That lot down at Phuoc Tre seem to be pretty good fighters.''

"Unlike the RD Team.'' Harley went on. "The CIDG down there aren't Montagnards, are they?''

"No. It's sort of unusual, but the Phuoc Tre CIDG are mainly ethnic Vietnamese. I understand that most CIDG troops are either Montagnards, Nungs, or Cambodians.''

After a few more questions, the session came to an end and it was time to be on their way to Phuoc Tre. Hamilton took Parelli and, in the back seat, two PF soldiers. Lan was driving his jeep, with his bodyguard riding beside him and, in the back seat, two girls who worked in the civil side of the district government. Both were possibly eighteen, very pretty, spoke no English at all, and, although given to young-girlish giggling, were very shy and inaccessible to

Americans. The district police chief, with Lan's civil deputy and two national policemen, was driving his green and white police jeep.

The Montagnards at Phuoc Tre had gathered in from little camps and settlements all over the mountainous part of northwest Phan Hoa Province and settled at Phuoc Tre to avoid the exactions of the VC and the hazards of war. They had built here new houses, but in the traditional manner: rectangular, mostly of wood with rice-straw thatched roofs and floors raised some distance off the ground on posts. Between the vertical posts the walls were made of woven bamboo mats or, in some cases, plywood or cardboard from C-ration cases. With the help of the Truong San team and using USAID cement and aluminum roofing, they had recently built a new dispensary and a schoolhouse. Today's ceremony was the solemn dedication of these two buildings.

They arrived at Phuoc Tre without incident about three o'clock. Since the settlement was on a hill, they could see from afar the crowd and commotion indicating that the festivities had already started. Hamilton also noticed a dark blue and white Pilatus Porter aircraft, with Air America markings, at the airstrip, and wondered what degree and type of outside dignitary had come for the show. They were greeted by the settlement chief, brown-complexioned but slender and wiry for a Montagnard; he was wearing the Truong San uniform of black pajamas and green jungle hat, and led them through the crowd to a covered stand that had been set up at the downhill side of the open space in front of the settlement headquarters building.

An open space, perhaps fifty yards square, of ocher-colored dry dirt, sloped gently from south to north. In the center was a massive post, about thirteen feet high, composed of numerous stout bamboo poles driven into the ground, lashed together with bamboo strips and bark fiber, and decorated with tufts of some kind of fiber dyed red, strips of colored cloth, mostly red and blue, and shiny discs of metal that Hamilton suspected of having once been the tops of tin cans. A cow buffalo was tethered by her head to the post by a massive bamboo strip, obviously nervous and unhappy. Around the edge of the open space was a happy, excited, constantly shifting crowd of stocky, brown, strong-featured Montagnards, the men mostly in shorts or loincloths (some with strips of geometric dark blue and red embroidery attached) and miscellaneous, mostly khaki, shirts, some with big, dark blue berets, others bareheaded; the women were all wearing very dark blue wraparound sarong-style skirts, with red and blue embroidered sashes and panels in front and back, "Chinese pajama" shirts, and dark blue turbans with a piece of red and yellow embroidered skullcap showing on top. The music sounded like offbeat tom-toms and an odd, wavering reedy flute. Thatched Montagnard houses, steep, dark green, jungle-covered hills, and brilliant blue sky formed the background.

In addition to those who had come with Hamilton, the party in the covered stand included the settlement chief, the leader of the Truong San team (a stocky and very competent-looking Montagnard), Captain Gherardi (CO of the Special Forces "A" Team at

Phuoc Tre; tall, lean, and bony, with the inevitable panoply of jump wings, green beret, and all), Captain Rodman of the eight-inch battery, fair-haired and stocky, and as the evident guests of honor, the national commissioner of Montagnard Affairs and his wife. The commissioner had the typical Montagnard heavy build and features, without any fat at all, brown complexion, and coarse black hair. He was wearing a bush jacket and trousers tailored out of a fine, dark gray material, good-quality shoes, and a lavender silk scarf at the neck. He greeted Lan and Hamilton with a very friendly smile and big handshakes and with no apparent effort to impress or awareness of any possible differences in race or status among them. His English was poor, and Hamilton noticed that his Vietnamese was not too fluent either.

The commissioner's wife was Vietnamese, possibly thirty, slender, ivory-skinned, and fine-featured. She was wearing Vietnamese costume: flowing black silk trousers and a close-fitting, long-sleeved, high-collared jacket with ankle-length panels in front and back, in a fine, dark slate-blue silk material, set off with earrings and necklace of small dark blue stones. Her greetings were polite and slightly remote, and Hamilton's initial impression was that here was an authentic Asiatic dragon lady. These, with three or four staff members, were evidently the passengers in the Pilatus Porter; it seemed that the Air America flight crew had elected to stay with their aircraft.

The stand and the various public buildings of the settlement were decorated with numerous small yellow and red Vietnamese flags, and in front of the stand were three large, covered jars with decorated lids and long, curved sipping tubes sticking out of them. From time to time, one or another Montagnard would come up to one of them and take a long draw at one of the tubes. When Hamilton was asked, even pressed, to try it, he found the contents to be a very fierce rice alcohol, of which he swallowed as little as he thought possible without giving offense. As the afternoon passed, he perceived that there was some connection between the consumption of this ferocious brew and the excitement and jollity of the Haru.

After a welcoming speech by the settlement chief, in fluent Vietnamese, and a reply by the commissioner in noticeably less-fluent Vietnamese (whatever his native dialect, it was not Haru), they took off for an inspection tour of the hamlet, with Lan, Hamilton, Gherardi, Rodman, and the police chief trailing along. Everything was in order; the place was certainly a lot tidier and cleaner than the average ethnic Vietnamese hamlet, and, of course, the new buildings looked very clean and modern, contrasting harshly with the traditional-style houses surrounding them.

Hamilton found himself walking beside Rodman, who asked, "What have they got in those jars?"

"Snake oil. White mule . . . I've got a hard head, but . . ."

"Oh . . . well, it seems to make the natives feel pretty good."

"Yeah, I noticed. Wait till they get around to killing that buffalo."

"I take it that's the high point of the ceremony?"

"I think so; at least they have to get pretty high first."

"Who's the one in the lavender scarf?"

"He's the national commissioner of Montagnard Affairs. It's equivalent to cabinet minister."

"Hummm. . . . He's got a nice-looking wife."

After they got back to the stand, and all were seated in their proper places, with the commissioner and his wife in the center of the front row, the music took on a different and more urgent cadence, and an ancient-looking Montagnard ceremoniously approached the commissioner. This man, whom Hamilton assumed was the tribal spirit priest or sorcerer, was wearing a dark blue turban, like those worn by Vietnamese elders, short-sleeved khaki shirt, loincloth, and an elaborate red and blue embroidered sash. He started a long, singsong incantation, paused to take a long draw on one of the jars, then passed the tube to the commissioner, who also drank; with further singsong, this was done with each of the other jars.

Gherardi, who was sitting next to Hamilton, leaned over and whispered, "I think they're initiating him into the tribe."

Hamilton nodded. Then the old man, still chanting, ceremoniously took off the commissioner's shoes and socks, picked up a small pottery container and poured the contents over his bare feet, and finally slipped a heavy brass wire bracelet onto the commissioner's right wrist. This apparently completed his initiation into the tribe, as the old man clasped hands for a moment with the commissioner, then backed away, stood for a moment before him, and gave the signal for the next phase of the ceremony.

The music changed pace again, and possibly a hundred Montagnards, both men and women, happy, excited, and a little high, formed a circle around the ceremonial post and the cow, and began a slow dance around it. Occasionally one of them, especially a younger man, would break away and execute a few steps on his own, then rejoin the circle. The chanting continued.

At another change in the pace of the music, four young men with long Montagnard knives stepped into the circle, cut the tendons of the now highly agitated buffalo cow, and pushed her over on her left side. Then one of them, with a flourish, drove his blade, which was about a foot long, into the animal's side. Blood and, after a moment, foamy bubbles came out. He had pierced the cow's lung.

Rodman, who came from New Mexico and regarded the Montagnards as being about on a level with blanket Indians, leaned over and murmured, "That's no way to kill a cow."

Hamilton replied, "They're better at killing VC."

"I hope so."

The crowd seemed to be interested at this moment only in the buffalo. Lan was leaning over saying something to the commissioner, who nodded and stood up, then, guided by Lan and the settlement chief and followed by his wife, the various ethnic Vietnamese officials, and all the Americans present, made his way out of the stand as unobtrusively as possible, around the crowd (which took no notice of

the departure), and up to a long, low building behind
the settlement headquarters. Hamilton was glad to be
spared the death and dismemberment of the cow
buffalo; he suspected that most of the other Americans and Vietnamese felt the same way. He glanced
at his watch; it was about five.

Within, a considerable, thoroughly Vietnamese feast
had been set out on long tables with benches: rice,
egg rolls, chicken with herbs, small slices of beef in
a sauce with what looked like Italian green beans,
dried fish flakes, little bowls of *nuoc mam*, and,
oddly, bottles of Tabasco sauce, probably promoted
from some U.S. Army mess hall. All was washed
down with green tea, Vietnamese beer, and, at the
main table, scotch provided by Lan, who now assumed the role of host. It was evidently now the
district's party in honor of the distinguished visitor.
Hamilton noticed Parelli at one of the other tables,
sitting next to the prettier of the two clerks from the
civil district office.

Hamilton liked rice and was genuinely fond of
Vietnamese cooking. The *nuoc mam* had been thoroughly doctored with lime juice, vinegar, hot pep-
pers, and a little sugar, which masked the underlying
fish-oil taste. He avoided the beer, which he had
found from sad experience did not agree with him,
and the chicken, which had been cut in the usual
Vietnamese style, across the bone; this requires sort-
ing out the bone from the meat with your tongue and
spitting out the little pieces of bone.

He found himself sitting next to the commissioner
and made the encouraging discovery that the guest of

honor spoke very good French, was pleasantly surprised that Hamilton was also fluent, and seemed glad of the opportunity to converse in a language in which he was more at ease than in English or Vietnamese. He was asking Hamilton, "Where did you learn to speak French?"

"In school, sir, and in France."

"Were you a student in France?"

"No, I was there with the army."

"Oh, is there American army in France?"

"At that time, yes, but not anymore."

"What did you think of the French?"

Something in his tone of voice made Hamilton cautious.

"They're a very interesting people."

"They did many good things in my country and not a few bad things also. Do you know where I learned to speak French?"

"No, sir."

"A little bit in one of their schools at Ban Me Thuot—they had a center there for the Rhade tribe—and mostly at Qui Nhon, in one of their prisons. I was two years in that prison."

"That must have been very unpleasant."

"Not so bad. I was fighting against them, and they put me in prison. Better than being shot."

On going into the meal, Hamilton had noticed that it was beginning to cloud over. Now, as the meal was winding up and Captain Lan was getting ready to make a toast, the pilot of the Porter, a tall, spare, fair-skinned man with long pale hair came in, squatted down behind the commissioner's and Hamilton's chairs, and advised that, with only an hour or so of daylight left and the weather making up, he would have to leave for Phan Hoa in an hour. Gherardi, who was sitting on Hamilton's other side, said that he could put the lot of them up in the Special Forces Camp if necessary, and would they care to join him there after dinner? The commissioner liked the idea, released the pilot, and asked him to be back about ten the next morning.

By the time the toasts and speeches were over, it was dark. Captain Rodman had to get back to his battery; the party that finally ended up at the bar of the Phuoc Tre camp (possibly two hundred yards separated the adjacent perimeters of the Montagnard settlement and the camp) consisted of the commissioner, his wife, Hamilton, Gherardi, Lan, the police chief, and three Special Forces sergeants. The others in the commissioner's party and those who had come down with Lan disappeared somewhere and showed up again the next morning, which was just as well, since the bar would have seemed crowded with any more people. One of the sergeants doubled as bartender, and Gherardi announced that, in honor of their distinguished visitor, the drinks were on the house. The commissioner, who had done quite well on rice alcohol, Vietnamese beer, and scotch, now switched to Bourbon and Coke. Hamilton asked for Bourbon and water, then caught Gherardi's ear and said, "Let me stand half of this."

"Out of your own pocket? Forget it. We've got a fund that pays for this. High-level official visitor from the indigenous government. Why do you think I invited 'em all over here?''

"Ah, so. . . . Just like the Royal Navy, eh?''

"I don't know about the Royal Navy, but do you have a drink?''

"I have one coming.''

The bar was paneled (if that's the word for it) in split bamboos, varnished to a golden brown, and decorated with foldouts from *Playboy* and cartoons out of the *PIO* magazine published by the 5th Special Forces Group. A record player produced a very fair imitation of danceable music. The commissioner was in a deep conversation with Lan and the police chief, so Hamilton asked his wife for a dance, which she accepted.

She danced well, had a shy smile, and, generally, on closer acquaintance, was not a dragon lady at all. Hamilton decided that the standoffishness had been mostly shyness, possibly compounded by distaste at the prospect of seeing the death and dismemberment of another buffalo. This could not have been the first Montagnard feast she had attended. Since she spoke only a very little French and hardly any English, they danced in silence, enjoying the music and letting it transport their spirits away from the grubby and perilous here and now to a more elegant world where civilized people dance to civilized music. Hamilton for the moment allowed himself not to be reminded that that more elegant world continued to exist only because its grubby and perilous outer ramparts were effectively defended, and that this required that at least a few who appreciated the civilities of life made it their business to man these ramparts.

After two dances, Hamilton decided that the commissioner might consider further dancing with his wife as unduly attentive, so when the music changed, he took the lady back to her seat. The commissioner had finished his conversation with Lan and the police chief and seemed disposed to exercise his French some more with Hamilton.

"How long have you been in Vietnam?"

"About five and a half months this tour, sir; this is my second tour."

"What were you doing the other tour?"

"Mostly in Saigon, sir; basically an office job."

"And this tour you have been all the time in this district?"

"That's right, sir."

"And with Captain Lan all the time?"

"Yes, sir. He's a very brave and competent officer."

Hamilton recounted to him the gist of the action where Lan had led his palace guard PF Platoon in a night counterattack against the NVA who had overrun Thanh Lanh hamlet. He finished: "If you should see Colonel Nhieu, sir, please tell him about this and that Captain Lan is one of the bravest and best Vietnamese officers with whom I have had dealings."

"Yes. I am going to Phan Hoa tomorrow, then up to visit some other tribes of my people in Phu Yen and Binh Dinh provinces, then back to Ban Me Thuot."

Hamilton knew that Ban Me Thuot was the seat of

the Rhade tribe and was more or less regarded as the capital of the southern Montagnards.

"Sir, I take it your office is at Ban Me Thuot?"

"Yes, it is a better place than Saigon; I am closer to my people there. . . . The war is very hard on my people. It is also very hard on the Vietnamese"—he glanced up at his wife, who was dancing decorously with Gherardi—"and I think also on the Americans and the French before them. Even those who are not killed or wounded are changed. We are all victims of the war."

"I know what you mean, sir, but is there any alternative to fighting it out?"

The commissioner shook his head and stared into his drink, as if thinking of very old things and gathering his thoughts. "No, we cannot surrender to them; if the government in Saigon wins, there is some chance that my people will be able to keep their land and their dignity and a little of their traditions. But . . . I was with the Vietminh once, when they were fighting the French—that was why they put me in prison—and I have seen what they do and how they think. In their scheme of things there is no room for my people to keep their old ways and their land. Oh, they would keep a few of us around, like a troupe of actors, to put on shows for propaganda to deceive the world, and the rest . . . I do not like to think of what would happen to my people. We are all victims of the war."

Hamilton had heard that a rather shadowy group of Montagnard leaders advocated establishment of an independent Montagnard state or states separate from both North and South Vietnam. It was sometimes alleged that this was a front group set up by the VC to muddy the waters and divide the opposition, or that it was backed by the French as part of some obscure scheme to preserve a measure of French influence in Southeast Asia. He did not, however, consider it appropriate to raise this matter with the commissioner, so he simply observed: "Yes, sir. The VC do some very ugly things to people who get in their way, and if they take over, they will be harsh rulers."

Since the commissioner's glass was empty and he had made no response to this, Hamilton got up and got them both refills. When he returned, Lan and the commissioner were again in conversation in Vietnamese, Gherardi was chatting with his sergeants, and the commissioner's wife just sitting, so Hamilton asked her for another dance. It was just as pleasant as before.

Finally, around midnight, the party broke up, and the various guests were found bunks here and there in one or the other massive bunkers which Gherardi had somehow acquired materials to build. Hamilton wished that he could find a way to tap that source for means to put up a bunker for his own people, and several other things.

At lunch the next day, Hamilton asked Parelli, "Well, how did you make out with the girls?"

"Sir, I didn't. As soon as the Dai-uy's party broke up, they went somewhere with the police chief and all, and I didn't see them until we all drove back here this morning. How did you make out with the dragon lady? I heard you were dancing with her all night.''

"Her husband was sitting right there, and he's a cabinet minister. I danced with her, she's an excellent dancer and speaks almost no English, and that's about as far as it went. Over.''

"I know I shouldn't say this, sir, but she seemed like a real good-looking head. I wonder why she married a Montagnard.''

"Parelli, you're letting your prejudices show. After all, Montagnard or not, he's a pretty important man.''

"I guess so, sir. They do seem pretty primitive, even compared to the Vietnamese. Whatever became of that buffalo?''

"They finally killed her. When we got out of Dai-uy Lan's party, they had cut her all up and distributed the pieces to the people, so all the Yards had buffalo steaks last night while we were eating the Dai-uy's chicken and rice. All that was left when I came out was a bloody spot on the ground.''

"Sir, I think I'd rather have chicken and rice, even with *nuoc mam*.''

"Have you ever tried buffalo steak?''

"No, sir, I'll stick to spaghetti.''

VII.

✖━✖━•━✖━✖━•━✖━✖━•━✖━✖━

OF ROKS
AND LOBSTERS

"Charlie, your lobsters are even better here than in Phan Hoa."

"Thank you. In any event, the view's better here, and I prefer the company."

Hamilton had finally been able to get up to Song Nao for lunch. There was a special meeting that afternoon at the Korean Regimental CP, so he and Harley had left Dong Hai as early as had seemed prudent, taking along several crossbows, and enjoyed the spectacular scenery along the coast road up to Song Nao. It had really been Doc Tinsley's turn to go, but with Sergeant Chambers in the hospital, it had seemed better to leave someone senior to Parelli in charge of the district. Lunch had consisted of grilled lobster, locally made French bread, rice, and a tomato-and-cucumber salad. Hamilton and Charlie Race were now sitting on a porch along the east side of the team house, enjoying a beer and the view across the bay of a hilly peninsula, blue water, and offshore islands.

"You know," Hamilton opined, "this would be an ideal place to build the Song Nao Hilton."

"No, there's an even nicer spot about ten miles north of here, which even has a beach."

"I think I know the place you mean; it looked very good from the helicopter coming down from Tuy Hoa."

"Only trouble right now is that it takes a company-size operation to get in there."

"Actually, there are dozens of superb locations for resort hotels all along this coast. If it weren't for the war, it could be the Riviera of the Orient, especially now that the air force has built a jet-capable airfield about every sixty miles along the coast. That would be a lot easier way for the people here to make a living than rice farming."

"Do you think it'll ever happen?" Race asked.

"I'm not buying any real estate along the coast," Hamilton said.

"I'm not either. . . . But look at it this way: If there weren't a war, and the whole coast were built up with very fancy resort hotels, the place would be wholly taken over by the middle-aged, timorous rich, and the likes of you and me couldn't afford to go near it. I shudder to think what the commercial airline fare out here must be, even from Japan, for instance, much less the States. As it is, at the price of occasionally being shot at, and living fairly low on the hog, we get to enjoy the best scenery in Asia, with transportation and lodging courtesy of Uncle Sam, and we even get paid for our trouble.''

"I'm glad someone in this province has such a positive mental attitude. I'll even admit that the topography of this whole area—and I have some really quite handsome mountains in the back part of my district—is a whole lot better than the Delta, but . . . I suppose you're right; at least it's some compensation for having to put up with . . . well, a whole lot of things.''

"Of which the VC are very far from being the most aggravating,'' Race offered. ''After all, they're only the enemy, which makes for a very simple relationship. . . . There are times when I wish I were in a U.S. unit, even if it did mean living like an animal most of the time.''

"I thought you had a pretty good counterpart.''

"I do. I get along fine with the Vietnamese. That's not it.''

"Oh . . . and here I came all the way up here in the hope that you'd tell me how you keep them off your back.''

"Well, part of it is, I have a civilian deputy, which helps. And I tell them as little as possible and, whenever possible, only what they want to hear. That saves them a lot of rewriting when they consolidate reports to go up to Nha Trang. You know, emphasize the positive. Also the VC have found out that the Koreans get nasty when there are incidents on Highway 1, or involving Korean units, but they generally stay out of the VC base areas over toward your side of the district. This tends to keep things quiet.''

Hamilton shifted the topic. "I wonder what this meeting's all about."

"The one at the Korean Regiment? I don't know. They haven't put on a large-scale operation in a long time, so I suspect this will be an operation briefing on whatever it is they have in mind."

"I noticed when I went by that they've been stockpiling ammunition and supplies at the battalion down the road from my place. I suppose it's necessary, but also telegraphs the punch."

"Except that it doesn't tell you where they're going to hit. You don't find that out—if you're the VC—until the choppers start moving out on the day of the operation, unless there's a leak. And I get the impression that the Koreans are pretty good at not having security leaks."

"Sometimes to the extent that they don't tell people who need to know about what they're going to do."

"Well, they invited us to the meeting. Let's go find out what they have to say."

The Song Nao District/Subsector compound was a large area of level ground next to the bay, adjoining Song Nao town and the Vietnamese Navy's Junk Force Base. It even included an airstrip suitable for light aircraft and helicopters. Captain Race had a comfortable team house, built mainly of two-by-fours and plywood; the various buildings used by the Vietnamese were cement with tin or aluminum roofs. Hamilton was of the opinion that its perimeter was altogether too long to be defended by the number of troops (two PF platoons, plus the subsector headquarters personnel) located there. En route to their jeeps, Race was showing him a new bunker he had built for his team. Hamilton inquired: "Where'd you get all the cement?"

"At the DeLong Pier at Vung Ngai port. It's a great big T-shaped prefab pier where they unload full-size ships. You go up there and talk to a Major Chapell who runs it. His office is in a little building way out on the end. Very often they get whole pallets of cement which are damaged in transit and considered unsalvageable. Tell him you need some cement for a civic-action project and if he has any damaged pallets, he will let you have all you can carry. Of course you have to bring your own trucks and the people to load them, and the Yang Cu pass between here and there, where Highway 1 goes up over the mountains, is kind of a bad place . . ."

"I know how to get to Vung Ngai, and I think I know where I can promote some trucks and warm bodies, but how do you find the DeLong Pier?"

"Navy people over at the Junk Base go up there all the time; they know where it is. I'm sure they'd be glad to go up with you. They don't like being sniped at on that road."

Hamilton glanced at his watch. "Is there time to talk to them now?"

"I don't think so. I'll talk with the navy and let you know how they think."

"I'd be very grateful if you would."

It was about a twenty-minute drive to the Korean Regiment's CP, through Song Nao town, along the shore by the bay, over a low range of hills, and finally among sand dunes to where the CP lay close to the shore. During the Vietminh war, the French had held Song Nao town in some strength, as the bay was, and is, a natural base for patrol-boat operations. Most of the houses, at least in the center of town, were one- and two-story buildings of stuccoed masonry, generally painted cream color with white trim. Their style and effect reminded Hamilton more than a little of the older, less fashionable type of resort town in southern France.

The hamlets along the shore by the bay had what Hamilton considered to be almost an exaggerated degree of "South Seas" picturesqueness: extremely tall coconut palms leaning gracefully out over the road toward the beach, neat, well-kept thatched houses, sharp-ended, gracefully curved boats pulled up on the beach or moored to pilings in the bay, people here and there working on boats or nets, or otherwise engaged, who took no special notice of their passage, all against a backdrop of bright sky and very blue water.

From the crest of the low range of hills beyond the bay, they were treated with a spacious view, to the west, of the dark, forbidding (and VC-infested) hills that separated Song Nao from Dong Hai; and on an arc from north through east to southeast, the bay, the coast, and the little offshore islands, all in various shades of green and blue and slate color.

The Korean Regiment's Command Post was located among the sand dunes and pine trees next to the beach not far from where the little river flowing down from Dong Hai empties into the South China

Sea. It included several one-story wooden buildings with tin roofs and a sizable helicopter pad, all surrounded by a high berm of sand and much barbed wire. Within, everything except the blowing sand was neat, well-ordered, and disciplined. It had been a long time since Hamilton and Race had been so frequently and so smartly saluted by the soldiers, starting with the impeccably turned-out MP at the gate. The buildings, although of very plain construction, were laid out with a hierarchical symmetry worthy of the imperial Altar of Heaven in Peking, focused on the regimental headquarters building and its two flagpoles with Korean and Vietnamese flags. Each structure was revetted with a parapet of sandbags laid with meticulous precision. Hamilton noticed without approval that the Koreans had dug in several armored personnel carriers around the perimeter berm; he disapproved of using tanks or other armored fighting vehicles in static defensive and palace guard roles. Not that the hilly country of most of this part of the province was too favorable to cross-country movement of armor.

Inside the headquarters building they were greeted by Major Jaeger, a tall, balding, slightly elderly Infantry officer who spoke Korean, and were directed to the regimental briefing room. It was plywood-paneled, with a low stage at one end, very sleek and trim for having been built by troop labor as a temporary building. Hamilton noticed, however, that the cement floor was much rougher than the really smooth cement slabs put down by the Vietnamese, even Lan's PF soldiers.

The gathering included the district chiefs and senior advisers of Dong Hai, Tuy Cau, and Song Nao districts, Major Jaeger, and a number of Korean officers, among whom Hamilton recognized and spoke to the commander of the battalion located just east of Dong Hai District. He had the impression that the others were mostly members of the regimental staff and commanders or representatives of subordinate units. After the customary greetings, the group sorted itself out by nationality: Vietnamese chatting with Vietnamese, Koreans with Koreans, and Americans with Americans. Hamilton, Lund, Race, and Jaeger were mostly discussing how unfortunate it was that Sergeant Chambers had been hit, and otherwise talking small shop, when a Korean lieutenant colonel came in and made an announcement in Korean, at which the Koreans, imitated by the others, sorted themselves out and stood in front of their seats. At another command, everyone came to attention, and Colonel Chong, the regimental commander, entered. He immediately gave what must have been leave to be seated, because the Koreans sat, followed by the others.

Colonel Chong was tall for a Korean, well muscled without appearing muscle-bound, with strong but not heavy features and larger than average eyes for a member of a small-eyed people. He gave the impression of being alert, forceful, and perfectly confident of his own authority. He made a short welcoming speech first in Korean then in accented but fluent English, with an apology to the Vietnamese for not being able to speak their language. The balance of his speech was to the effect that the meeting was to brief them on an operation about to be conducted by his regiment and to obtain their collaboration in certain parts of the overall scheme. Then he sat down.

The next speaker, a major, was the regimental intelligence officer. Since he didn't understand a word of Korean, Hamilton sat back to appreciate the style and method of delivery, which was almost a caricature of the purest Fort Benning Method of Instruction, complete with two assistant instructors, one to change briefing charts and shift acetate overlays on maps, and the other to handle a long, red-tipped white pointer. All three were perfectly turned out and rehearsed; their movements were as precisely synchronized as a first-class ballet, but without hint of gesticulation or flourishes, completely and classically virile and military. The thought struck Hamilton that, in addition to its practical end, this ritual also served, probably quite subconsciously, the purpose of a war dance: to gain favor with the inscrutable gods of battle by performing the prescribed rites with zeal and precision.

Then the assistant instructor, a captain, who had had charge of the pointer, delivered an English translation of the briefing: First a discussion of the terrain in the northwestern part of Dong Hai District (this was the first indication Hamilton had had of where the operation was going to take place, and he began paying a great deal closer attention); then the weather prediction and related items such as times for sunrise and sunset and the moon phases. This was followed by a summary of non-Korean friendly forces in the northern part of Phan Hoa Province and the estimate of the enemy situation. It appeared that the Koreans had information which they deemed reliable, indicating that the regimental CP and one battalion of the 299th NVA Regiment were located near a stream junction in a small valley about ten miles northwest of Dong Hai town. They had less precise information and seemed, at least for present purposes, much less interested in the locations of the other two battalions of that regiment and of the 58th VC Provincial Force Battalion. This presentation was followed by a translation in Vietnamese by the other assistant instructor.

The second part of the briefing was given by the operations officer, and followed the same style and pattern: first in Korean, then English and Vietnamese translations. The operations officer had a strong and resonant voice, and the delivery was, if possible, even more precise, virile, and military than the intelligence officer's.

Two regiments of the division were to be inserted by helicopter encircling a considerable area around the probable location of the 299th's CP and battalion, then search the area and destroy any enemy forces encountered. Captain Lan was invited to participate by moving two Regional Force companies into blocking positions astride two probable avenues of escape from the area to be encircled. Given the size of the companies and the area to be covered, all of it steep hills overgrown with heavy brush, Hamilton privately decided that ''screening'' was a better word than ''blocking'' for what would actually happen. Tuy Cau and Song Nao districts were involved only in the sense that most of the Korean troops in both districts would be temporarily pulled out for the operation, with platoons holding down the various company-size strongpoints in those districts.

There was no invitation to provide RF or PF troops as temporary garrisons for these localities. When the Koreans installed themselves, they habitually built elaborate and very well-designed fortifications; it was clear that they had no desire to entrust their handiwork, even temporarily, to their allies. Moreover, the date of the operation was not announced; when Captain Lan asked when it would start, Colonel Chong replied that the date had not been set. Lan agreed to move his RF companies as requested, but made the point that it would be very difficult to coordinate timing unless he knew the date of the operation; he was assured that he would be given "adequate" advance notice of the start of the operation.

After some further discussion it was agreed that any VC or civilians captured in the operation would be turned over to Lan, but the Koreans insisted on keeping any NVA prisoners. In his closing remarks, Colonel Chong thanked the American and Vietnamese participants for their assurances of cooperation and stated that he would not take up their time with the S1 and S4 parts of the plan, in which they were not involved.

"It's amazing," Hamilton remarked to Captain Lund after the meeting, "that you can actually fight a real live war by coordination and without any unity of command."

"I know, but it works, which is a real credit to the

good sense and willingness to cooperate of everyone concerned.''

"And I suppose that it wouldn't be feasible politically to have a combined command below about the Saigon level, if there.''

"I don't think they really have a combined command even there.''

"Do you sometimes get the impression that your people and mine, the RF and PF and so on, are fighting one war, and the Koreans and the Special Forces are each fighting a wholly distinct, separate war, even though all three wars are being fought at the same time, against the same enemy, and in the same area?''

"That's about what it amounts to. If the Koreans weren't here, things would be pretty bad, though.''

"Of course. . . . Well, I'd probably best be heading back to Dong Hai and see what's going on.''

Lieutenant Colonel Kim, commander of the Korean battalion just east of Dong Hai District, joined them. He was of about average height for a Korean, slender, with a finely boned face and a generally cheerful manner. He spoke very good English. Hamilton and Lund both saluted him and wished him good afternoon.

"Good afternoon, gentlemen," Kim replied. "This afternoon, in about one hour, there is a Special Services show from Korea for the soldiers at my battalion. If you wish, maybe you come and see it. I think you may find it interesting.''

Lund and Hamilton both accepted the invitation. Kim had also invited Lan and Lieutenant Dao. They all traveled together in five jeeps, one Korean, two Vietnamese, and two American, and arrived without incident.

The battalion command post was located on the side of a hill near the crossroads where the road up to Dong Hai branches off Route 1. The perimeter was surrounded by a great deal of barbed wire and a number of obviously very well-built bunkers. Within, a ceremonial axis led up the hillside to a bunker housing the battalion command post and Colonel Kim's quarters with the usual two flagpoles in front. Other, lesser bunkers were symmetrically arranged in descending hierarchical order each side of the central axis. The lower part of the hill, which was bare of trees, formed a natural amphitheater; here a small stage had been set up, and several hundred Korean soldiers had gathered to enjoy the show. It was the largest number of Korean soldiers that Hamilton had seen together at one place. They all had their helmets (with mottled camouflage covers) and individual weapons, and were sitting on the dry yellowish ground by platoons and companies. Many of them had cameras. The atmosphere was quiet, relaxed, and cheerful.

About a third of the way up the ceremonial axis, a group of folding chairs had been set up for Colonel Kim, his guests and staff, including the company commanders. Even from this little elevation, there was a very pleasing view of hills to the north, west, and south, and eastward of the sea beyond an extent of flat rice land, with Highway 1, a small hamlet, and some trees in the foreground. Colonel Kim's arrival was not marked by any special show of respect or deference, but it was clear that the show had been held up until he arrived. It began immediately after they were seated.

The troupe consisted of four girls, a master of ceremonies, and a technician who looked after the loudspeakers, microphones, and other sound equipment; the musical accompaniment was taped. Generally, the show alternated between American nightclub song-and-dance acts, sometimes with the lyrics in Korean, and traditional Korean songs and dances. The girls were pretty in a stocky, slightly moonfaced way, and reasonably talented, the costumes stylish, and the music lively; but it was hardly the first time that Hamilton had seen East Asian variants of American nightclub acts. For the traditional Korean presentations, the girls wore the very long bell-shaped skirts, short jackets, and elaborate hair ornaments of the national costume. The music had a gentle, lilting, nostalgic singsong which Hamilton found very much to his taste. Both types of acts were enthusiastically applauded by the Korean troops. Hamilton also noticed that a platoon of Popular Force had somehow been included, and were enjoying the show; he reflected that their lives consisted generally of long stretches of boredom punctuated by short periods of excitement of the least pleasant kind, and that this was probably their first entertainment in a very long time.

After the show the troops moved out by platoons and companies, and in about five minutes the little amphitheater was empty. Hamilton joined Kim, Lund, Lan, Dao, several Korean officers, and the members of the troupe for a gathering over Korean beer, green tea, and soda pop. It was held in the officers' mess hall and club, a semi-underground building about halfway up the ceremonial axis, which had a nice view out toward the sea.

The girls all spoke English to some degree; they had performed at U.S. Army officers and NCO clubs in Korea. They were much more at ease chatting with the Americans than with the Korean officers; Hamilton suspected that there was an element here of intra-Korean class consciousness, male supremacy, or both. The girls were equally at ease with Lan and Dao, so the problem, whatever it was, was Korean. He had noticed similar reticence when various colleagues had brought along Chinese or Vietnamese girlfriends to parties in Saigon attended by Vietnamese officers and officials.

Hamilton expressed his appreciation and gratitude both to Colonel Kim and to the members of the troupe, with particular emphasis on how much he had enjoyed the Korean music, politely declined another beer, and departed. He wanted to get back to Dong Hai by nightfall. Harley was waiting at the jeep.

They were out of the gate of the Korean perimeter before Harley spoke: "Well, sir, how did you like the girls?"

"Not bad if you like the type."

"Are they staying there tonight, sir?"

"I gather they have to go on up to Vung Ngai tonight."

"They're not driving, I hope. I wouldn't want

good-looking stuff like that to get caught on the road at night by the VC.''

"I think they have a helicopter. . . . How did you like the show?''

"Real good, sir. Is that the traditional Korean singing?''

"That's what Colonel Kim says. How do you like it?''

"Not bad, sir. It's sure different from what the Vietnamese do.''

"Well, they're quite different countries.''

There was a pause in the conversation as Harley, who was driving, threaded through the last hamlet in Tuy Cau District before they crossed the invisible line into Hamilton's district.

"Sir, one of the Koreans said they have a big push coming up.''

"That's what the meeting at regiment was all about, but it's supposed to be a big secret.''

"With all the ammunition and supplies they have stacked up, sir?''

"Well . . . I know. Did he tell you when they're going in?''

"No, sir. Didn't they tell you at the meeting?''

"I'm afraid not. They're pretty security-conscious.''

"Is it you or the Dai-uy they don't trust, sir?''

"Probably a little of both.''

Suddenly there were shots from the hill to their left. Hamilton saw spurts of dirt in the road in front of them and heard the nasty whine of a ricochet. Harley gunned the jeep, and before Hamilton was able to get the muzzle of his carbine pointed back to the rear, they were around a bend and out of the sniper's field of fire. They slowed down.

"Dammit it all, Harley, that's the last time we go anywhere without a rear gunner. . . . That was damn quick thinking."

They stopped in the next hamlet with a PF Platoon, but the platoon leader spoke no English, and Hamilton's Vietnamese was not good enough to convince him of the desirability of stalking the sniper. Of course it was getting toward sundown.

It was nearly dark when they finally rolled into the Dong Hai compound. It had been a long afternoon, and the supper, even if it was chicken, not lobster, tasted very good.

VIII.

×—×—×—×—×—×—×—×—×—×

COLONEL CHONG'S
PICNIC

The big hill west of Dong Hai is connected by a narrow, bare, saddleback ridge to another hill which forms the southeast corner of an extensive and complex tangle of hills covered with scrub brush and jungle, whose sterling qualities as a lair for guerrillas had not been overlooked by the VC and NVA. A well-defined trail runs along the crest of the saddleback, around the east side of a small bare knob, and into the brush, generally following the crest of the ridge a little distance down the east side. In many places the trail is sunken about three feet below the surface, and the brush arches overhead, giving it somewhat the aspect of a tunnel.

The 608 Company's "blocking" position was about three quarters of a mile up this trail, astride an area where about four prominent trails converged, including two from the northwest and one which led eastward, down into the valley north of Dong Hai and thence across that valley to the equally forbidding hills between Dong Hai and Song Nao. This position was several miles from the point of insertion of the nearest Korean unit; the apparent objective was to prevent the escape of any enemy troops which had avoided the Korean encirclement and might attempt to leave the general area by this group of trails. The 607 Company, whose normal location was a small hill in the middle of the valley about a mile north of Dong Hai, had the mission of blocking a similar trail junction about two miles further north on this same general ridge line.

Captain Lan had decided to accompany 608 Company as it moved out to its assigned area, and Hamilton and Parelli had come along. Lieutenant Colonel Kim had come by in his chopper late the previous evening to pass the word that the operation was about to begin; Lan had advised 608 Company, and, shortly after breakfast, they had walked up the hill and moved out with the company. The company commander moved out behind the leading platoon; behind him was Lan with his bodyguard and a radio operator, then Hamilton and Parelli with the team's radio. From the top of the big hill and first part of the trail, they had had a fine view of the great number of helicopters carrying the Koreans and their equipment (including sling-loaded artillery) into position. Most of the choppers were CH-47s, looking like Greyhound buses with a set of rotor blades at each end. Equally impressive were the air strikes being delivered on the suspected enemy command post by several kinds of jet fighters, followed by the old, piston-engined A-1s (sometimes irreverently known as "Super-SPADs"). Each aircraft came in to the attack in a shallow dive, then pulled up, gracefully circled around, and struck again; the third time around, this process was completed with low strafing runs. Even at a distance of several miles, the heavy *whump-whump* of bombs could be heard and felt. As a taxpayer, Hamilton quietly hoped that the Koreans had been correct in their estimate of the enemy's location.

Now, as they hiked along the section of trail inside the brush, they could still hear and feel explosions of bombs, whistling jets, and the throbbing *thump-thump-thump* of the helicopters. From the speed with which the column was moving, Hamilton concluded that the RF troops were fairly confident that they were not immediately likely to bump into the enemy; when they sensed enemy ahead, they habitually took their time and moved with caution. The day was clear and not yet extremely warm.

After several weeks devoted mostly to bureaucratic coordination and such necessary but uninspiring actions as checking distribution of supplies to refugees, it was satisfying to be moving out once again on an operation with troops, even if the prospect for contact was slight and the action, if any, would be fought dismounted and with weapons that were older than most of the soldiers. It would have been even better, of course, to be in command of the operation, and to have fully trained troops with modern equipment and with whom he had a common language, but it was still preferable to visiting refugee camps or trying to cope with the apparent refusal of the civil bureaucrats at Phan Hoa even to attempt to comprehend any view of the problem other than their own, or to discuss any problem on any terms other than the neat, completely artificial stereotypes promulgated from Saigon. And, with luck, in about four months he would be working for Colonel Sprague's outfit . . .

Suddenly the column stopped. A moment later there were several shots up ahead, a shouted command, and the lead platoon began running down the trail, followed by the RF Company commander, Lan, Hamilton, and their radio operators and bodyguards. Soon they emerged into a more open area, and it was apparent what had happened: The point of the column had run into a VC trail-security element. One VC had been killed—his body lay to one side of the trail—and one had been captured. The prisoner was standing in the middle of the trail, visibly shaking with fear and excitement while one of the RF soldiers was tying his arms behind his back by a lashing just above the elbows. Apparently a third VC had made off; the leading platoon had fanned out and was searching for him. Both the dead VC and the prisoner were young—possibly eighteen—and both were wearing black pajama shirts and shorts, no headgear, blue and white rubber shower shoes, and belts with canteens, grenade and cartridge pouches, and a ball of cooked rice about the size of an orange rolled up in a piece of cloth. The prisoner's belt was made out of an old leather strap, and his rice ball was in a piece of mottled light green parachute cloth; the dead VC had a very old U.S. Army-type pistol belt, and his rice ball was done up in an OD handkerchief. Both had been armed with M-1 carbines. At a glance the stocks on both weapons seemed to be in very poor condition, but the metal parts were free of rust and serviceable. Lan spoke to the prisoner, who had calmed down a little, but the reply was not, apparently, satisfactory, as Lan slapped him briskly on the face. This was followed by more questions, and apparently satisfactory answers, interrupted after a little while by another flurry of shots down the hill to their right; they had found the third VC.

Shortly, two RF soldiers came laboring up the slope carrying the third VC, who had been shot in the shoulder and legs. He was still alive and conscious, but was bleeding badly. Lan unslung his carbine and chambered a round. Hamilton laid a hand on his arm.

"No, Dai-uy; maybe he talk."

Lan thought for a moment, nodded, reslung his carbine, and spoke briefly to one of the RF. Shortly, the RF Company medic was there bandaging the wounded man, and the first prisoner was being taken away down the trail. Hamilton got on the radio with Tinsley and called in an urgent medevac, stating only that they had had an accident and had "one VN military" with gunshot wounds—no need to announce to the world that they had made a clean sweep of the VC security element on this particular trail—to be picked up at the big hill.

Meanwhile, Lan was squatting next to the wounded man, talking with him in a very gentle, almost bedside manner. The VC was barely conscious and merely mumbled in reply. Lan shook his head and gave another order.

"Did they say anything?" Hamilton asked.

"Not much. Maybe VC District Company." He grinned. "We get all three of them. Maybe VC not know we're here. Set up ambush."

"Very good, Dai-uy. I call one medevac for this one."

"I don't know, I think maybe he die, but . . . okay, I send him to big hill for medevac. Maybe I send one sergeant with him."

"Okay, I tell medevac to come to the big hill."

Hamilton, Lan, and the RF Company commander set up the two platoons (the company's third platoon was holding down the big hill) in well-concealed, mutually supporting ambushes covering both trails from the northwest, the trail eastward down the hill and the trail along which they had come, and double-checked to make sure that they had communications with the big hill and with the mortars at the subsector compound. Meanwhile, the wounded prisoner and the dead VC had been carried back down the trail, each in a hammock slung under a pole with a bearer at each end. The RF Company medic went with them, and the captured weapons and equipment were taken along.

After a final look-round, Hamilton told Lan, "Well, Dai-uy, I guess that's about all we can do. Let's go back to the big hill and try to make sure that VC and your sergeant get on the medevac."

Lan nodded, and they headed back down the trail. At the big hill there was a hassle with the chopper pilot, first because Hamilton had not announced that the patient was a VC, and second because he wanted one of the RF Company's NCOs on the chopper to guard the prisoner and try to get a first crack at interrogating him. After Hamilton explained why he had not wanted to announce to the world that he had a wounded VC, and why he needed whatever information this prisoner had while it was fresh, the pilot capitulated. Unfortunately, this particular VC did not regain sufficient consciousness to make any sense until after he was taken over by the sector intelligence people, and Lan's sergeant got no information from him. The sergeant spent the night with cousins at Phan Hoa and came back to Dong Hai the next day on the Vespa scooter bus.

While on the big hill, Hamilton had seen a helicopter at the subsector pad with its engine shut down. This was unusual, and indicated that someone with enough status to have a chopper at his disposal, for the day at least, had come to call. Hamilton and Lan, with their people, had therefore hurried back down the hill to the compound. The visitors were Major Jaeger and Major Cho, the regimental operations officer who had briefed them a few days before. Tinsley had provided cold beer for them and coffee and soda pop for the chopper crew (who had rules about mixing beer and flying). Hamilton briefed them on the morning's proceedings so far and inquired on how the Koreans were doing.

"Nothing remarkable so far," Jaeger replied. "All units report being inserted in their proper places, two or three minor contacts and, so far, only four detainees, apparently charcoal cutters and not VC.''

"Sir, I assume that you'll be sending them here for interrogation as soon as you can.''

"Maybe you and Captain Lan come out to the first battalion's fire base and talk to them there,'' Major Cho suggested. "That is where they are.''

"I'd be very glad to"—if nothing else, it would be interesting to see how the Koreans operated in the field—"but as you know, we don't have a chopper, and I expect it would take about two days to walk in there.''

Major Cho smiled. He had several gold teeth. "Is no problem; we take you in our chopper.''

"Wonderful. That's very kind of you.''

Hamilton refrained from observing that it was one of Uncle Sam's choppers; after all, it had been put at the Koreans' disposal, not his. Hamilton took along Parelli with the radio, and Lan took his radio operator and bodyguard. The chopper was a command and control (C&C) ship with an impressive array of radios, but they managed to get everyone on board, and although the pilot, a warrant officer, had looked a little doubtful, he made no objection. By the time they installed themselves in the chopper, the engine was again started up, and after some moments of idling to warm up, it changed to a more purposeful-sounding pitch, and they lifted off.

As always, the view from the chopper was superb: flat valleys, now yellowish brown with rice ready for harvesting, gray-thatched houses surrounded by trees and banana plants, whitewashed or gray cement grave monuments here and there on the hillsides, the bare brown top of the big hill with its little yellow and red flag snapping defiantly in the breeze, and beyond, to the west, tangled dark green hills as far as could be seen. As they passed the big hill, someone on top waved at them, and Hamilton, who was sitting in the door, waved in reply. If anyone had a right to fly his flag with pride, it was the Regional Force on that hill. As the chopper, still climbing, turned northwest, Hamilton caught a glimpse, far to the east, of the blue waters of the South China Sea.

In ten minutes they were at the 1st Battalion's fire base on top of a hill about eight miles northwest of Dong Hai. At first Hamilton wondered how it had been possible for the Koreans to clear the top of the hill and generally do so much on the first day of the operation, but then he saw that this spot had undoubtedly been used several times before by U.S. and Korean troops operating in the area, so it had not been any great task to check the place for booby traps, clear out the trenches, reroof the bunkers, install new barbed wire, put out trip flares and claymore mines, and generally set up shop. The hilltop was occupied by Colonel Kim's command post, a platoon of 4.2″ mortars, and four 105mm howitzers. As the hill was slightly higher than the surrounding terrain (no doubt the reason for its selection for use as a fire base), and the ground sloped away sharply on three sides, the observation and view of closer and more distant green hills and sky were extensive and impressive. Such a view is also very deceptive, as there are many folds in the ground and hidden avenues of movement, and the brush and forest can conceal a large enemy force.

Colonel Kim's executive officer met the chopper and escorted them to the CP bunker, which consisted of two convex containers buried to about half their height, then covered with sandbags; inside were the usual array of maps and radios, and Colonel Kim, who briefed them on the situation. Generally his battalion's portion of the line of encirclement was about one mile north of the fire base. He had two rifle companies on line there. They had successfully linked up with each other and with the other units on each flank, and were beginning to move forward, searching as they went. One company was securing the fire base and acting as reserve, and one company was scattered out among the various permanent strongpoints held by his troops in Tuy Cau district. Two of the detainees had been captured at the edge of the fire-base perimeter, and the other two in the jungle, by one of the companies on line. All four were here at the fire base. They had had no other contacts.

The detainees were squatting on a bare piece of ground about halfway between the CP bunker and the nearest of the mortars, guarded by a very bored-looking Korean soldier. Their brush hooks and other possessions were stacked in a pile in front of them. All four were of indeterminate age and dressed in the usual peasant work costume of black shorts and pajama shirt, shower shoes, and conical palm-leaf hats. They had not been tied up. They stood up respectfully and took off their hats when Lan approached. If any of them had any fear or other emotion except weary indifference, it was not evident in their stance or expression.

Lan quickly examined the papers and other items which had been taken from them, talked briefly with each one out of hearing of the others, then started back toward Colonel Kim's bunker. Outside, he stopped and turned to Hamilton, glanced around to make sure no one was within earshot, and said very quietly, "Two of those men are informants of mine. The other two, I don't know, maybe VC, maybe just cut wood."

"You've got to protect their cover. It would also be nice to have a longer talk with the other two. I suggest we tell the Koreans that we think they may be VC and we would like to hold them at Dong Hai for maybe two days for investigation. Then you can turn your two loose and, if the other two are VC, send them in to Phan Hoa."

Lan paused for a moment, apparently translating and weighing this suggestion; it was the second time since Hamilton had been at Dong Hai that his advice had been sought. Lan nodded and they went into the bunker. Colonel Kim looked at Lan inquiringly.

"I think maybe local VC," Lan said. "They speak local dialect, not North Vietnamese. Maybe send to Dong Hai?"

Kim nodded and said something in Korean to one of his officers, then answered, "Okay, I send next chopper, but please you hold them until this operation is finished; they have been inside this fire base."

"How long you go on operation?"

"Maybe five more days."

"Okay, I hold them."

They were taken to Dong Hai that afternoon by a chopper which had brought supplies into the fire base; Lan sent his radio operator with them, with instructions to have them held until his return.

When Hamilton and Lan came out of the bunker, Major Jaeger and Major Cho were outside, preparing to depart in their chopper. Jaeger was giving the signal to the helicopter pilot to crank up when the mortar crews suddenly went into action; in a very few moments they had several shells on the way. Looking in the direction of fire, Hamilton saw them striking along the lower part of a hill about two miles northeast. Someone had contact. They all trooped into the bunker and found out that one of Kim's companies had discovered a recently abandoned collection of huts in the jungle, apparently a VC or NVA base of some kind, and had contact with an estimated enemy platoon in bunkers along the stream where the mortar shells were going in. Colonel Kim, Major Cho, and several other Korean officers were standing in front of the map in excited conference, ignoring Lan, Hamilton, Parelli, and Major Jaeger. Hamilton extracted his map of the area from his right thigh pocket and began thinking out loud, mostly to Lan, but also to Jaeger and Parelli:

"If the Koreans came down the hill from here . . . and whoever was in the camp bolted, they probably went downstream this way. . . . I would suppose that the people engaging the Koreans here are a covering and decoy force with a mission, among other things, of drawing the Koreans away from the escape route of whoever was in the VC base.''

Major Jaeger cut in: ''Why do you think they went downstream?''

''Move faster that way; also it leads to this trail here, which leads into some very heavy jungle along this stream. . . . Now, if we could insert about a squad here, around the hill from where the action is—and the mortar shelling will cover up most of the noise of the chopper—we could work down this ridge and ambush this trail either where it crosses this stream or at this junction.''

''And if the VC don't do what you think they're going to?''

''We stay put until the Koreans push up the trail.''

''Do you know if those trails are where the map shows them?''

''Yes, sir, I VR'd the area about a month ago with an L-19 from Phan Hoa.''

''Who do you propose to send on this venture?''

''Ideally it should be part of Colonel Kim's recon platoon. I'd be very glad to go along, if I can get someone to interpret.''

''Is there an LZ over in here?''

''No, but it's fairly low brush in places—apparently cleared off some years ago by the Montagnards—and the C&C ship has a cable rig.''

''What do you think, Dai-uy?'' Major Jaeger was evidently very much aware that, as senior U.S. officer present, he had some responsibility in the matter.

Lan's reply was positive: ''Sir, I think number one.''

"Okay, I'll see what I can do with Colonel Kim."

He joined the group of Korean officers at the map board. There followed a long discussion, mostly in Korean, while Hamilton wondered what the Koreans' reaction would be to his intrusion into their conduct of the battle; he further wondered why he had been such a damn fool as to volunteer himself to go on this venture (Major Jaeger's word seemed the politest way of putting it) without a properly trained team to go in with him, and if there was some reasonably graceful way to wriggle off the hook. Eventually, Major Jaeger reported:

"Colonel Kim says he doesn't very much like it, but he'll let you take five of his people, a forward observer who also speaks English, a radio operator, and three soldiers. He prefers the idea of watching the place where you wanted to set up the ambush from a vantage point—if you can find one—and beating up the area with the mortars and artillery when they come through, rather than trying to ambush something that may be bigger than you can handle. Frankly, I think he's right. You can only put in about six people at one time with a chopper—and even that's stretching it—and if the chopper goes back for a second load, it's sure to be seen and the whole operation compromised."

Hamilton agreed and the details were quickly settled. In addition to the five Koreans, the party would consist of Hamilton and Parelli (who had immediately volunteered to go) with his radio. Major Jaeger would monitor Hamilton's frequency on a radio borrowed from the Koreans. It was agreed that operating in two languages was going to be hard enough, so Lan was to remain at the fire base or go down the hill and help the Koreans with any documents they might find in the abandoned enemy camp. Several mortar and artillery concentrations were plotted in the target area, so that all that the forward observer had to do was call in the numbers. The Korean company in that area was to be alerted, and Hamilton's party was to throw a yellow smoke grenade as a recognition signal; also the company commander was to have a radio on the same frequency as the forward observer. Major Cho agreed to hold the chopper ready, at least until sundown, in case they got into trouble and had to be extracted.

The forward observer, a lieutenant, spoke good English. He, his radio operator, and two of the other Koreans had M-16s, the last Korean had an M-79, and Hamilton and Parelli had M-2 carbines. Each member of the party had several hand grenades, and the Koreans brought along four claymore mines. Hamilton carefully briefed the whole team—at least two of the other Koreans understood a little English—and the lieutenant translated into Korean while Hamilton briefed the pilot of the chopper. After a hasty equipment and radio check, they mounted up in the chopper and moved out. The chopper took a circuitous route to the intended LZ, following stream lines and gullies well away from the contact, and flying breathtakingly close to the tops of the trees.

Fortunately, the pilot found the right hillside and was able to hover close enough to a partly overgrown clearing so that they could jump down without recourse to the cable rig. They quickly moved to the taller brush on the downhill side of the open space, the chopper was on its way, and they stayed well concealed and motionless for several minutes, watching and listening. There were no unusual or alarming sounds, so they began working their way downhill as quietly as possible. Hamilton judged that they were possibly two hundred meters from a trail by a stream line that led into the trail junction which they were going to stake out. They were in fairly open brush, possibly fifteen feet high, which got thicker farther down the hill. He had not yet decided whether to use this trail or to push through the brush parallel to it; he could move much faster on the trail, but the risks were vastly greater. The decision would depend on whether the trail seemed to have been recently used (and hence probably watched) and how great an obstacle to movement would be offered by the brush each side of it. After all, the sooner he had his stakeout in place, the better the chance of catching something. He was pleased at the Koreans; they were tough and knowledgeable of this kind of work, and they grasped and reacted quickly and correctly to his signals and to the situation. Obviously, they had been very thoroughly trained.

It took about twenty minutes to work their way downhill to the trail, which ran through heavy brush and did not seem to have been used recently. It was clear that they would have to use the trail to get to their destination in time to accomplish anything. So they set off, with one of the Koreans as point, followed at a distance of several meters by Hamilton, then Parelli, the lieutenant, the Korean radio operator, and the Korean with the M-79, with the fifth Korean as rear point. The point man took his time, moving with skill, caution, and alertness; even so, they were moving much faster and more quietly than would have been possible by pushing through the brush.

After about ten minutes of stop-and-go cautious movement, the point man suddenly stopped, then faded off the left side of the trail, which was downhill. Hamilton and the others did the same. Fortunately, the brush at this point was manageable enough that they could get off the trail and take up concealed firing positions quickly and silently. It had been agreed that, unless definitely fired upon, the others would fire only if Hamilton fired. So they lay silent, motionless, in the hot stuffy jungle, waiting for whatever had disturbed the point.

Hamilton was just beginning to wonder whether the point had been seeing things when he heard footsteps and saw two NVA soldiers coming up the trail; they were wearing the usual uniform of greenish, ocherous brown shirt, trousers, and round hat, "Ho Chi Minh" sandals, web equipment, and rucksacks. One had an AK-47, the other an SKS. They were walking very fast, almost running, with no attempt at silence or caution. Reluctantly, Hamilton let them go by; picking two NVA off a trail was hardly worth opening fire and compromising the whole exercise, and he was not close enough to grab or knife them. Their hasty and incautious movement indicated that probably Hamilton's party had not been detected and also that this trail was in use by the NVA.

After allowing a couple of minutes for the two NVA to get well clear, Hamilton gave the agreed double-click signal to move out, and the point man, followed by the others, wormed his way back onto the trail and again moved out, this time even more cautiously. The trail ran along the lower part of the north slope of a steep ridge, at the downhill, east end of which was the stream and trail junction they hoped to stake out. It took an hour of cautious movement to cover the six hundred or so meters to this area, even though they saw no further signs of the enemy, and whatever noise they made was periodically muffled by mortar firing on the other side of the ridge.

Their trail ran down into a flat area of almost swampy bottomland which had once been cleared but was now covered with dense, brushy, secondary jungle. Although ideal for an ambush, it did not afford a field of observation for calling down mortar fire on the enemy from a safe distance. The other trail ran straight for possibly thirty meters from its intersection with the trail they had used. Hamilton decided to lay an ambush at this point, hit the lead element of any sizable enemy force that came through, and call down the mortars and artillery on the area of the stream crossing and the branch of the trail leading southwest from there in the hope of disrupting the rest of the column. He explained this to the lieutenant, who agreed to the plan. As the required concentrations were already plotted, there was no need for either of them to get on the radio, other than to turn the set on and squeeze the "push to talk" button twice as the signal that they were in place and ready to go.

Hamilton and the lieutenant selected firing positions just to the north of the trail junction, each with his radio operator in a firing position close by. The Korean with the M-79 was slightly behind them, also with a good view down the trail, and the other two Koreans were staked out to watch the other branch of this trail and the trail by which they had come. One claymore was set up covering each of these trails, and the other two were set up to rake the trail in front of Hamilton and his group. Theoretically, they were all too close together, especially for a daylight action, but Hamilton decided that in this case the advantages of being able to fight back-to-back as a unit and, if necessary, to make an orderly getaway, especially in the dark and in this very close country, argued against getting too spread out. Timing on when and whether to fire the two claymores covering the other two trails was up to the Koreans guarding those trails; Hamilton would fire the two claymores covering the main trail as the signal to open fire. All this was accomplished and everything concealed in a very few minutes, and they settled down in watchful silence to wait for the enemy, meanwhile providing nourishment for numerous mosquitoes and other insect life. In the distance they could hear the *whump* of incoming mortars and, occasionally, the rattle of small-arms and automatic-weapons fire. Hamilton glanced at his watch, then at the sky, of which a thin strip was visible above the trail. There were about three hours of daylight left.

After about forty of the longest and least comfortable minutes that Hamilton could remember, the Korean to his right rear, who was watching the trail down which they had come, made a single click with his tongue—the agreed alert signal. A few moments later they heard footsteps on the trail, and shortly thereafter the same two NVA soldiers—or two that looked just like them—came down the trail at the same fast walk, turned onto the main trail heading north, and soon were out of sight.

Another twenty minutes passed. An NVA soldier with an SKS stepped into Hamilton's field of fire and started walking with slow and cautious alertness toward him; he felt certain that they were going to be detected, and could almost feel the Korean lieutenant next to him tense and prepare to fire. He gave the one-click signal, but very soft. When the NVA was about twelve meters from their position and Hamilton's hand was beginning to close down on the firing device for one of the claymores, he saw two more NVA come around the bend, followed by others, some with heavy rucksacks and a few carrying double loads coolie-fashion with flat bamboo dummy sticks. He held his fire. The NVA point man went past them and turned north up the main trail.

Hamilton could see now that the first three men in the column, although burdened with heavy packs, were carrying their weapons—two AK-47s and an SKS—at the ready; behind were at least four more with weapons, if any, slung, and carrying loads with dummy sticks. There was a twig in the path marking the near side of the fan of coverage of the nearer claymore; when the first man in the column was about to step on this twig, Hamilton fired the claymores and everyone opened fire down the trail and into the brush each side of it. The Korean radio operator was talking fast into his radio. Suddenly the trail was clear of movement; there were several bodies and abandoned dummy sticks with their loads, but the survivors of the first fusillade had jumped into the brush.

Hamilton and his party at once ceased firing—no point in giving an unseen enemy an aiming point— except for the Korean with the M-79 who fired about four grenades into the brush each side of the trail, where they exploded well above the ground. Someone on the left side of the trail fired a short burst at them with an AK-47, which drew a long burst from the lieutenant's M-16, then silence. Hamilton could see no movement in the brush either side of the trail. Then the mortar shells started coming down on the stream junction; they were unpleasantly close.

Hamilton shouted to the lieutenant over the din, "Let's get the hell out of here."

The lieutenant nodded and said something in Korean to his men. The man with the M-79 fired a couple of more rounds at each side of the trail; Hamilton turned his head and noticed that the trail-security men were policing up their claymores. Apparently the one on his left had shot the NVA point man rather than wasting a claymore on him.

The lieutenant turned to Hamilton and said, "Okay. We go now."

They pitched out two fragmentation grenades and one white-phosphorous grenade, stood up, and legged it up the trail they had come by. Hamilton had counted five bodies in the trail, which, with the point man, made six for sure, plus whatever damage was caused by the mortars and M-79 grenades. They stopped at a bend about two hundred meters up the trail, counted noses, got off the trail on the uphill side, and waited for two minutes, watching and listening for indications of pursuit. All they heard were the mortars beating up the trail and stream crossing and they saw no enemy in pursuit.

The lieutenant was again on his radio, adjusting the mortar fire northward to cover the area of the ambush and to discourage any efforts at pursuit. Now was no time to be on the trail. Hamilton called Major Jaeger and asked to have the chopper come by to pick them up at the LZ where they had been inserted in about an hour, then worked out a general compass bearing which he hoped would take them to the LZ. He felt very tired, but as he didn't care to spend the night out in the jungle after having stirred up the NVA, or to take the considerable risks of being overrun by advancing infantry, even if friendly, there was no better plan than to push on up the hill to the LZ as rapidly as possible without making too much noise. In the jungle, invisibility and haste are inverse functions: The faster you move, the more noise and stir you make.

The hill seemed a great deal steeper going up than

it had coming down, but they eventually found the LZ, made contact with the chopper, popped a yellow smoke, and were picked up without interference by the enemy. On the chopper, the lieutenant agreed to write up any necessary reports. Hamilton got his name and later wrote a highly laudatory letter of appreciation to him through ''channels''—in this case Major Jaeger. He also resisted the temptation to add a paragraph thanking the Koreans for the best hunting he had had in a long time.

IX.

THE CEMENT CONVOY

The MACV billets at Vung Ngai were at the edge of the city, across the street from the beach, in a three-story building of white stucco that was probably intended originally as a hotel. The bar was on the top floor, commanding a handsome view of curving beach and palm trees with the two headlands forming the bay stretching out to the east. At night the view was punctuated by the lights on the several ships at anchor and around several Allied installations, especially on the north side of the bay.

Hamilton was sitting at a small table a little way from the bar with Major George Brandon; they had been company commanders in the same tank battalion at Fort Hood, and had fortuitously encountered one another at the bar here. Brandon was fair-haired and slender but very tough and had a reputation for insisting that everything be done in the most thorough and professional manner possible. He was also a loyal friend.

"Well, congratulations on your promotion, *Major* Hamilton."

"Thank you. The list finally came out. I guess that shows they'll promote anybody these days."

"You're better than that, and we both know it, but I know what you mean."

"They're promoting too many people too soon and too fast, and when this thing finally comes to an end and they cut the army down to its normal size, they'll have a hell of a hump in the middle grades, just the same as they had after Korea."

"And they've got captains running around who know less than you and I knew when we were promoted to first lieutenant. A lot of these characters will go on up without ever having had any real experience with troops."

"They did the same thing in World War II and Korea, which is one of the things wrong with the army today."

"Hamilton, your morale is damn near as bad as mine."

"Well, what have they got you doing, if that's not an indiscreet or painful question?"

"I'm the S3 adviser here at Sector; I suppose it's interesting enough, but . . . well, you know how it is."

"I do. When's your DEROS?"

"About three more months, thank God."

"And then what?"

"I'm getting out of the army."

"You're what?"

"You heard me. I've already sent in my papers."

"What moved you to this? I'd always regarded you as the most professional of professionals."

"Exactly that. First they send us over here to fight a goddamn war which we're not supposed to win and are not permitted to win. At that point I see no patriotic duty in sticking around while the politicians play footsie with other people's lives to ensure their own reelection. At that point you have to look at the army as a career and a way of life only, and not by way of civic duty. An army as it ought to be run would be an extremely rewarding profession, but today's army has corrupted itself to the point where you can't breathe anymore. Not monetary corruption, not people with their hands in the till—we haven't sunk that low—but corruption of the spirit. And the evils are incurable, because the people on the outside, including the civilian leadership, don't know and can't find out what's wrong; the generals, who do know, have got where they are as a result of the present system and are therefore the last people to be interested in changing a system by which they have prospered and profited."

"You seem to have given this a lot of thought, George."

"You don't put in your papers at my age without much reflection and a damn good reason. . . . There are two fundamental and very closely related evils which are poisoning the whole officer corps and in fact the whole army: First, the efficiency report. You and I both know that, with the inflated ratings being given, just one less-than-outstanding rating, especially if you're not a ring knocker, means that you're done for professionally when it comes to going to the staff colleges or ever making full colonel. This means that each rating officer has the power of professional death over each rated officer, with no recourse, because there is no way that you can reclaim a merely satisfactory rating. Most rating officers are very fair and extremely tolerant of abrasive subordinates, but there are enough of the other kind—the insecure bastards who can't tolerate an honest difference of professional opinion and use the efficiency report as a control measure to bolster their own inadequate leadership—so that the system statistically favors the smiling yes-man, who, no matter what, tells the boss what he wants to hear rather than what he ought to hear, and it disfavors the officer who is guilty of an indiscreet display of independent thinking, moral courage, or professional integrity. In short, it forces an officer to choose between whether being in the army is a career or a profession.

"Well, we've had the system, with minor variants, since just after World War II, which is why, with honorable exceptions, we have a bunch of mealy mouthed politicians who long ago made the decision between integrity and advancement, for generals. Also, I am convinced that this system is one of the major reasons why the so-called decision-making process has disappeared into that monstrous swamp of structures upon structures of staffs and agencies in the Defense Department and the Department of the Army. You have a system that favors the avoidance of decision-making and responsibility and what do you do at the level where decisions have to be made and the results justified to Congress and the people? Anyone with the courage to make a decision solely on the basis of his own professional knowledge and competence, and then stand up for it, never gets beyond the grade of full colonel, at best—the few generals who were exceptions to this rule got fired by Superman. So you conduct an elaborate mass of repetitive studies, preferably with a lot of carefully rigged computer inputs, then staff it and get comments from everybody in the world, comment on the comments, put on a lot of elaborate briefings, and finally have a review board of about twenty generals—that spreads the blame around—to make a recommendation, which is then further reviewed, and, with any luck, the decision will be imposed from the outside by Congress or the Bureau of the Budget, or become unnecessary with the passage of time. And in the meantime, everyone who had a hand in it has been reassigned and can't be found.

"The real evil of this is that it requires such a colossal number of officers to man all these structures upon structures. I suspect that at any one time, at least 80 percent of the combat-arms officers of the army over the grade of captain are sitting in division or higher staffs or in one or another of a whole variety of paper-shuffling bureaucratic empires, mostly in the so-called R&D business; anywhere and everywhere except learning how to command troops in the field. Which means that you and I can look forward to spending at least twelve out of the next fifteen years perfecting our skill as bureaucrats and forgetting what a field soldier smells like."

He paused, stared briefly into his glass, and took a sip, then went on:

"The second evil is that they tell too many lies. Now, going into battle and getting killed is a pretty absolute sort of thing, and the one absolutely necessary right of the combat soldier, ever since the Macedonian Phalanx, is not to be lied to by his officers. I don't mean the civilian politicians; after all, integrity in politics is like chastity in a whorehouse, and always has been, and nobody should let himself get upset by it. Unfortunately, first the generals and now those who would like to be generals someday seem to have adopted the politician's ethic on matters of truth, honor, and integrity, without relinquishing their claim to a moral and legal authority based on a much stricter set of standards.

"For example, they put out all this talk about professionalism, and then make it very clear, by the efficiency report system and in a great many other ways, that they absolutely do not trust the professional integrity and competence of their own officer corps. And they make a lot of noise about "one army" and then treat the Reserve and the National Guard like dirt. Probably worst of all, they put out a lot of propaganda about equal treatment for West Point graduates, non-West Point Regulars, and non-Regular career officers. Just check the percentages that go to the War College or make general. Why it should still be necessary to have first-class, second-class, and third-class citizens all within the same body of career officers is an absolute mystery to me. Even worse than these evils themselves is the notion that by issuing an official pronouncement that they do not exist, which everyone is bound as a matter of discipline to agree with, they are thereby made invisible and immune from corrective action. It is also a serious abuse of authority to compel everyone to agree with and act on one of these officially pronounced falsehoods.''

''But if you abolish the efficiency report,'' Hamilton interjected, ''what basis would you use for selecting people for promotions and so on?''

''The British use competitive examinations, which may be something of a mandarin system, but at least it doesn't require a man to decide between integrity and advancement. There are all sorts of rules and regulations giving commanders authority to say, 'Damn it, I'm the boss, we do it my way,' and make it stick, without recourse to the efficiency report as a control device.''

''I hope you don't believe that things are very different in companies on the outside.''

''There's one very big difference: The army deals in human life and national survival, but business is just for money. It's the difference between asking a soldier to walk out into the jungle and die and asking a delivery man to take a load of coal down the street to a customer. Also, in business, if you tell too many lies, or cheat your customers or employees too much, you don't stay in business very long.''

''What are you planning to do?''

"I don't know yet—probably take a nice long vacation, then start looking for a job."

"You're still a bachelor, aren't you?"

Brandon laughed, then replied, "I see you're concerned about my being able to support my family and meet my obligations—still making a noise like a company commander. Be advised that I am still a bachelor; in fact, I'm writing to at least three different girlfriends, each of whom would probably be very glad to become Mrs. Brandon, but I think there's safety in numbers."

"You want to be careful what you write."

"Oh, always. . . . But I rant and rave. Please accept my apologies for this long tirade and tell me what brings you to our fair city."

"Mostly cement. I was told that the people down at the DeLong Pier occasionally give away damaged pallets of cement for use in civic-action projects. We have a log-and-sand bunker at one corner of the compound that's just about rotted out and needs to be rebuilt, the powers that be are putting the steam on us to build a district operations center, without, of course, supplying the necessary materials, and I have long hankered for a decent team bunker to hide in during mortar attacks.

"Of course you have to bring your own trucks and labor to load them, which took a bit of wheeling and dealing and a couple of false starts, but as it finally worked out, I borrowed three five-ton trucks with drivers from the eight-inch battery down the road from me, and hired about a dozen civilians out of the refugee camp to do the loading. Since it's out of the province, the district chief couldn't send any of his RF or PF soldiers.''

"What did you hire them with?"

"Imprest fund. I hope it's a legal expenditure. . . . The artillery sent a duster to escort us as far as the crossroads where the road up to my place goes into Highway 1, and at Song Nao we picked up a truck-load of Junk Force sailors and a jeep with a couple of U.S. Navy advisory types, mainly because they know how to get to the DeLong Pier. Are you familiar with the south side of Yang Cu Pass?"

"Not on the ground. I know where it is, and I've heard it's a bad place; Koreans had some trouble there recently. Apparently at one time the VC used some of the inlets along the coast there for maritime infiltration.''

"We got held up by a Korean roadblock some distance south of the pass. It seems they had a couple of bad mining incidents this morning in the pass and closed the road until they cleared the area. While we were sitting there waiting for the Koreans to decide to let us go on, a whole battalion of them walked by in the opposite direction. It was a very curious effect, almost as if one were looking at a pale sunset reflection of what the Imperial Japanese Army must have looked like on the march.''

"I know just what you mean," Brandon said. "I wouldn't care to have them coming after me.''

"Just when we were about to give up and head back to Song Nao, they let us through and we headed up the pass. One Korean truck and one civilian bus had been blown up; they had taken away the dead and wounded, of course, but the wrecks and some of the odds and ends on the bus were still smoldering when we drove past. Not exactly encouraging. And even on a clear day, the topography doesn't help; it's kind of a grim place. When you're a child, you hear the phrase in the psalm about the valley of the shadow of you-know-what. As you grow older, your image of this gets clearer and more elaborate, then one day you drive into the south end of the Yang Cu Pass, and a little voice in the back of your head says softly, 'Mac, you're here.' It's that kind of place.''

"It doesn't sound like you had a very strong convoy to be fooling around on that piece of road, even if the Koreans did decide it was clear."

"We didn't," Hamilton said. "We passed a platoon of Koreans walking up the pass and were very glad to give them a lift."

"Anything happen on the way in?"

"Of course not. You always worry more about the goblins that aren't there. But I shall be very glad when we're out of that place southbound tomorrow."

"I take it you're going up to the DeLong Pier in the morning?"

"That's the plan."

They ordered a refill on the drinks, then sat for a little while in silence. It was a damn shame that Brandon was leaving the army. Everything he had said was true, of course, but Hamilton had views about resigning in the middle of a war, however unpleasant things got, and he did not feel that the antics of the political leadership had yet got to the point where the old bonds of loyalty and fealty no longer required him to stay on. He was reserving judgment on what to do if his request for transfer to Colonel Sprague's outfit didn't go through.

The drinks came, Hamilton insisted on paying for them, then asked, "What are you going to do if they won't let you out?"

"I'm almost sure they can't. I'm just a reservist, you know."

"Well, there's one advantage of being a second-class citizen."

"Big deal if you wanted to make the army a career."

"Really, though, we're very lucky. After all, most everyone signs up in a great glow of enthusiasm and idealism for a perfect army that exists only in his own imagination, and by the time he finds out how the place is really run, he's got a wife and children and creditors and can't quit."

"A lot of them do quit, though; only they just don't put in their papers until fifteen years later. You've met the type."

"Oh, yes, altogether too many of them. Once a good man is thoroughly trapped and broken, he can be molded into a docile and obedient bureaucrat. Some of them may even show a little flash of the old fire in combat."

"Combat is a very incidental part of the army's business. The main thing is making yourself and your rating officer look good, especially on paper and for the record. . . . Frankly, I prefer dealing with someone whose main ambition is to hang on and collect his pension than with some greedy hotshot who thinks he's going to be a general someday."

"George, you must have some really unpleasant people to work for here."

"It's not that bad. The military here are pretty straight; all the hotshots are running around with the U.S. units, faking their body counts and writing themselves up for medals. As the S3, I have very little to do with the civilian scum here."

"Did you say faking body counts?"

"I did. I used to think they were sacred also, and on the MACV side they still are, at least in this part of the world, but . . . you know how it is when you have a brigade commander who's trying to impress his division commander. He makes it a big statistical competition between his battalions as to who can report the biggest body count. Like PT test scores and rifle marksmanship."

"It's hard to believe that U.S. Army officers would actually fake operational reports in combat, and if a body count isn't an operational report, what is?"

"I know. You don't have any U.S. units in your province. I do, and occasionally some company commander or battalion S3 whom I know from somewhere stops by and cries on my shoulder."

"That's pretty bad."

"Well, what do you expect? When you tell people to fight a war, but they're not supposed to win it, and you tell all the battalion and brigade commanders that their performance in six months of command will determine whether they make general or not, what becomes the most important thing?"

"Especially with the high standards of truthfulness which seem to prevail at the highest political and military levels."

"Exactly. The saddest part is that 90 percent of them, at least up through the colonels, really want to be on the up-and-up, and only cheat when they have to. All it takes is the wrong kind of emphasis down from the top, and a few ambitious politicians on the make, to turn the whole thing into a real can of worms."

"George, you're depressed. You need to go on R&R and get away from it all for a while."

"I've already been, thank you."

"Where did you go?"

"Australia. It's a wonderful place: friendly people who speak real English and actually seem to like Americans, lots of girls, some of them really good-looking, none of them whores, and most of them more than willing to have all kinds of a good time. I'm seriously thinking of settling there when I get out of the army. Have you been there yet?"

"No. You're about the tenth person who's been there and says it's wonderful. But I think I'll go to Bangkok this time."

"How come? I didn't know you liked slopes."

"It's not that. I don't like paying for it, directly anyway, and I find it difficult to communicate without a common language. Anyway, for this trip I have something much better lined up, I think. . . . The reason for going to Bangkok is this: It's the last bastion of old-fashioned Oriental monarchy in all its splendor, with all sorts of magnificent palaces and temples to see, and frankly, the way things are going, I don't see too much hope of the friendlies holding on to the place for more than about another five years. Australia is going to last a hell of a lot longer than that. Also I like curry."

"I see your point. Only thing is, if we back out of Southeast Asia, the Australians aren't going to feel all that damn friendly anymore."

"I suppose you're right, but there's not much I can do about it."

"Of course not. The world's a dreadful place, but what the hell. . . . By the way, your old friend Karla Bergman is here."

"Oh? What's she up to?"

Hamilton and Karla had had an affair at Fort Hood. Hamilton didn't know how much Brandon knew about it.

"She's still working for the Red Cross," Brandon replied. "She was sleeping with one of the doctors over at the hospital, but he went back to the States about two weeks ago, and I don't think she's found a replacement. Occasionally she turns up here at the club in the evenings."

"I take it you're not interested?"

"Not my style. For one thing, she's taller than I am. She's big and blond and Nordic, and anyway I'm too short to start anything new."

"Well, if I don't manage to see her tonight or tomorrow, say hello to her for me."

"I will. I'm sure she remembers you with great affection."

"Do you care for a refill?"

"No, thank you. It's about time for the movie. I don't know what they're showing; would you care to find out?"

"I'd better not. It's been a long day, and tomorrow probably won't be much better. Shall I see you in the morning?"

"Unless you go blind during the night. I usually eat breakfast at seven."

"Well, good night. Have fun at the movie."

Hamilton sat for a while, toying with the ice in his glass. Brandon's disillusionment with the army was disturbing. George was a really dedicated professional who, like Hamilton, regarded being an army officer as a special and almost sacred calling, somewhat like Holy Orders. The evils that he saw in the army were undoubtedly there, although it had not occurred to Hamilton before that the working of the efficiency report system was the underlying cause of so much that was visibly wrong with the army. With an effort, Hamilton dismissed these thoughts; after all, there was still a war to fight, and the politicians hadn't yet completely sold the army down the river. He looked up. Karla had come in, seen him, and was walking across to his table. She was nearly as tall as Hamilton, and, as Brandon had put it, big and blond and Nordic, but not fat. Their affair had been more fun and physical than passionate or emotional. She looked very strong and dashing in her light blue Red Cross uniform.

"Karla, it's great to see you again."

"Charlie, you don't know how much I've missed you."

When they embraced, her body made it clear that whatever had taken place since they parted had not quenched or changed her direct, earthy reaction to Hamilton or, he suspected, to any other male animal she took a liking to. Oh, well. Neither one of them mentioned that, since an exchange of Christmas cards, neither had written the other, or that each had unblushingly enjoyed other adventures with other partners in the interim. She had a placid, practical acceptance of life as it was, and thoroughly enjoyed its pleasures as they came without regret or jealousy.

"Sit down and have a drink, and tell me what you've been doing all these months."

"I've a better idea, Charlie. Let's go up to my room and talk. I've a bottle of real Cognac up there, not this rot-gut stuff they have at the bar."

"You know I could never resist you and Cognac, and now, with moonlight and palm trees thrown in . . ."

She laughed, quietly but triumphantly, and they walked out.

Her room was at the front of the building on the second floor, a plain, high-ceilinged white-plastered box with a red tile floor and a window looking out over the bay. In addition to the usual government-supplied rattan furniture and iron cot, she had a medium-size stereo and matching record and liquor cabinet in some light-colored local wood. The effect was cool and bare, but practical and comfortable. As soon as they were inside the door they kissed, long and slow and deep. After they separated, she went

over to the liquor cabinet and got out the Cognac and
two glasses.

"You still like your Cognac straight, don't you?"

"Is there any other way?"

"Of course not. Sit down and be comfortable.
Take off those boots if you like. Do you mind if I get
out of this uniform?"

"You know I much prefer you with no clothes on
at all."

She pulled the curtains, and they undressed. Her
body was just as he had remembered it, tanned,
muscular, well proportioned, full-breasted, and re-
sponsive. Neither had forgotten any of the little techniques and caresses which make the difference between
an act and an art. It was some time before they got
around to sipping their Cognac.

"Thank you, Charlie, that was fun."

"Thank *you*; you're the nicest thing that's happened to me in a long time, and you serve excellent
Cognac."

"I wish you weren't going back to that subsector
of yours tomorrow."

"Nor I; actually I'm stretching things by coming
up here for even one day."

"I'm glad you did."

"So am I."

At breakfast the next morning with Karla and George
Brandon, Hamilton looked a little pale and felt the
need for quite a little bit more than the usual amount
of coffee. Karla was radiant, and Brandon, who saw
everything and said nothing, was amused.

*   *   *

Everything went as planned at the DeLong Pier. Hamilton got two truckloads of cement and most of a truckload of two-by-eight planks for roofing beams and the like. He had brought along two Thompson submachine guns and several crossbows as trade goods, but these were not required. Nevertheless, he gave one of the crossbows to the officer in charge of the pier, Major Chapell. After all, he might have to come back for more cement later; in fact, since Karla was at Vung Ngai, he had every intention of doing so as soon as possible.

They left about two P.M. Although they made fairly good time on the road, considering the heavy loads in two of the trucks, it was nightfall when they pulled into the Dong Hai subsector compound; they had had no incidents en route.

"Well, sir, how was the trip?" It was Doc Tinsley.

"As you can see, we got some cement and lumber, and didn't get shot at. I ran into some old friends at Vung Ngai, which was very pleasant, but I don't like that Yang Cu Pass."

"I've heard it's a bad place, sir. By the way, you have some mail."

The letter was from Liz Parnell announcing that she very definitely could meet him in Bangkok for his R&R. It was a tender and happy letter, and it made him feel like an absolute heel. And his rationalization, mostly of the "She's a free agent and so am I" variety, didn't seem to help much. With alarm he began to wonder if he might be falling in love. He was very grateful for the cold beer that Tinsley brought him.

X.

A LONG WALK IN THE SUNSHINE

Hamilton was feeling rather pleased with himself. Lan's PF troops had not wasted any time in putting to use their share of the cement from Vung Ngai (one-third had been split off for Captain Rodman's eight-inch battery as rental for the trucks). A foundation for the new district operations center had been dug, a considerable detail was now busy mixing cement, sand, and water and molding the result into building blocks, and there were even grounds to hope that there would be enough left over to build a team bunker for Hamilton.

Also, the most recent monthly meeting at Phan Hoa had been Lieutenant Colonel Dace's last; he had taken a six-month extension to get command of a U.S. artillery battalion somewhere not far from Kontum, and would be leaving in about three days. Dace's replacement, an Infantry lieutenant colonel named Withrow, had not arrived at Phan Hoa in time for the meeting; all that Hamilton had been able to glean from the grapevine was that Withrow was white, not a ring knocker, and on his first tour to Vietnam. In the absence of facts to the contrary, one was at least permitted to hope that the new colonel would be a little less sharp of tongue than the old one.

Captain Gherardi, commander of the Special Forces "A" Team at Phuoc Tre, had stopped by for a visit while en route back from one of his infrequent trips to Phan Hoa city. Since this involved something of a detour from the most direct route into Phuoc Tre, it was not a common event. Hamilton and Gherardi were sitting in the relatively cool, dark interior of Hamilton's dining-cum-radio room.

Hamilton was curious. "To what do we owe the honor of your visit?" he asked.

"Just thought I'd stop by and say hello. . . . I suppose you'd heard that the 182d Airborne Brigade is planning an operation in these parts."

"No, I hadn't. It seems a little soon after the Koreans; the NVA who missed getting caught by that exercise must still be lying pretty low."

"They also haven't had the chance to dig new tunnels and generally repair the damage. Anyway, they're planning to set up their CP at Phuoc Tre and operate generally on my side of the river. I briefed them on several areas over there which they might want to go into. Most of them are places you can't get into with a walk-in operation by two CIDG companies, which is about the most that my people can take out into the field and still leave something behind to secure the camp and the hill behind it.''

"I know what you mean," Hamilton said. "If they're bigger than you are, which is likely to be the case around here if you're out with only two companies, you're in real trouble without something big to back you up, and if they're smaller, you fiddle around with their rear guard while the main body quietly walks away from you and then disappears. And it takes several battalions to put an encirclement on an area big enough to be worth fooling with, and a lot of helicopter assets to put them in simultaneously.''

"It's not all one way, though. They can't be everywhere and see everything, and they definitely don't have the means to communicate rapidly what they do see. The trick is to get your operation out of the immediate area of the camp and into the jungle without their seeing and reporting it, which is mostly a question of getting well clear of the camp before daylight. Once you're into an area where they think they're relatively secure, you can do quite a lot of damage until the word gets out that there's something wrong and everybody holes up. We ambush them at least as often as they ambush us. So far we've been running about a five-to-one kill ratio, and a little better on weapons.''

"I suppose the big risk is getting ambushed on the way home after you've gone out and stirred things up.''

"That does happen, but with a two-company operation and inside the artillery fan, it's not likely to be a disaster if they do pop an ambush on part of your column. Remember they have to keep their battalions spread out by companies and platoons most of the time, and only bring 'em together when they have a big operation planned. By the time they find out where I am and decide to get a whole battalion together to intercept me on the way home, I'm already moving, and by the time they can have their troops together and in place to cut me off or spring an ambush, I'm already back in camp fat and sassy. After all, they don't walk any faster than we do. Anything smaller than a whole battalion I can handle with a two-company operation.''

"You said there were places you couldn't get into.''

"There are a couple of base areas back there with bunkers and everything else that are always held in some strength, and if I go out there with two companies and stay around long enough to fight my way into the place, especially with these lightly armed CIDG troops, we're going to take quite a few casualties, and give the bad guys plenty of time to get a battalion or more together and climb up my backside. Which is not habit forming.''

"Hardly. I suppose you'll be helping the Airborne with this operation?''

"Oh, yes. We'll be securing their CP and fire bases and probably attaching about half a platoon to each airborne company for scouts, guides, and whatnot. If things work out, and I can borrow the choppers, there are a couple of company-size raids I'd like to try. Do you think your Dai-uy wants to get involved in this thing?''

"I know he'll be very glad to provide a holding

and interrogation point for any prisoners and detainees you all pick up; it's about the only way we get information. Otherwise, I don't know. We're spread pretty thin just securing places that have to be secured all the time. But it is his district, and I do think it would be a very good idea, just as a matter of protocol if nothing else, for someone from the Airborne, preferably the S3, to come up here sometime before it starts to brief him on it and invite him to join the party. I assume that our discussion so far has been for U.S. ears only?''

"More or less," Gherardi said. "The operation has been cleared with the province chief. Whether he passed the word down through VN channels I don't know."

"Neither do I. Lan hasn't said anything to me about it, and I make it a point not to pry into his relationship with Colonel Nhieu. But just from the point of view of keeping everyone happy, it would be a good idea for someone from the Airborne to come down here before things start and tell us about it officially."

"I see what you mean, and I'll take it up with the Airborne next time I see them."

"Thank you very much," Hamilton said. "By the way, when does the fun begin?"

"The Airborne moves in in about a week. Day after tomorrow I'm taking out two companies and a recon platoon for what amounts to a diversionary operation in the opposite direction. Would you care to come along for the ride?"

"At the moment I'm the only officer here, and my

senior NCO is in the hospital, so I probably shouldn't.
. . . How long are you going to be out?''

"It's just an overnight operation. We'll be moving
out from camp about three A.M. day after tomorrow,
stay out that day and all night, and walk back in the
next day.''

"That means two nights away from this place.''

"You stay away that long when you go to Phan
Hoa, don't you?''

"That's a command performance, though. But what
the hell, no one objects to my staying up all night on
an ambush somewhere, except the Dai-uy, that is,
and after their go-round with the Koreans, I suspect
that the bad guys aren't going to be raising too much
trouble for a little while. Should I bring along a radio
operator, and what's the uniform? I'm going stir-
crazy in this goddamn compound.''

"It might help to bring along a radio operator,''
Gherardi said. "All of our people will be wearing tiger
suits and round hats. And I know what you mean; if I
had your job I'd go out of my mind. By the way, I
heard you were out and about with the Koreans
during their last operation.''

"Well,'' said Hamilton, "after they'd stirred things
up, we managed to talk them into letting us set up an
ambush on one of the obvious escape routes.''

"Did you get anything?''

"Oh, yes. We ran into what looked like a platoon,
popped the ambush, called in some mortars, and then
cleared out, since there were only seven of us—me
and my radio operator and five Koreans.''

"You must be getting hard up for excitement, to be doing things like that."

"Someone once said that war consists of long stretches of uncomfortable boredom punctuated by short spells of excitement of the least pleasant kind."

"I'll say that's a fair definition. I guess I'd better send someone up here to pick you up tomorrow afternoon; that way we save tying up your jeep for two days doing nothing. Will you be needing to borrow tiger suits? Hopefully we have your size."

"I acquired one some time ago; I don't know about my radio operator. We can sort that out tomorrow."

"Why not? I guess I've done about as much damage as I can here and ought to be moving on. Thank you very much for the beer."

"You're quite welcome. Anytime. And see you tomorrow."

It was fortunate that somewhere, somehow, Harley had been able to promote a tiger suit; he was a big man, and the Phuoc Tre camp didn't have on hand anything even close to his size. He was also carrying his M-14 rifle and a radio. Hamilton, as usual, had his M-2 carbine and the usual battle harness: pistol belt, load-carrying suspenders, two canteens, two ammo pouches, each with four "banana clips" for his carbine, map, compass, Bowie knife, several grenades, first-aid packet, gloves, and rope, plus a poncho for overnight.

The column moved out just after three A.M. in almost complete darkness, with the recon platoon

leading, followed by two companies. The command
group, consisting of the commander of the leading
company, the LLDB camp commander, Gherardi,
and Hamilton, each with his radio operator, followed
the first platoon of the lead company. A Special
Forces sergeant, with radio, accompanied the recon
platoon, and another was with the second company in
the column. All the troops had been very carefully
checked to make sure that they carried nothing that
rattled or made any other avoidable noise. The perimeter lights had not been turned on that night; the
men had fallen in and moved out in almost complete
silence and darkness, and were moving slowly and at
fairly close intervals so no one would lose the column.

On leaving the camp, they turned left, then left
again through a little draw between the adjacent perimeters of the camp and Captain Rodman's eight-
inch battery. Once clear of the perimeters, they headed
southwest across about half a mile of gently rising
open country, moving as quickly as possible without
losing anyone or making any great amount of noise.
Hamilton could see the loom of a big hill ahead of
them. He knew that the hill was covered with fairly
heavy scrub jungle and was not under permanent
occupation by any friendly forces. The plan was to
go over the side of this hill, across the little valley
beyond it, and be on the crest of a saddle between
two hills behind it before daylight, then lay up for a
short rest and something to eat, and try to find out if
they had been spotted. That meant climbing two
sizable hills before breakfast.

Soon they were inside the jungle, working up a

steep, irregular path. The darkness out in the open
was nothing compared to the utter blackness inside
the jungle. Even though Hamilton made it a point to
stay fit and the column was not moving very fast, he
had difficulty keeping up. Everyone seemed to have
caught a sense of the necessity for stealth and speed
and for getting well clear of the camp and into the
jungle before daylight. A good part of the way they
were pulling themselves up with their hands, so Hamilton slung his carbine and put on the pair of heavy
leather gloves he had been carrying for just this
purpose; he had long ago learned not to grab things
in the jungle at night with his bare hands. There was
a much better, easier trail over this hill about five
hundred meters farther west, but, as the obvious
avenue of movement from the camp to the little
valley behind the hill, it was almost certain to be
watched. With a little wind rustling the trees, there
was reason to hope that whoever was watching the
other trail would not hear or see them pass on this
one.

At the top of the climb, where the trail passed over
the shoulder of the hill, they had a few yards of
relatively easy level going, then started down. Here
the column went very fast and Hamilton had even
more difficulty keeping up without making a great
deal of noise. Their path was a steep and rocky dry
streambed, and in many places tangled vines grew
right across the path, making it necessary to slide
through feetfirst, which, in nearly total darkness and
in a rocky streambed, is not much fun. Eventually
they got to the bottom, sore, scratched, sweating,

and ill-tempered, crossed a muddy little stream with about two inches of water in it, pushed through some heavy bottomland brush interspersed with clumps of impassable bamboo, and started up the other side, again by way of a rocky and overgrown streambed. Not for the first time that morning, Hamilton wondered by what folly he had let himself in for all this. Behind him, Harley was keeping up, apparently without any trouble, even though he was carrying a radio and a heavier weapon, if several fewer years.

After what seemed like an interminable struggle up over rocks and through brush and vines, with the sides of the streambed seeming to get deeper and deeper, they pulled themselves one by one out of the streambed, up an almost vertical bank about eight feet high, and set off diagonally uphill on a somewhat easier track, rendered even easier by the faint beginnings of the coming of day. They were moving fairly fast, and Hamilton wondered how the people in the second company in column, who were no doubt still in the creekbed, could keep up enough not to go astray.

Shortly after daylight, the column closed up and settled into a defensive perimeter astride the saddle they had been making for, with outpost ambushes some distance out in either direction. So far there had been no sign of the enemy, very little had been said, and there had been no radio traffic. Everyone was off the trail and sufficiently concealed so that any but a very alert and observant VC could probably have walked all the way through the position without being aware of their presence—provided he stayed on the

trail. Each of the outpost ambushes had a pistol with
a silencer to dispose of any single VC coming up the
trail who seemed to be taking an undue interest in his
surroundings. Otherwise small parties were to be let
through without being shot up. It was still far too
soon to start diverting the enemy's attention.

Hamilton was making breakfast out of a chocolate
bar and a little water. Lan had politely declined to
accompany him on the operation, stating that Colonel
Nhieu required him to stay at the subsector headquarters, especially at night. From what he had seen of
the more junior officers on the subsector staff, Hamilton could hardly fault this rule. He had not advised
sector of his own impending absence, in part because
he had no convenient way to do so without discussing the whole matter on the radio for everyone to
hear, but mainly lest they forbid him to go. If Tinsley
were asked at night about Hamilton's absence, he was
simply to advise that Hamilton was out on an ambush; otherwise, that he was down at Phuoc Tre
coordinating with the CIDG. All of which was more
or less true. Hamilton also reflected that it was a
sorry state of affairs when a combat-arms officer
damn near had to go AWOL to get a crack at the
enemy. He had no doubts that Tinsley and Parelli
would cope very adequately with any enemy activities at the subsector during his absence.

The CIDG troops were visibly younger and fitter
than Lan's RF troops. Most of them were ethnic
Vietnamese; the few Montagnards were conspicuous
with their darker complexions and heavy features. At
least among the troops, there seemed to be no "feel-

ings" between the two groups, which spoke very well for the leadership of all concerned. The LLDB camp commander, a captain, was middle-aged, tough, and ugly; he knew his business and took no nonsense from anyone. The company commander of the lead company was small and wiry and seemed to say very little.

About half an hour after full daylight, they began moving out again. At six o'clock the radios had been turned on. When the time came to move out, all that the camp commander had to do was break the squelch twice with his "push to talk" button. The company commanders and the recon platoon leader had been briefed on the plan. Each broke squelch once to acknowledge. This was also the signal to Phuoc Tre that the operation had arrived at the saddle without incident and was now moving out according to plan. The plan was to walk in another six miles or so and lay a set of interlocking ambushes on a group of trails that connected a VC base area in the mountains west of Phan Hoa city to a larger base area generally west of Dong Hai.

Initially, they went straight down the south side of the hill. It was another unpleasant scramble down a dry watercourse, albeit aided by daylight. They were moving slowly, spread out and with caution, complete with security elements on both flanks and at both ends of the column. As an additional measure, they were deliberately avoiding known trails and traveling by map, compass, and such substitutes for trails as ridge lines and watercourses.

During the briefing before the operation, Hamilton

had asked what to do when they encountered a well-used trail in VC country. Gherardi had replied, "First of all, I've laid out our route so as to cross as few known major trails as possible. And there's a regular drill when we do run across one. First the column stops and gets down. Then the recon platoon very carefully checks out the trail for fifty to a hundred meters each side of where we cut it, and reports. Next, the leading platoon of the lead company stakes out a security ambush on the trail about fifty meters each side of where we're going to cross it. After the rest of the lead company is across, the lead platoon of the second company takes over the ambushes and the old platoon tacks onto the tail end of its own company. When the last of the column is through, the ambush platoon takes over as rear guard for the whole column. People in the middle cross over by twos and threes but only when they have the all-clear signal from the security ambushes. Once when we were about two thirds of the way across a trail, we had to stop and let a whole company of NVA walk through on the trail; they never knew we were there. I had my scouts trail them to where they stopped for the night, and then gave 'em a dose of eight-inch."

"I bet that hurt."

"Well, when we looked over the area the next morning, we counted eleven bodies and collected eight weapons, six of them pretty well smashed. Apparently when the eight-inch hit them, they bugged out, and hadn't got up enough courage to come back and police up the bodies when we got there. So we staked the place out and gave 'em another dose of eight-inch when they came back to pick up the pieces after the first time. Then we got the hell out of there.''

"You guys fight dirty.''

"Is there any other way?''

"Not that I know of, at least assuming that you want to win the war and keep your own casualties down.''

It was midafternoon before they got to the area where they intended to operate, all of it very laborious scrambling mostly up and down hot, stuffy, rocky, overgrown dry watercourses, punctuated by the short, tense halts required by the trail-crossing procedure. At one point, a single VC had come up the trail, spotted the ambush, and been shot down by the man with the pistol with the silencer. He had had an old M-1 carbine, two hand grenades, and papers indicating that he was "liaison cadre'' (VC for runner) for the Phan Hoa city committee. The body was quickly concealed and the column moved on, taking along the weapons and papers. Most of the other trails that they crossed showed signs of more or less recent use, evidently by the VC, but otherwise they had no contact before arriving at their objective area.

This location had been carefully selected. It was a hill, one of many, a knob at the east end of a ridge between two steep, narrow valleys. The entire area was covered with heavy scrub jungle, thickest in the valleys and lower slopes, and thinning a little along the ridge lines. The highest part of the knob had been used as a fire base during an operation by U.S.

troops about eight months before and was not yet so overgrown as to prevent its use by helicopters for evacuation of casualties or, if need be, extraction of the whole force.

Three trails formed a triangle around the central knob. Gherardi planned to lay platoon-size ambushes on the trails passing north and east of the knob, and a two-platoon-size ambush on the main trail on the south side of the ridge, with the balance of his force in reserve further up the hill in the general vicinity of the old fire base.

Their approach to the area was by way of a dry watercourse which ran straight up the north side of the ridge to the vicinity of the fork in the trail from the west. Since parts of all three trails were open to observation from the air, it did not seem likely that the enemy would use them during the daytime, so, when they arrived at the fork, they began using the trails. A squad from the recon platoon, with a Special Forces sergeant and a radio, went a little ways west on the main trail and set up a concealed outpost to give warning of any enemy force coming from this side. The lead company, preceded by another recon squad, and including the command group, went down the right fork; their mission was to set up the two-platoon ambush on this trail, with the recon squad manning two outposts further down the hill, and the third platoon of the company making part of the reserve. The second company was to take the trail along the north side of the hill, set up ambushes there and along the north-south trail, with the third recon squad manning outposts on that side.

It seemed to Hamilton as they moved along the trail that the jungle was unusually quiet, that the accustomed sounds of bird and insect were oddly absent. From the middle of the column it was, of course, very hard to judge, and he decided that it might well be that the wildlife simply avoided well-used trails and were more likely to be encountered on the abandoned watercourses and other unused places they had been using. But the column was moving unusually slowly, as if the point men were also uneasy. Suddenly there was an explosion ahead, followed by a heavy rattle of fire, then silence; everyone was off the trail and into the brush, crouching. The camp commander was alternately talking and listening to his radio, and Gherardi was on his radio, apparently with the sergeant with the lead element. A grenade or booby trap had exploded in the trail, killing the point man, and the point squad was pinned down along the trail by an estimated enemy platoon. Several CIDG soldiers had found an open spot and were setting up a pair of 60mm mortars. After a hurried consultation between Hamilton, Gherardi, and the camp commander, it was decided to attack straight ahead along the trail with the lead company and to send the second company around the north side of the hill to cut off the enemy's retreat, or attack him in the flank and rear over the top of the hill if he stayed put.

There was more firing ahead, as the lead platoon of the lead company got into action to relieve the point squad, and the two little mortars started firing. While Gherardi and the camp commander were radioing out the orders for the attack, Hamilton was on Harley's radio with Phuoc Tre (using one of their call signs, not his own), advising them of the contact and the probable need for a dustoff, and requesting a forward observer aircraft, if available. It had been arranged for Rodman's eight-inch battery to be on this frequency and to have two of their cannon laid in the direction of this hill. Rodman advised that he had monitored, and did they need any support? So Hamilton inquired:

"Gherardi, do you think we need any eight-inch yet?"

"For one platoon? Let's save it for later."

Rodman was so advised. Meanwhile, the remaining two platoons of the lead company had spread out astride the trail and were advancing through the brush. The command group pushed back onto the trail and followed them. Ahead there was considerable small-arms firing, including a fair number of rounds that came snapping through the brush around them, and the loud *whump-whump-whump* of the 60mm mortars beating up the enemy's position and the branch of the trail going down the hill. If what was up ahead was the rear guard, they were not ignoring the probable avenue of escape of the main body. At a bend in the trail it became evident that whoever it was had no immediate intention of falling back. After taking several casualties, the advancing skirmish line stopped and went down into firing positions in order to more effectively return the fire of an enemy who had numerous automatic weapons and no apparent lack of ammunition or determination. Gherardi radioed further instructions to the other company, telling them to attack over the top of the hill and down onto the enemy's flank, then called for eight-inch three hundred meters in front of their forward position. With further exhortation by the camp commander, their company commander, and two of the Special Forces sergeants, the company astride the trail again began to advance, this time by crawling and occasional short rushes, making all possible use of any protection offered by folds in the ground or the occasional fallen tree.

About four minutes later the first two rounds of eight-inch came in. Hamilton estimated that they were about two hundred meters too far east; Rodman was evidently taking no chances on dropping these ponderous shells on friendly heads. Even so, five hundred meters away, the sound was impressive and the blast of each explosion could be felt. After a quick consultation with Gherardi, Hamilton brought the next volley a cautious one hundred meters closer; the 60mm mortars could take care of the close-in stuff. The next two rounds of eight-inch were considerably nearer; the enemy was apparently feeling the heat, as his rate of fire slackened off, and the CIDG each side of the trail began moving forward somewhat faster. Shortly, there was further firing on their left; the other company, coming over the hill, had made contact with the enemy's flank. At that point the enemy made off down the hill, and the battle was over in a rush. Gherardi and Hamilton directed the mortars and eight-inch onto the enemy's probable routes of withdrawal. They decided to regroup on the hill, sort things out, and get set for the night, as a tail-end pursuit could only result in losing the enemy or walking into a trap.

Three CIDG, including the point man, had been killed, and there were eight wounded requiring evacuation. A sweep of the enemy's position turned up seven bodies and two wounded, plus two AK-47s, one SKS, assorted grenades, demolitions, web equipment, and papers. Between the papers and what could be gotten from one of the two wounded, they determined that they had been in contact with a full company of the 4th Battalion of the 299th NVA Regiment, and that another company of that battalion would be coming east along the trail that night. Unless, of course, they had got the word that the CIDG were in the area in some force, in which case they would be either diverted or substantially reinforced.

One of the Special Forces sergeants was calling a dustoff for all ten wounded, plus transportation to take out the bodies of the three dead CIDG. The dead NVA were left in place; in a day or so their comrades would find them and bury them. Elements of the recon platoon were sent out to outpost each of the trails leading to the hill, and the rest of the column took up a defensive position at the old fire-base area, first making a thorough check of the area for booby traps.

"Well, sir, they know where we are, and when those choppers come in for the wounded, the whole damn world will know. This hilltop is likely to get rather noisy tonight."

It was Gherardi; he was dirty, sweat-stained, and looked very tired.

Hamilton, who felt as if he looked about the same, replied, ''Well, on the one hand, we're here, and it's a good strong position, and if things really get ugly there's a chance that they can get us out by chopper. Between the eight-inch and the Spooky, I really don't sweat a ground attack, provided our ammunition holds. Also the troops are probably darn near as tired as I am, and could use a rest before the night's activities begin. With the pre-dug foxholes up here, we should be at least in fair shape if they beat the place up with mortars.

''On the other hand, I definitely like the idea of slipping quietly away after the enemy has decided that we're going to spend the night here, let him waste a lot of ammunition on an empty hill, then give him a big dose of eight-inch after he overruns it.''

Their deliberations were interrupted by the arrival of the L-19 with the forward observer. Hamilton asked him to make a VR of the area within two kilometers of their location. He went on: ''There's no doubt that we're under observation, but that FO will keep them from moving anything serious against us before dark, which is another hour and a half. So if we're going to slip away, the best time will be shortly after nightfall, when, hopefully, their observers can no longer see us, but before they've had time to move against us in strength.''

''Which means that, in the meantime, whichever we decide to do we'd better start setting up a night defensive position here. Also get some chow and some rest. And if we do decide to make it, the best way is down the south side of the hill; it's away from the camp, which is the direction they will be least suspecting us to take.''

"I'd rather go west along this ridge, so we stay on high and fairly defensible ground and have some chance of making it to an open place if we have to be taken out by chopper. Also I have doubts about communications with Phuoc Tre from the south side of this ridge.''

So, after consulting with the camp commander, they selected a hump on the ridge about six hundred meters west of their present position, and decided to move out shortly after dark. Eventually, the dustoff choppers arrived and took away the wounded; there was also a supply chopper with ammunition, claymore mines, and some concertina wire, which took away the captured weapons and the bodies of the three dead CIDG. The weather was warm and bright, and the view from the top of the hill, as they each ate a can of C rations for dinner, was superb, if not at all informative. Hamilton was sitting between Harley and Gherardi.

"Well, Harley,'' Hamilton inquired, "how are you making it?''

"Just fine, sir, except I haven't seen anything worth shooting at yet.''

"We'll see what we can do about that. Did you bring along your bayonet?''

"Oh, yes, sir, but I'm not sure I want to get close enough to use it.''

Since most of the serious digging had already been

done, it did not take the two companies very long to make a respectable defensive position out of the old fire base, except for lack of overhead cover, for which materials were lacking (none of the scrub brush in the area was big enough to make into bunker roofing timbers).

Toward sunset the weather began making up; it would be another night of wind and probably rain, which would facilitate concealed movements by both sides. About half an hour before sundown, the FO, who was in any event running low of fuel, asked to be released because of the weather, and of course they let him go. Runners were slipped out to the outposts with word as to when to move; additionally, the squad outposted at the trail fork was sent to reconnoiter and occupy the knoll where they would spend the night. Shortly after sundown the reconnaissance squad reported themselves in place and the area apparently clear of the enemy. The camp commander also sent out a detail to cut some ten-foot bamboo poles, initially to move the coils of concertina wire, but also in case they had to move any wounded any distance.

At sunset the platoon and squad leaders were briefed on the plan, and as soon as it was thoroughly dark, the troops, most of whom had had about an hour's rest, policed up the concertina wire and claymore mines, stuffed the mines into rucksacks, tied the coils of wire to the poles to be carried by two men each, and formed up to move out.

It took very little time to cover the six hundred meters to their new position. It was a high-speed

trail, and the troops didn't have to be told the advantages of not getting caught by the enemy en route
from one defensive position to another. The Special
Forces sergeant with the recon squad had already
planned the layout of the position, and each platoon
was met by one of the scouts who led it directly to its
proper sector. The command group and the mortars
were set up in the center of the position. Claymores
were set out, but not the concertina, as that would
make too much noise and stir. About half an hour
after the last elements had closed and the outposts
set, it started drizzling.

The night was dismally wet and uncomfortable.
Shortly before three A.M., about fifty mortar rounds
were fired onto their old position. It was too rainy
and windy, especially in the brush, to make a guess
as to where the enemy mortars were located, and
they heard no small-arms firing to indicate that the
enemy was attempting a ground attack on their former position. Otherwise, the night was quiet, and
those who were not on watch had no difficulty
sleeping.

They moved out about half an hour after daybreak.
Since the enemy knew they were in the area, the
direct routes back to Phuoc Tre could lead to trouble,
and since the Airborne was planning to go into the
area west of the camp, they made a long detour to the
east; a good part of their route went through the
western edge of Tuy Cau District. This was out of
their authorized area of operations (AO) and had not
been coordinated with Tuy Cau or the Koreans, so
there was some risk of being spotted and shot up by

friendly aircraft and artillery, but Charlie also knew their AO boundary and wasn't likely to be looking for them outside it. Inside the Phuoc Tre AO they traveled in the same style as they had used coming in, staying off the regular trails, but once outside the AO, they hiked boldly up the trails, which saved time and effort.

Twice en route they had to stop to let through small parties of VC; in each case the group of VC were too numerous to take out with pistol and silencer, and too small to risk disclosing their position by shooting them up. They also encountered three apparently innocent woodcutters on one of the trails in the back part of Tuy Cau. Since it was possible that they were VC trail watchers or agents of Lieutenant Dao, they brought them in.

About two hours before sundown one of Gherardi's sergeants drove Hamilton and Harley into the Dong Hai compound. Hamilton noticed with some alarm a chopper on the pad, shut down. If the new boss had come out to visit him, only to find that he had slipped off on this thoroughly illegal venture with the CIDG, things were going to be grim, indeed. It turned out, however, to be a Lieutenant Colonel Ellis, the S3 of the Airborne Brigade, who had come to brief him and Lan on the coming operation. He greeted Hamilton in a friendly way and made no issue about having to wait for him, or on the lack of polish in Hamilton's briefing for him of the operation just concluded. He also agreed without demur not to rat to Sector about Hamilton's having been out with the CIDG.

After they left, Hamilton indulged himself in a shower and a cold beer. Harley had showered during the briefing. After Tinsley summarized the very little that had happened during Hamilton's absence, he said, "Sir, if you don't mind my saying so, you look a little tired."

"It's the farthest I've walked in a long time. I'm going to have sore legs for a week. Hopefully, Sector didn't find out where we were."

"Sir, no one asked where you were."

"Sometimes it's comfortable to be unimportant."

XI.

━━━━✦━━━✦━━━✦━━━✦━━━✦━━━━

BANGKOK AND AYUTTHAYA

"Well, how was your trip from Dong Hai?"

It was Liz. She and Hamilton were sitting at a small table under a large, bright umbrella next to the pool at the Imperial Hotel in Bangkok. Liz was wearing a scanty, bright green bikini, large sunglasses, and a pale tan floppy beach hat; Hamilton had on close-fitting dark green swim briefs. Each had a bottle of the excellent and quite potent local Singha beer. As arranged, they had met at the hotel, taken a room, and joyously reestablished their status as lovers, then decided to spend the hour or so that remained of the afternoon by the pool, before changing for dinner and whatever evening excursions they might think up.

"Complicated but not exciting," Hamilton replied. "I left Dong Hai yesterday morning by the supply chopper, showed my face as briefly as I dared at

Phan Hoa Sector, and caught a ride to the air base. From there I got a ride on a C-123 to Cam Ranh Bay and the so-called R&R Center. Cam Ranh Bay, especially the peninsula between the bay and the South China Sea, is really beautiful, and has what looks like a very nice beach, but the R&R Center, which is also a replacement center for people arriving and departing from in-country, is a dismally uncomfortable collection of wooden barracks in the sand dunes, with practically no local security and nothing at all to do. Even if I hadn't been en route to seeing the most delightful creature I know and in one of the most enjoyable of places, I would have been glad to leave.''

"Careful, Charlie, flattery will get you everywhere.''

Hamilton topped off their beer glasses, took a sip, and went on: "The flight in was an old DC-7 belonging to one of the charter airlines—still a lot more comfortable than those strap seats in a C-123, and it got us here. Do they put civilians through all that rigmarole with changing scrip for real money, briefings, and the rest?''

"Since I've never gone on a military R&R, I'm not familiar with what they have you do, or do to you; I did have to go through customs and change my scrip for green, amid solemn warnings of dire punishment if I brought any green back into Vietnam.''

"Other than that, how was your trip?''

"Charlie, it was so simple. One of the people at the office drove me out to Tan Son Nhut, I got on one of Air Vietnam's Caravelles, and in about an hour I was here.''

"That's the best part.''

"The best part is being with you, anywhere, but especially in Bangkok."

"Why Bangkok?"

"I don't know. Maybe I should have said anywhere away from Saigon. I've only been here since this morning, but I think I'm going to like the place, and it's awfully good to get away from all the noise and pressures in Saigon."

"I thought you said you liked being a war correspondent."

"I do, I really do, but it's nice to get away from it for a little while. I'm sure that if I were stuck here in Bangkok I'd either get very bored or immediately start snooping around for some good lively copy, especially if you weren't here to keep me company. . . . By the way, I noticed that everyone here seems to be so very prim and proper, even the GIs and their floozies. How come?"

"Well, the Thais have a curious viewpoint. You can play at any kind of fun and games you want to, indoors and with the shades drawn. It's really a rather wide-open town, but any kind of outdoor hugging and mauling, even holding hands, is considered a public display of affection, PDA for short, and offends their sense of propriety and decorum."

"Is that why you didn't kiss me in the lobby?"

"We made up for that later, didn't we?"

"Ummmm . . . didn't we?"

She grinned, a relaxed, happy, satisfied grin that came very near to being a leer. Then she sipped her beer and went on: "This is excellent beer. How come they make so much better beer than the Vietnamese?"

"I suspect it's because the Thais learned brewing from the English, and the Vietnamese learned from the French. Outside of Alsace, French beer is rather like the German attempts at red wine."

"You know, I've never been to Europe. But I'd always been told that the Germans made pretty good wine."

"They do. They make excellent white wine, and their red wines aren't anywhere nearly as bad as Vietnamese beer, but .. ."

They sat for a while in silence, enjoying the beer, the slanting sunlight, and being together. The hotel building, modern, four stories of white stucco, looked over one side of the pool; a one-story wing, housing the hotel's barbershop and massage parlor, was across one end. The other two sides were enclosed by a ten-foot stuccoed wall; between this wall and the terrace around the pool were narrow beds of dark green, flowering shrubs. In the far corner, carefully sited so the shadow of the main building would never fall on it, was the "spirit house," a miniature Buddhist temple, lacy and ornate in red, white, and gold. Aside from two Americans, also in swimsuits, apparently soldiers or junior officers, who were taking in the last of the afternoon sun, and a discreet bar waiter in a high-collared white jacket, they had the pool to themselves.

Eventually Liz observed, "This is such a nice place. I think I could spend our whole time here without leaving the hotel."

"So could I, but there's too much to see that exists

nowhere else in the world, to say nothing of all that lovely shopping.''

"Of course you're right, but I'm going to pay my own way when it comes to the shopping. Otherwise, I'd feel even more like a kept woman; I'm also going to insist on paying my half of the hotel bill.''

"That independent streak could get expensive.''

"That's all right; they pay me fairly well. And, well, you know . . . a long time ago I promised myself I'd never let myself get dependent and emotionally involved. When you're around, it's very hard to keep that promise.''

"I'm sorry. Shall I discreetly disappear?''

"Oh, Charlie, don't even say that. I like being with you—especially in bed. You're strong and gentle and so very good to me. I've been looking forward to this trip for a long time, and I'm going to enjoy it all the way if I can, and let the bits and pieces take care of themselves. God knows, if I hadn't had you to look forward to, and this trip, I don't know what would have become of me in Saigon. . . . But, you see, that's all the more reason why I have to keep to the little symbols of being independent.''

"You know I've missed you, and the thought of our being together here in Bangkok . . . well, let me say that, without it, it would have been a whole lot harder not to come unglued up there in Dong Hai. But I wouldn't want you to get any more deeply involved in this thing than you want to, and end up getting hurt.''

"Oh, Charlie, you're always so melodramatic, and

so gallant. But look here, we're grown children now, so I hope we can play house together for a week, and enjoy it thoroughly, without putting too many dents in each other's vanity when or if it does come to an end. At worst, I know that you're cautious enough to let me down gently.''

Hamilton couldn't think of an appropriate reply, so he laughed and suggested that they change for dinner. He was relieved that she accepted, verbally at least, that this affair might be no more than another affair, although a very pleasant one, and was trying to avoid too much of an emotional commitment, which would make the inevitable termination much less complicated. But he had also had too much experience with the workings of female emotions to have much optimism as to how long this attitude would last. They finished their beer and went upstairs.

Once inside their room, he took her in his arms and kissed her, meanwhile undoing the back of the bra to her bikini. They separated for a moment and it dropped to the floor. Her hands, which had been caressing up and down his back, slid down and began working off his swim briefs. In a moment, they were both naked, kissing, arms entwined and caressing.

They paused for a moment, and Hamilton suggested: ''Shower time?''

''Why not . . . let me get my shower cap.''

So he went and turned on and adjusted the shower. In a moment she joined him, looking somehow very neat and hygienic in her shower cap. The ivory whiteness of skin where she had been wearing the bikini contrasted crisply with the golden tan of the rest of her body. The shower took some time, as each one washed the other, gently, caressingly, and all over. Afterward, they rinsed down, toweled off, and stepped back into the bedroom. For a long while they lay on the bed entwined, caressing and stroking each other, and then made love. Just at the moment when Hamilton was beginning to lose control of his reflexes, Liz dug her fingers into his shoulders and began having a climax, so the timing was as close to perfect as it ever gets. For several minutes afterward they remained together, warm, relaxed, and satisfied.

Eventually, Liz observed, "Affectionate little beast, aren't I?"

"You're wonderful . . . and that was beautiful."

"Do you say that to all the girls you seduce?"

Hamilton laughed and rolled off, then replied, "What else is there to say, especially when it's true?"

"Charlie, as a technician you're superb, but you've got to invent a better exit line."

"Have you any suggestions?"

"Not right now, but I'll think about it."

The sun had set and the brief tropic twilight had turned into night when they came down for dinner. Liz was wearing a sleeveless slate-blue silk sheath and her jade necklace and earrings. Hamilton had on his one dark gray tropical-weight suit, white button-down shirt, a sober dark crimson silk tie with a small blue and white paisley pattern in it, and dark gray suede shoes. He liked the jaunty grace with which her lean body and legs moved within the dress, and was not unaware of the admiring and envious glances of several Americans and some of the hotel staff as they passed through the lobby into the dining room. They had decided to dine at the hotel, which is justly famous for its Kobe steaks, then take in the first part of the nightclub act there. Both felt the need for a good night's sleep, and Hamilton had plans for a fairly busy day on the morrow. Also, both of them had been around enough not to feel any compulsion to stay up most of the night in a series of indifferent nightclubs just to prove to themselves that they were really on vacation.

It may have been Hamilton's coat and necktie, in contrast to the sport shirts worn by most of his compatriots, or it may have been that Liz was visibly not one of the Thai or Chinese whores who generally attach themselves to the great majority of GIs on R&R, but the headwaiter was very cordial and gave them an excellent table, just the right distance from the little stage where the nightclub act would later appear, and the service was even better than Hamilton remembered from the last time he had been here.

A Kobe steak comes from cattle that are kept in stalls all their lives, hand fed and rubbed down daily to ensure the extreme tenderness of their meat. The steak is marinated, spiced, tenderly grilled, and generally fussed over to produce one of the really major culinary delights. Here it was accompanied by tender French fried potatoes and an excellent green salad. Since the offerings on the wine list were not of a quality to justify their prices, the meal was accompanied by more Singha beer.

When the steaks arrived, Liz observed admiringly,

"Charlie, this is the most magnificent steak I've ever seen."

"It does make one realize the difference between food and food. Also that it's been a long time since lunch."

"You, too? You seem to do fairly well on an empty stomach."

"Only when inspired by something very special, like you."

For a while they ate in silence. It seemed a pity that conversation should be allowed to interfere with appreciation of the Kobe steaks. The room was low and dimly lit, with a dark carpet, large black leather chairs for the diners, and round tables with white tablecloths reaching nearly to the floor. About half the other diners seemed to be Americans on R&R, only a few of them with Thai or Chinese girls; there were also businessmen of several nationalities, but predominantly Japanese, two middle-age couples from the West, probably vacationing, and two tables occupied by what Hamilton took to be pilots and stewardesses of the Japanese airline. No Thai or local Chinese appeared to be present among the diners. Hamilton admitted to finding the sleek, discreet, quietly expensive atmosphere very much to his taste.

For dessert they had fresh papaya with lime juice; the nightclub act arrived at the same time as dessert. It was a Filipino band with a girl singer. The band, composed of five mop-headed, skinny youths, cranked out the usual East Asian imitation of American popular music. The girl, whose bony Latin features betrayed more than a little Spanish ancestry, bounced around and sang with great gusto and charm, and was even on-key most of the time.

Liz leaned over and whispered, "She looks exactly like a girl I went to high school with, only she was Italian."

"I think this one's mostly Spanish; after all, the Islands were a Spanish colony for several centuries. Anyway, it's a pleasant switch from moon faces and button noses."

"Charlie, you're letting your prejudices show."

"Sorry, it's just that I'm queer for round-eyes, especially you."

"Some of these Thai girls are very good-looking."

"I've noticed, but I haven't seen any as attractive as you, and you speak English."

After dinner, they each had a Cognac (hang the expense) and eventually went up to bed, where they made love once more, and quickly went to sleep.

Next morning, they had coffee, fresh pineapple, and sweet rolls in a sunlit "coffee shop" overlooking the pool. Hamilton had laid on a tour of the Royal Palace and its adjacent Wat Phra Keo temple complex, which are only open to the public at certain times on certain days, for that afternoon, so they decided to have a try at shopping that morning. He had telephoned the firm he had done some business with on his previous visits to Bangkok and arranged to have a car come by to pick them up.

Shortly after breakfast, the driver turned up. He was a sleek young Chinese in the usual business uniform of white shirt and dark trousers, with a Datsun Bluebird car. He seemed a little put out that Hamilton had a girl with him; after all, this eliminated the opportunity to do a little pimping on the side. But he hurled the car through the swirling traffic with skill and daring, in a style reminiscent of the more aggressive type of Roman taxi driver.

Bangkok is a big, clean, modern city, with few tall buildings, many parks and boulevards, and considerable distances. In addition to the Royal Palace and the various temples, which are unmatched anywhere, the city has many handsome public buildings of relatively recent date and no great specific interest to the visitor. Their destination was in an older, predominantly Chinese section of town, built up in the usual Chinese style with buildings of two stories, the lower one an open-front shop, the upper, usually with a balcony in front, living quarters for the family. But the Eastern Silk and Gem Company, their destination, was a more elaborate, Victorian-looking stone building.

Inside, they were taken in charge by a Thai-Chinese girl who spoke excellent English and plied them with Singha beer and what Hamilton defined as the high-speed soft sell. Except for one piece of Thai silk, enough for a dress, a like amount of Thai cotton, and a black star sapphire pin that cost about forty dollars, Liz insisted on paying for everything she bought. Aside from a large set of bronze tableware "for my trousseau" and a piece of heavy, nubby black silk for Hamilton to have made up into a tuxedo jacket and cummerbund, her purchases were gifts for her parents, aunts, uncles, and cousins: silk and cotton for dresses, bronzeware and black star sapphire and niello jewelry for the women, cuff links and niello lighters and cigarette cases for the men. Hamilton was buying the same kinds of items for members of his family. Despite the difference in backgrounds, he found their tastes to be remarkably similar; in most cases each bought a piece of cloth off the same bolt.

"I hope you're buying something for your girlfriends back in the States," Liz said.

"What gave you the idea I had any?"

"Well, you must. I hate to think of the idea of you going off to war and not having someone pining for you and writing you tear-stained letters every week."

The salesgirl had discreetly drifted away.

"I have never received a tear-stained letter in my life . . . and the others were demoted to the grade of mere pen pals when I met you."

"I'm sorry, I shouldn't pry, and if I caught one of your pen pals, I'd probably try to claw her eyes out . . . and it's your money."

Hamilton bought two more pieces of silk, selected with expert assistance from Liz. In all, it was a profitable morning for the Eastern Silk and Gem Company. Since Hamilton was an old customer and the total of their purchases was rather large, they gave him a 15 percent discount and accepted their personal checks on stateside banks without any fuss. They also recommended a tailor shop, no doubt run by a relative. The sleek young Chinese with the Datsun took them there, had a brief word with the tailor, and stayed around while Hamilton was measured. The tailor promised to deliver the jacket to their hotel for a fitting the evening of the next day, and they were back to the hotel in time for lunch.

After they said good-bye to the driver, Liz observed, "I like the way they do business, but the markup must be tremendous for them to be able to provide all that free transportation and beer, plus a discount."

"Absolutely, but also all of them are probably members of the family, including the lad who was driving the car and the gal in the store, who could very well be brother and sister, so they don't have to pay them very much. And you and I are pretty good customers; we walk in with a good notion of what we want to buy, buy it quickly and in quantity, and don't waste their time with fiddling and haggling. We could probably have got all this stuff at about two-thirds what we paid for it, but it would take us four days to haggle them down to our price."

"Which wouldn't leave any time for sight-seeing."

"Exactly. And in any event, what we did pay is still quite a lot less than the price of comparable goods in the States—if you could get them there at all."

Lunch consisted of what by Thai standards was a very mild curry of chicken and superbly done long-grained Thai rice. The Thais claim that they have the best rice in the world.

After their dishes arrived at the table, Liz said, "It seemed to me that there were an awful lot of police and soldiers out and about."

"Don't forget," Hamilton pointed out, "Thailand

is pretty close to the war. Also the army is an important institution here. The economy is founded on rice, but the Thais' political unity and national pride are really based on three institutions: the monarchy, Buddhism, and the army. It's the only country in all of Southeast Asia that was never anyone's colony, which has spared them a lot of complicated hang-ups and the disruption of their traditional institutions. The police, I understand, are a branch of the army."

"And I suppose that the monarchy and Buddhism are pretty thoroughly tied in with each other."

"Oh, yes. You sometimes get the impression that the Buddhist church, if I may use that term, constitutes a stronger tie between the king and his people than the civil government does."

"I noticed that even those Chinese at the store this morning seemed to be very proud of being Thais and of everything made in Thailand."

"They are justly proud of their country, the fact that it was never a colony, its artistic and religious heritage, and its excellent rice, *and* they have a self-assurance about the whole thing which keeps them away from the strident xenophobias that afflict most of the former colonies. Even the local Chinese, who have been pretty harshly persecuted at times, seem to have the same spirit, but without ever backing off an inch from their own quite different and equally impressive cultural heritage."

"Where do you find out all these things?" Liz asked.

"I've been here before and I do my homework."

"An officer and gentleman who's also a scholar

and a connoisseur of fine wines and fast women. I'm impressed."

Hamilton laughed. "That's the nicest thing anyone has said to me all day. And I will admit to superior taste in my selection of feminine companions."

Liz grinned and replied, "Charlie, sometimes you spread it on a little thick."

"I just calls 'em like I sees 'em."

For dessert they had papaya with lime juice again, followed by black coffee. Hamilton went upstairs to get his jacket and necktie, which are required for visitors to the Royal Palace, and his camera. Liz browsed the two or three boutique shops in the hotel lobby.

The tour company showed up at two o'clock in the form of a Volkswagen minibus with a driver and the guide. The driver, a Thai, wore a khaki short-sleeved shirt and trousers; the guide, wearing a bright green uniform in the style of an airline hostess, was an attractive and slightly stocky girl of about twenty. Hamilton couldn't decide whether she was Thai, Chinese, or a mix (many Chinese immigrants married Thai women), but she spoke excellent English and, as it turned out, was well informed on the things they were going to see.

In addition to Liz and Hamilton, the party from the hotel included one of the couples they had seen at dinner and two GIs, one of whom brought along his Chinese girlfriend. Hamilton wondered how many times this girl had been through the Royal Palace and the Wat Phra Keo with various GIs; he suspected that by now she probably knew the guide's spiel as well as the guide. On the bus already were two Japanese, apparently businessmen, with cameras.

If your taste in architecture runs to stark, functional simplicity and the suppression of all ornament, you will not enjoy the incomparable splendors of the coronation and funeral halls of the Royal Palace and the Wat Phra Keo, inside and out. Not that the vibrant, sinuous, flamelike carved ornamentation in color and gilding is ever permitted to overwhelm and obscure the strong and elegant proportions and dramatic rooflines of these buildings; in relation to the scale of the buildings, the ornamentation is discreet and well controlled. Both the coronation and funeral halls show a striking alternation of plain white wall, dazzling in the tropical sunlight, and jewel-like ornamentation at cornices, around windows and doors, and especially at the gable ends. Due to the accumulation of shrines, royal-tomb monuments, and other structures, the overall layout of the Wat Phra Keo is, like so many holy places, obscure and confusing; the effect is more that of a rich storehouse of exotic treasures than of a grand monumental design.

They rode back to the hotel in silence; after such a surfeit of visual splendors and delights, there was little to say. Finally, back at the hotel, Liz observed, "You know, that's sort of like a dream. I wouldn't have believed it if I hadn't seen it, and even though I have, I'm still not sure I believe it."

"That's one reason why I keep coming back to Bangkok."

They enjoyed a swim and a cold beer by the pool (the tropical sunlight at the Royal Palace had been warm as well as bright), then dressed for dinner. Hamilton had chosen a restaurant, almost strictly for tourists, that combined very good Thai food with a floor show of traditional Thai music and dances, most of which are stylized renditions of incidents from the Ramayana. Thailand has been a strongly Buddhist country for many centuries, but without rejecting the Ramayana and many other legends and beliefs derived from the underlying Brahminism. The style of costume, music, and dance is similar to that found in Bali, Cambodia, and elsewhere in Southeast Asia where the Indian cultural heritage has predominated: the music with simple tunes and complicated rhythms played on variants of the xylophone, richly decorated costumes including pointed helmet-crowns and stiff shoulder pieces with flame-shaped finials, and the dance consisting of rather simple footwork and sinuous, graceful, highly stylized gestures with arms, fingers, and head.

Liz and Hamilton stayed through the whole show, nursing their after-dinner drinks, decided that any sort of ordinary nightclub would be an anticlimax, and took a taxi back to the hotel. It was becoming apparent that Liz shared Hamilton's lack of enthusiasm for nightclubs.

The enchantments of exotic sound and color and movement were still in their heads as they undressed and entwined and caressed each other and made love. Afterward, they remained joined for a little while, savoring the delicate after-pleasure of being together. In the half light, Hamilton could see Liz's blissful, dreamy expression.

"What a beautiful and lovely way to end a beautiful and lovely day," she murmured.

"Liz, that's so true, and you're so poetic."

"If you like it, you can use it for an exit line."

They laughed, and Liz, who was on top, rolled off.

Ayutthaya was the capital of the Thai kingdom until it was besieged, taken, and destroyed by the Burmese in 1767. It was not rebuilt and the capital was moved some distance down the Chao Phraya River to Bangkok. What remains at the site are three piously restored, toweringly graceful white stupas, assorted ruins, and an ornate but handsome modern temple.

Liz and Hamilton had a car with guide and driver for the whole day for this trip; it was expensive, but Hamilton, who spent almost nothing at Dong Hai, considered it a vastly better expenditure than night-clubbing and whoring. The guide was the same girl who had shown them around the Royal Palace and the Wat Phra Keo the day before.

They left the hotel about nine, and it took about an hour and a half to reach the old city. After leaving the city, the route is by way of a very good straight road (courtesy of the U.S. Army Corps of Engineers) across rich, flat, water-soaked rice land; this is the heart of Thailand.

As soon as they were clear of the city, Liz remarked, "The land looks a lot like the Delta around Can Tho, but the people are different, and so are the houses. It's not just wraparound skirts versus pajamas and a different type of hat, or the way they do their hair; the people are darker and stockier. They almost look like the ethnic Cambodians.''

''Shhh, don't ever say that. Accusing a Thai of looking like a Cambodian is like accusing a Jew of looking like an Arab. The Thais, I'm told, have a saying that if you see a snake and a Cambodian, you kill the Cambodian first. They have not been the best of neighbors.''

''I'm sorry; I didn't mean to offend. It's just that both groups seem to be darker and more powerfully built than the Vietnamese.''

In the rearview mirror Hamilton noticed that the guide, who was riding in the front seat, had taken in this exchange and was grinning. So he asked her, ''Isn't that true about the Thais and the Cambodians?''

''Sir, I think so. The Cambodians go to war many times against the Thai people in the old time. Maybe good friends now. There are many Buddhas in the Cambodian style in Thailand, and also one of the temples at the Wat Po. Maybe you see it?''

''This trip not yet; I think we take in the temple tour day after tomorrow.''

''Oh, good. Then you see many beautiful things.''

''I know. I was here before. That's why I came back. There are many beautiful things and I like the Thai people.''

''Thank you, sir. We are happy to welcome guests and to show them the beautiful things in our country.''

That might have been part of the prescribed spiel, but it sounded as if she meant it.

As Liz had observed, the houses were also different from those in Vietnam. The Vietnamese rural house is built on a low earth platform with mud-plastered walls and a thatch roof; the Thai equivalent is all wood, on pilings, and with a thatch roof.

"Liz, aside from being with you, the best part is riding around out in the country without having to make a military operation out of it."

"It is a pleasant switch."

The subject died. Comparing Thailand and Vietnam was a reminder that in a very few more days both of them would have to return to the hazards and hardships of war and separation from each other. Hamilton sensed that these four days were going to be the golden pinnacle of their affair, that anything between them that came after would be something of an anticlimax, and that Liz, perhaps subconsciously, also felt this. All the more reason to banish gloomy forebodings and enjoy the glorious moment.

The three great white stupas were magnificent against the sky, amid overgrown ruins which in no way competed with the stupas, but added a note of nostalgic melancholy, even under a brilliant sky. They scrambled around the ruins, photographed the stupas, and accompanied the guide on a pious visit to the modern temple. The souvenirs for sale outside were not impressive. On a previous trip Hamilton had acquired a magnificent Thai sword here, but nothing of that kind was now visible. But the stupas could be seen for a long time as they drove away.

The main streets of the modern town of Ayutthaya, which is several miles from the ruins, are composed of two-story Chinese house-shops, with a cluster of

Thai-style wood houses around the edge of town. The wide main street had an air of desolate somnolence, not unlike the siesta hour in Italy or Spain. The guide picked out a Chinese shop, no doubt run by a relative, where they had lunch. She ate with Liz and Hamilton; the driver declined and disappeared somewhere for his meal. The Thais have a very strong sense of social hierarchy, and the driver probably felt more comfortable not getting out of his depth.

The restaurant was open to the street, with a blue and white tile floor, white plastered walls with photographs of Sun Yat-sen and the king of Thailand, small marble-topped tables and metal chairs. They had a soup with lettuce and noodles and small pieces of chicken in it, and some egg rolls, washed down with green Chinese tea. It was simple but tasty everyday Chinese cooking, and the bill for all three of them was just under a dollar. By the time they had finished and returned to the car, the driver reappeared, and they set off for the summer palace of the kings of Thailand, the other main feature of the tour.

The main palace and its formal gardens are an average example of what Hamilton defined as Riviera Rococo; much better specimens can be seen in Monaco and Bavaria. There is also a Chinese pavilion, exotic, ornate, massive, and dark, to be admired more for craftsmanlike elaboration of ornament than for beauty of line or proportion. But the real jewel here is a little temple pavilion set in the center of an artificial pond, in the purest and most flamboyant Thai style. It is a cross-shaped building with multiple

roofs, a central spire, and a disciplined profusion of
sinuous, flamelike ornament, most of it gilded. The
effect is almost more a work of jewelry than of
architecture, but the decoration is never allowed to
obscure its purity of line and excellence of proportion.

They took the full tour, of course. Refusal to visit
the main palace and the Chinese pavilion would have
given offense, especially in view of the guide's rev-
erent views on the monarchy of her country and
probable ethnic background. Liz was enchanted with
the little temple pavilion, and the guide, who was
careful and cagey about expressing opinions, did not
seem reluctant to go back for further examination of
it.

It was after four when they were finally on the
road back to Bangkok. For many miles as they rolled
across the flat, green plain, they could see the three
stupas of old Ayutthaya white and splendid in the
slanting sunlight against a backdrop of towering slate-
blue clouds.

The remaining days and nights passed all too
quickly. They visited the Marble Temple and the
Wat Po, each in its own way as magnificent as the
Wat Phra Keo, if not quite so holy to devout Bud-
dhists (Wat Phra Keo is the holiest place in Thai-
land). They climbed the mighty spire of the Wat
Arun, the Temple of Dawn, and took the "Canal
Tour" through the teeming, colorful waterways of
Dhonburi, across the river from Bangkok proper.
They ate the hot Thai curries and long-grain rice, and
drank much Singha beer. They even found a little
time to swim and sun themselves by the pool. And at

night they made love, joyously, tenderly, passionately, and frequently, with all the refinements of technique and art that imagination or experience could suggest, or good taste permit.

On the morning of the last day, there were tears at parting but no regrets, and Liz insisted on paying half the hotel bill.

"After all, Charlie, I'm going to have to get along without you for quite a little while now, so I have to begin reasserting my independence."

"I was trying to avoid thinking of going back to Dong Hai and that narrow, lonely little cot. With luck I may be in Saigon in March or April."

"Wonderful! What is it, another school?"

"No, a new job, in Saigon. I extended and they may cut three months off my sentence at Dong Hai."

"That's even better. What kind of job is it?"

"Desk job. And I very likely may not get it."

"Knowing you, it's probably something very spooky that you can't tell me about. At least you won't have to worry about a place to stay."

"You're right. But don't bet on it until it happens."

"You can't keep me from hoping."

Thus their parting was on a reasonably cheerful note. In the airplane en route back to Cam Ranh, Hamilton reflected that living with Liz in Saigon, with both of them working and under various pressures, couldn't be the same as playing house with her on vacation in Bangkok. Of course not. But still a lot better than a narrow cot at Dong Hai. It was going to be a long dry spell.

XII.

TET, 1968, PHAN HOA CITY

"What's this about your leaving us and taking up some desk job in Saigon? I thought you claimed to be a field soldier."

It was Lieutenant Colonel Withrow. His tone was less than half jocular. The orders for Hamilton's transfer to Colonel Sprague's outfit after nine months up-country, and approving his extension, had arrived while he was in Bangkok.

"That's right, sir," Hamilton replied.

"Well, whose idea was it to transfer you before you had completed your full tour in this command?"

"Sir, that was in the original request for extension, which was submitted through channels and sent forward from here with a recommendation for approval signed by Colonel Dace."

Withrow, while trying to think up a reply to this, made something of a show of ruffling through the collection of papers relating to Hamilton's transfer. He was of medium height and build, with receding hair, a large, oval, slightly soft-looking pale face, and small, neat hands. He had been in the army since 1951, had not served in Korea, had not commanded a battalion, and had spent most of the last ten years in staff jobs of one kind or another; this was his first tour in Vietnam. Finally, apparently satisfied that Hamilton had not been lying to him, he looked up and inquired, in a notably less hostile manner, "What sort of outfit is this Concept Analysis Team?"

The fact that Withrow had doubted his word to the degree of going through the papers in an attempt to prove him a liar did not sit well with Hamilton, who had old-fashioned views on the subject of personal honor and, he hoped, enough wit not to make statements subject to being shown up as false. The day had long since gone by, however, when one could challenge one's colonel to a duel over such a point of honor, or even attempt the various bureaucratic equivalents, so Hamilton merely replied, "Sir, it has a classified mission."

"Oh, a spook outfit? That's right, you used to be in some kind of fancy spook outfit in France, didn't you?"

"That's right, sir."

"You can have your Mickey Mouse outfits. I'll just stick to good old plain field soldiering, thank you."

Hamilton resisted the temptation to inquire how it was, then, that Withrow had managed not to volunteer for duty in Korea at a time when infantry lieutenants had been in very high demand, and had not become involved in the present war any sooner. "Each to his own taste, sir. And there's really not that much field soldiering up in the subsectors."

"There is if you make it. You should get that district chief of yours up off his ass and out on some operations like they do in Tuy Cau. Push the VC. Take the initiative."

"Sir, as you know, Captain Lan doesn't work for me, he works for the province chief. Also, sir, in the last six months, Dong Hai District has produced about half the body count and weapons captured for the whole province, not counting operations by the Koreans and the CIDG; and all this with very few casualties. Out in front of the Koreans it's a little different ball game than it is in Tuy Cau."

"That's still no excuse for not pushing the enemy. You're my representative up there and I'm going to hold you responsible for results. You've still got about two months to go here, so don't start phasing out yet."

Hamilton wondered whether Withrow was going to add that he was also Hamilton's rating officer and that, since their overlap was more than two months, he would be rating Hamilton, and as Hamilton was looking to his career, he had better produce the desired results. But this was left to implication.

"I do the best I can, sir."

"You've got to do better than that."

With this, Withrow grinned and stood up. Apparently, he believed in terminating interviews on a positive note. Hamilton took it up:

"I'll give it a try, sir."

Hamilton had caught a flight from Cam Ranh to Phan Hoa shortly after his arrival from Bangkok, so he did not have to stay overnight at Cam Ranh. By the time he had got from the air force base across the river and through town to the area of the MACV and sector compounds and finished with his talk with Colonel Withrow, it was clear that there would be no way he could get up to Dong Hai before the morrow. Fortunately, the extra bunk in Captain Clark's room was available, so, with Clark's permission, he stayed there, with the intention of getting a ride of some kind up to Dong Hai in the morning.

Hamilton also had supper with Captain Clark, who inquired, soon after they sat down, "How was Bangkok?"

"Oh, delightful, as always."

"And the girls?"

"Reasonably cute, I guess, if you like whores who don't speak much English and probably have diseases."

"If you don't like the girls, why go there?"

"Well, there are other things to do and see, and . . . I have friends there."

"Oh? . . . then you didn't spend all your time visiting temples and shopping for black star sapphires?"

"You have to set aside a little time for eating and sleeping and healthy indoor exercise. When are you going on R&R?"

"In about two weeks, to Hong Kong. I don't have

your talent for getting good-looking round-eyes to enliven my travels.''

"What talent and what round-eyes?''

Hamilton was curious about who knew how much about what.

"You know,'' Clark replied, "I do sometimes make liaison visits to the A&L Company advisers in other provinces, including the one up at Vung Ngai. He said something about your being on fairly good terms with one of the Red Cross girls up there.''

"You don't believe all that gossip, do you?'' Not that Hamilton really gave a damn, but he considered it vulgar to boast of his infrequent successes with girls, and preferred to keep such matters as discreet as possible. He changed the subject: "If you're looking for good-looking round-eyes, why not go to Australia instead of Hong Kong?''

"There are lots of round-eyes in the States and I'm not prejudiced against slopes; there's also a lot of shopping I want to do in Hong Kong.''

"It's your R&R, not mine,'' Hamilton said. "What are the chances on getting a ride up to Dong Hai tomorrow?''

"There shouldn't be any difficulty. The truce for Tet went into effect last night at six o'clock and remains in effect for three days. And tomorrow's our regular day for the supply chopper.''

"That's right, it's Tet again. I suppose I'll have to go to a lot of parties with and for the Vietnamese.''

"Colonel Nhieu's party for us was last night, so you missed that. I don't know what your district chief has planned. He was at the party last night, but

I didn't talk with him—any more than just to say hello and wish him a happy lunar new year, or whatever it is you say."

"If he's still here in town, maybe I could get a ride with him."

"I'm almost certain he went back up to Dong Hai this morning. Colonel Nhieu is pretty strict on the subject of absentee district chiefs. And the chopper will be going up that way anyway."

"Anything exciting happen here while I was away?"

"No. Nothing that I know of, outside of minor stuff, since the Airborne finished their operation in your district, and you know more about that than I do."

After supper Hamilton stayed away from the bar, wrote two or three letters, and turned in early. He woke up shortly after midnight, decided that what he was hearing was probably firecrackers in celebration of Tet, and was about to go back to sleep when someone began hammering on the alarm gong in the compound. Hamilton quickly dressed, borrowed a pistol from Clark (who also had a carbine), and headed for the radio bunker. Once outside, the rattle of small-arms fire and thump of heavier explosions made it clear that someone, somewhere east or northeast of the compound, had a serious contact. At the radio bunker, Hamilton found himself temporarily the senior man present, sent Clark to look for Colonel Withrow, and began taking reports from the subsectors and other stations in the net. Phu Xuong Subsector, across the river, had been mortared and was receiving sporadic small-arms fire but for the moment was not under serious attack. The air force base had heard firing, evidently the action at Phu Xuong Subsector, but had not been attacked. The Phan Cao Subsector team and the 38th Regiment adviser stayed at the MACV compound, so there was no report from them, but the U.S. artillery battery, northeast of the city on Highway 1 next to the Phan Cao Subsector compound, was under attack by an estimated battalion and was partially overrun; they also reported hearing heavy firing around the subsector compound and the adjacent province prison, which contained about twelve hundred prisoners, mostly VC. The outlying subsectors, Cung Hoa, Tuy Cau, Dong Hai, and Song Nao, all had negative reports.

As soon as he had all this, Hamilton put it together in the prescribed format and had it called in to next higher headquarters, which was at Nha Trang, and found out that a Spooky was already on its way to the U.S. artillery battery. At this point Colonel Withrow and Major Scammell, the sector S3 adviser, arrived. Withrow was in full battle kit, including helmet, flak jacket, and load-carrying harness; Major Scammell made do with a helmet and pistol belt with pistol.

As soon as he was inside the bunker, Withrow demanded, "What the hell's going on, Hamilton?"

"Sir, we've got trouble." He briefed Withrow and Scammell on the situation as it then stood, including the fact that he had put it all in a spot report to Nha Trang, and then went on: "There appears to be trouble all over, especially province capitals and major U.S. bases. Qui Nhon, Tuy Hoa, Vung Ngai, and even Nha Trang are all reporting serious contacts with at least a battalion and sometimes more, but nothing much going on in the back country."

"Why did you send out that spot report without my seeing it?" Withrow demanded. "Dammit all, no reports go out of here without my seeing them."

"Yes, sir. It's a MACV regulation that any initial enemy contact be reported immediately and by the fastest means. If you wish to amend the spot report, I'm sure we can do that, sir."

"Let me see it."

He examined the report for a little while and set it down.

"I guess it's all right. . . . By the way, where's your helmet and weapon and your other equipment?"

"In Dong Hai, sir."

"Oh . . . of course. What about this compound here?"

"Captain Hodgen reports that everyone's up and armed, in bunkers or manning the perimeter, and no contact or movement outside the perimeter. I've been here in the bunker since the alarm was rung, so I haven't gone out and checked him yet."

Hodgen was the detachment commander, responsible for mess and administration of the military part of the MACV team, as well as local security. About this time Sergeant Major Barlow, the team sergeant major, tall, thin, and gray, came in. Withrow turned to him.

"Sergeant Major," he said, "let's go check the perimeter security."

Major Scammell broke in: "Colonel, we should try

to get teams out to the Sector CP, the civilian compound, the 38th Regiment, and Phan Cao Subsector, so we know what's going on and can help the Vietnamese."

"Okay, you take care of that. But if we get overrun here, we can't help anyone. I've got to check my local security."

Withrow and the sergeant major swept out. Scammell glanced at Hamilton, shook his head slightly and sighed, then observed: "Getting people up to sector and the civilian compound, and even the 38th Regiment just down the street, isn't going to be a problem unless they've got the whole damn beach area infiltrated. And we should send someone over to the PF training center. Also no problem. But Major MacCabe's on emergency leave, and I don't know whom to send to Phan Cao Subsector, which is where the action is, and I damn well don't know how to get someone across to the other side of the city if the place is under siege."

"That subsector may or may not be under close siege," Hamilton replied. "My guess is that the enemy will be concentrating on the province prison. In any event, the friendlies in the subsector compound will be reporting what's going on to Colonel Nhieu's people at sector. As soon as we get someone up there to find out what's happening on the Vietnamese side, we can make a decision as to whether to try to get in there tonight, and if so, how best to do it. If some of MacCabe's people are around who know the town better than I do, I'm willing to make a try at getting in there, after we find out what's going on."

Scammell was a burly infantryman with many years in airborne units. He had a gruff manner, close-cropped dark hair, a broken nose, and features more rugged than handsome. He agreed with Hamilton, and it was decided that Colonel Withrow, Hodgen, and the sergeant major would stay at the MACV compound, and that Scammell and Hamilton would go up to sector with enough people and vehicles so that Scammell could stay there with Colonel Nhieu, and Hamilton would be able to try to get through to Phan Cao Subsector. Then Scammell got busy getting out teams to the civilian compound (which was in the same perimeter as the sector compound), 38th Regiment headquarters, and the PF training center. The artillery battery called in and reported that they had eliminated the enemy penetration, that the enemy force were clearly NVA, and that they seemed now to be attacking the province prison.

Colonel Withrow and the sergeant major returned with Captain Hodgen. Withrow raised no objection to Scammell's plan for getting into Phan Cao Subsector, and in about ten minutes they moved out in two jeeps. Scammell with a sergeant and a radio operator in one, and Hamilton with two of MacCabe's sergeants and a radio operator in the other. Hamilton had borrowed Clark's battle harness and carbine and returned the pistol.

The trip up the beach road to the sector compound took place without incident and there was no difficulty in being admitted to the sector compound, whose perimeter was fully manned and on the alert. Inside, in Colonel Nhieu's command and radio bunker, there was a considerable crowd of radio operators, operations clerks, staff officers, and so on; rather more people than Hamilton would have considered efficient, but no one seemed unduly excited, and Colonel Nhieu, tall for a Vietnamese, lean, and with an ascetic-looking triangular face, was quietly but very definitely in charge. He greeted Scammell and Hamilton and briefed them on the situation. Phan Cao Subsector compound had been mortared earlier without much damage, but was not now under attack. The Regional Force Company guarding the prison was holding—at least for now. He had had no reports of enemy penetration into Phan Hoa city proper.

The Spooky would help take the pressure off the prison, but would require an American observer on the ground and in touch with the defending Vietnamese. It was agreed (Hamilton never ceased to be surprised at how many tactical decisions were arrived at by a coordinated consensus of opinion rather than by the fiat of command) that the Phan Cao Subsector compound was the obvious location for this observer, and Colonel Nhieu immediately agreed to provide a three-quarter-ton truck and a squad of soldiers to escort Hamilton and his party in an attempt to run through the city to that location. Hamilton's plan was to drive through town as fast as he could without headlights, relying on speed and firepower to brush past any opposition, and resort to the stealthy, dismounted approach only if one of the vehicles was disabled.

Hamilton, the other three Americans, and the Vietnamese lieutenant in charge of the escort, who understood English, went over the plan carefully, including selection of the route, agreed signals, emergency actions, and the like, then checked weapons and equipment and set out. Sector was to advise the National Police, theoretically guarding the city, and the subsector commander only after Hamilton had left the sector compound, so that the enemy, who was no doubt monitoring, would have as little reaction time as possible. Both vehicles were stripped of windshields and all canvas.

The lead vehicle was the jeep with Hamilton and one of MacCabe's sergeants, who was driving, with two RF soldiers in the back seat, one with a carbine, the other with an M-79. The other two Americans, with a spare radio, were riding in the truck with the lieutenant and six other RF soldiers. The armament of the truck included a Browning machine gun and two more M-79s.

The first leg of their route was across the straight causeway connecting the beach with Phan Hoa city; they got across without incident and sped up the wide, deserted main street of the city. Off to their right there was suddenly a series of bloodcurdling screams, followed by some shooting—by the sound, probably AK-47s. The sergeant, sitting next to Hamilton, slacked up a little on the accelerator, as if querying whether they should stop and investigate.

Hamilton shook his head. "We got a job to do. Keep moving."

At the main traffic circle, they passed the bodies of

two National Policemen; they had been shot and beheaded. From a side street on their left they were briefly taken under fire by what sounded like an RPD and two or three AK-47s on full automatic. The volume of return fire was impressive, and no one in Hamilton's jeep was hit during the exchange.

As they were approaching the intersection of the main street with Highway 1, Hamilton saw shadowy figures trying to pull a coil of concertina wire across the road. He fired a long burst with his carbine straight ahead at them, and the machine gun on the truck, which was following very close, blasted close over his head. When the dazzle of the muzzle flashes cleared, the shadowy figures were gone. The driver slowed, was nearly run into by the truck, swerved around the end of the coil of wire, and ran over something soft. Hamilton glanced down and saw the body of an NVA soldier. At this point they took and returned heavy but generally inaccurate fire from both sides but mostly from the right. Hamilton heard a distinct clang and saw the spark as a bullet struck the hood of the jeep. A moment later there was a groan behind him and one of the RF soldiers slumped down, followed by the roar of a hand grenade going off behind the truck. There had also been several loud explosions of M-79 grenades striking here and there on both sides of the street. They rushed on, the tepid night air in their faces. Farther away, out in the city, were occasional shots and short bursts of fire.

About halfway up the portion of Highway 1 between its intersection with the main street and the turnoff for the subsector, a bridge crosses a little stream. Hamilton saw lights on the bridge, turned to the sergeant, and said, "Headlights. High beam."

In the flood of light he could see four or five NVA soldiers on the bridge. As one of them rushed out into the center of the roadway, holding up his hand, Hamilton let him have it with his carbine; the machine gun on the truck again cut loose. They raced over the bridge, smashing through a light barricade, and rushed on; as they went over, the RFs in the truck pitched two hand grenades over the side of the bridge, which exploded in the streambed. The driver cut the headlights and slowed down a little to let his night vision return. Hamilton could hear the anguished, heavy breathing of the wounded soldier behind him, and reflected that at least this man hadn't been killed.

As they approached the turn for the subsector compound, they again cut on the headlights and were relieved to see two RF soldiers in steel helmets, with carbines and flashlights, signaling them to make the turn, then stop. They stopped, and the two RFs, evidently not wishing to stay out all night, swung on board the truck, and they rolled into the compound.

In addition to the wounded soldier in the back seat of Hamilton's jeep, two RFs in the truck had been wounded and one killed; each vehicle had been hit in several places and one of the rear tires of the truck was ruined. Hamilton left the junior of the two sergeants, who was a medic, and the Vietnamese to cope with the casualties, and headed straight for the subsector command bunker. There was heavy firing around the prison, about four hundred meters west of their location.

Captain Ngo, the Phan Cao district chief, was stocky, middle-age, and homely. His English was not very good, and he seemed shaken and very relieved that Hamilton had arrived. They conversed in French; Ngo's French was only a little better than his English. One of the two radios which Hamilton had brought had collected a bullet, but the other one worked, so he called in to sector and advised them that he had made it to the subsector and that Phan Hoa city seemed to be full of NVA troops. Scammell passed on the good news that the Spooky was expected in about five minutes and would come up on the MACV frequency. Hamilton explained this to Ngo and asked him to have someone at the prison help with observing and adjusting the Spooky's fire. Ngo agreed and immediately called the prison on a field telephone; apparently the enemy had not taken the precaution of cutting the line. Of course, it would be no more difficult to tap the line than to monitor Ngo's radio frequency.

A few minutes later the Spooky came up on Hamilton's frequency: "Sleepy Onion Bravo, this is Spook three three. Over."

"Spook three three, this is Bravo. Nice to have you with us. Over."

Hamilton had some difficulty in talking the Spooky in and adjusting flares, since Ngo, the only contact with the defenders in the prison, wouldn't come out of his bunker, and Hamilton had to stay outside where he had a good view of the area. Eventually, he put one of Major MacCabe's sergeants on the radio to talk with the Spooky and squatted by the door of the bunker, shouting alternately in English and French with the sergeant and Captain Ngo. The third flare was right where they wanted it, but the NVA attacking the prison were uncommonly tenacious when confronted by the awesome firepower of the Spooky's miniguns. Hamilton's previous experience had been that the enemy normally broke off an attack at once when they found out that a Spooky was supporting the defenders. This time, however, it took six or seven long bursts, reportedly squarely on the enemy's positions, before the NVA faded back, made a brief and not very effective repeat attack on the artillery battery, then apparently cut across Highway 1 north of the battery and infiltrated into the city from the north.

The next day Scammell and Colonel Nhieu planned, coordinated, and launched an operation to clear the NVA out of the city, using the two available battalions of the 38th Regiment, one Korean battalion, artillery of three nationalities, army gunships and rocket-firing L-19s (an L-19 can carry six 2.75-inch rockets), and quite a lot of Tac Air. It took three days of fairly serious fighting to clear the city; neither side had had much training or experience in house-to-house fighting, but they learned fast. Some of the gunship pilots later said that they were going to write a Field Manual on Employment of Armed Helicopters in Combat in Towns. The 5th Battalion of the 299th NVA Regiment and the VC Phan Cao District Company were just about wiped out. The town was thoroughly smashed up in some areas, and there were considerable friendly and civilian casualties, although not so many as might have been expected: Both the ARVN and ROK worked methodically and avoided risks, and the civilians had gone into the bunkers under their houses and other hiding places the first night and, generally, stayed there until it was over. Most of the civilian casualties were local people in some way connected with the government or employed by the Americans, and their families, who were hunted down and systematically murdered by the VC, beginning the first night of their incursion into the city.

During this operation Hamilton and Captain Ngo and his PF troops were mostly engaged in securing cleared areas, guarding prisoners, helping civilians, and identifying victims. Sometimes the mopping up got vicious, as pockets of NVA bypassed by the ARVN troops turned up either trying to escape or simply trying to sell their lives for the highest possible price. In one house they found one of the maids who worked at the MACV compound, her husband and four children all dead; the children had been shot and the parents beheaded. Two NVA found hiding under some debris in a house next door were not invited to surrender.

Finally, about noon of the fourth day, Hamilton made it back to the MACV compound and returned Clark's carbine and web equipment.

"I'm sorry this stuff's in such a mess. At least I cleaned the carbine."

"That's all right. From what I hear, you had more use for it than I did."

"Did you all have any trouble out here on the beach?"

"The PF training center got mortared once, and that was about it."

"And Colonel Withrow?"

"Hasn't been outside the compound. Major Scammell's been running the show."

"So I noticed. . . . What's the chances on a chopper up to Dong Hai? I don't want people to get the idea that I'm the permanent Phan Cao Subsector adviser, the trouble here seems to have calmed down for the time being, and I'd like to get back up there, if for no other reason than to get into some clean socks."

Before he left, Hamilton submitted papers recommending MacCabe's two sergeants, the radio operator, and the RF lieutenant for Silver Stars for their parts in the run through Phan Hoa city. Eventually, the RF lieutenant got a Silver Star, the three Americans got Bronze Stars with "V" device. No one put Hamilton in for anything.

"Sir, it's good to have you back. How was R&R?" It was Tinsley.

"Bangkok was delightful. Phan Hoa city was rather more noisy than my taste runs to."

"It's been very quiet here, sir."

"That's why I came back."

XIII.

━━✕━━━○━━━✕━━━○━━✕━━━✕━━━○━━✕━━

HOW CAPTAIN CLARK
OPERATED

By the end of February the fury of the enemy's Tet offensive had spent itself. Except at Hue, in the far northern part of South Vietnam, where it took three weeks of very difficult fighting to evict the enemy from the citadel, none of the places taken in the first few hours of the attack were held for more than a few days. This was done at a cost of thinning out the government U.S. and Allied regular troops holding the countryside, with some loss of control in the hamlets and villages. From the military point of view, however, it was a disaster of the first magnitude for the VC and NVA. Substantially all their combat-ready battalions were committed, very often in ill-coordinated frontal assaults against resolute, well-entrenched troops backed up with overwhelmingly superior artillery and air support, and in many cases, even when these assaults did not take their objectives, the enemy would hang on grimly to what they had taken and be destroyed in place, rather than fading back and conserving their strength for the next time, as had been their custom. The sacrilege of violating the Tet and the ruthless and systematic slaughter of people connected with the government or employed by the Allied forces, and their wives and children, especially at a time supposedly devoted to reconciliation and family reunions, profoundly shocked and alienated the great majority of the Vietnamese.

In Phan Hoa Province the action was almost entirely in and around Phan Hoa city. Five nights after the initial onslaught, the 4th Battalion of the 299th NVA launched an attack southward across the open sand dunes next to the beach against the provincial PF training center and the headquarters of the 38th Regiment. The defenders stood their ground and were not overrun. Between them, the Spooky, various types of artillery, and a Korean battalion which cut off the enemy's retreat, there was very little left of the 4th of the 299th by noon the next day. Several nights later, a third battalion-size attack, on the Phu Xuong side of the river, was also hacked up and repelled; in this case, however, the attacking unit, a VC provincial force battalion, faded back while it was still dark and thus avoided encirclement and annihilation. There was hardly any enemy action during this period in the four outlying districts.

Major Scammell and Captain Clark had come up to Dong Hai on the morning supply chopper. After escorting them into his living-cum-radio room and providing coffee, Hamilton inquired, "To what do I owe the honor of your visit?"

"Just a staff visit." Major Scammell replied. "I haven't been up here in a long time, and it's nice to get away from Phan Hoa once in a while."

"Is there anything you're particularly interested in seeing? We've completed the District Operations Center building, including furniture, and rebuilt two of the perimeter bunkers. On the civil side, nothing much has happened since the trouble started three weeks ago. What's been going on in Phan Hoa?"

"After a while I suppose we should have a look at your District Operations Center and bunkers, so I can assure Colonel Withrow that they really are there. Harry MacCabe is back from emergency leave; the lucky dog arranged not to be here when all the trouble happened. Two of the CORDS people lost their nerve and resigned—the agriculture adviser and the Chieu Hoi adviser. Said they hadn't been hired to be shot at."

"What the hell did they expect? Even from the garbled accounts in the newspapers it's not hard to figure out that some of the natives out here are a little restless."

"I guess their idea was to draw whatever the civilian equivalent is of hazardous-duty pay, but without any hazards. Anyway, the other civilians are still here, which is more or less to their credit."

"One also wonders how many of the military would be on their way home if they could."

"Charlie, that's why we have a military organization."

"I suppose that's also why we can't get a civilian deputy for this place."

"If you were a civilian and had a choice, would you take the job?"

"Of course not."

There was a pause. Scammell took a sip of coffee, stared for a moment at the cup, and went on. "I wonder what the enemy's trying to accomplish by all these attacks on cities and bases. They're certainly losing a lot of people. Is it just to prove to the world that they can still hit pretty hard, or what?"

"They believe their own propaganda too much. You know they have a doctrine of the General Uprising, when the people in mass will rise in wrath against their oppressors and gloriously put Ho Chi Minh in power. I think that they really believed that if they hit hard enough, the government and the ARVN would come apart and the people would rise in mass to their support. Well, it didn't happen. From what I hear, generally, the ARVN, including the RF and the PF and the CIDG and everyone else, stood their ground and fought like tigers; the government manifestly hasn't come apart; and the people, as always, got down in their holes and stayed there until the shooting was over with. What they planned to do with us and the Koreans, if the Vietnamese came unglued, I don't know. As it was, they got their clocks cleaned."

"They sure did," Clark said. "There are so many AK-47s and SKSs floating around Phan Hoa air base that you can't hardly give 'em away. Same with

NVA uniforms and even belt buckles. I guess we'll have to go back to trading with crossbows.''

''That's why you're such a good supply officer,'' Hamilton said. ''You never think of anything except scrounging up supplies for the supported units.''

''It's more or less my job.''

''By the way, have you made any progress toward getting me a better radio?''

Clark glanced at Scammell, shook his head almost imperceptibly, and replied, ''Nothing to speak of.''

''Oh. . . . I'm almost too short to care, but even then it would be nice to get something respectable for my replacement.''

''I'll let you know if something turns up.''

They finished their coffee, declined refills, and went outside to look at the new construction. The District Operations Center was a plain but handsome one-story rectangular building, built of cement blocks plastered over with more cement and painted, with a wood and sheet-aluminum roof. Lan's PF organization included a carpenter and several masons, who had directed the work and achieved a very finished result. The cement floor was extremely smooth, the walls were a cool light green inside and out, with darker green trim. In lieu of glass, the window openings had bars made of the long iron rods used in artillery ammunition boxes, and neat wooden shutters, also made from ammunition boxes. A Korean 105mm battery next to the battalion headquarters down the road had donated the boxes, which also served as raw material for the door and most of the desks and chairs inside the building. Captain Lan had joined them and took pleasure in showing them his new building. Neither of the visitors was so indiscreet as to inquire whence had come the cement or other materials, or to comment on the considerable number of bags of cement—about half a pallet load—neatly stacked on the porch of the subsector headquarters building.

After their tour of the compound, while Major Scammell was using the not very elegant men's room, Clark took Hamilton aside and stated very quietly, "I can get you a VRC-46 radio and some batteries."

"Good. What's it going to cost me? I have some old NVA uniforms here, a couple of belt buckles, and a few crossbows."

"What about the .45 you got from Sergeant Thurwell?"

This weapon had a curious history. On a recent CIDG operation which Hamilton had accompanied, they had picked off a VC courier who was carrying an M-1 carbine, which Gherardi had given to Hamilton. Several days later, one of the helicopter pilots expressed the need for a shoulder weapon to augment the issue-type .38-caliber revolver that he carried. As Hamilton needed a pistol, they had no difficulty agreeing to exchange the VC's carbine and some ammunition for the pilot's privately owned, short-barrel .38 (not, of course, the government-issue weapon). About two weeks after that, while Sergeant Thurwell, the detachment supply sergeant, was making one of his weekly runs to the subsectors on the supply chopper, he traded a very well preserved .45 pistol for the .38 revolver. This was really what Hamilton had wanted,

as there were a great many excursions (such as trips
to Phan Hoa) where a pistol was a much more convenient weapon than his carbine, even with the folding
stock. But he had very little faith in the accuracy and
stopping power of a snub-nosed .38 revolver.

"You guys drive a hard bargain," he said to Clark.
"You don't know how tough it is to get a radio."

"It appears that I'm finding out. I really did want
to hang on to that pistol. Are you sure that you can't
do business with some of the other trade goods? I can
even get you a Thompson gun."

"I'm just the middleman in this one. I'll have to
check it out, but I know this guy's getting short and
is really looking for something he can take home
with him."

"He'll go to jail if they catch him taking home a
Thompson gun. At the moment I don't have any
SKSs or bolt-action rifles on hand, but I may be able
to promote one down at Phuoc Tre."

"I'll have a look-see for someone who wants to
trade a .45 for a Thompson gun, but I'm not too
hopeful. After all, .45s that aren't signed for out of
somebody's arms room aren't too common."

"Tell you what. I'll take the radio. I need it. Send
it up here with word whether your man will take the
Thompson gun instead of the .45, but if he won't,
I'll part with the pistol. I'll even throw in two crossbows and an NVA belt buckle just to show that I'm
not stingy."

"Okay, I'll see what I can do on that basis. By the
way, where did you get the Thompson gun?"

"They captured it from the VC some time ago. It's in fairly good condition."

"Would some other type of pistol do you as well as a .45?"

"I suppose so, if that's what it takes to get that radio. Were you thinking of trading the Thompson gun for a pistol for me?"

"Something like that. Before this last VC offensive, everyone was looking for bolt-action rifles or other things they could take home, but now there seems to be a little more interest in weapons you can fight with, including Thompson guns."

"It's an excellent weapon if you don't have to carry it any great distance. And I have about five magazines for it."

"Ummm . . . I think I can do something for you on that."

"I'd be very grateful, especially for a radio."

Major Scammell returned, so Hamilton changed the subject.

"How was R&R?" he asked.

"Delightful. It's really quite scenic in Hong Kong, the restaurants are excellent, the natives are friendly— or seem to be—and you can go bankrupt saving money on all the bargains they have for sale."

"Good. I hope you didn't spend all your money. Will you join us for lunch?"

There were six of them at lunch: Hamilton, Scammell, Clark, Tinsley, Parelli, and Harley. It consisted mostly of steak and rice.

Scammell announced that Sergeant Chambers had come back from the hospital, but would not be returning to Dong Hai, then went on: "His shoulder's still a little stiff from the wound, so he's going to be the mess sergeant at the MACV compound. He's been a mess sergeant before, you know."

"I hadn't, but I'm sure he'll do you a very good job. Will I be getting a replacement for him?"

"There's a Sergeant Riordan coming in. I think you'll be getting him. All I know about him is that he's been in the army a long time; he's an infantry-man but not airborne. You know I'm really not sup-posed to be involved with the personnel side of things, so I don't get anything more than bits and pieces and rumors."

"Which is more than I get."

"I know. Nobody tells anybody anything. I've been a commander or an S3 most of my career, and I've never been anywhere where personnel management—trying to get hold of the right kind of people, fitting people and jobs together, and then trying to get 'em to do what they're supposed to do with a minimum of problems—isn't always the hard-est part of the job. Any moron who knows the format and can read a map can put together a tactically sound operations plan or a workable training sched-ule. It's the people that give you the gray hairs. That and all the penny-ante little things that Higher Head-quarters is always inventing and emphasizing to keep you from doing the important part of your job."

Hamilton was more than a little surprised at Scammell's thus unburdening himself, especially with three enlisted men present, so he merely replied, "I know what you mean."

"Of course you do. There's no way of changing it, so there's not much point in grumbling about it. . . . This is excellent steak. You didn't get this from the mess fund, did you?"

"No. This was donated by the eight-inch battery down at Phuoc Tre. Periodically they get more rations than they can eat up, so they pass on some to us."

"Sounds like a good arrangement."

"I like it."

After lunch the supply chopper came back, and Scammell and Clark departed. Back at Phan Hoa city, Scammell gave Colonel Withrow a favorable report on the new bunkers and District Operations Center and on the general state of things at Dong Hai.

Meanwhile, Clark looked up Sergeant Thurwell. After some preliminary discussion Clark inquired, "Just how badly do you need that .45?"

"I really need it, sir."

"You know, it's a government weapon, even if no one's signed for it, so if they catch you trying to take it back to the States, you could be in real trouble."

"Er . . . Sir, that's not exactly the problem. . . . Thing is, I'm signed for the damn thing and I'm getting kind of short . . ."

"Why the hell did you give it away if you were signed for it?"

"Sir, I really needed that .38 to put together a deal I was working on—you know how it is—and I felt sure I could promote another .45 to replace this one, or something. Maybe write it off as a combat loss. But now I don't know . . ."

"Dammit . . . Major Hamilton needs a pistol of some kind up there, as well as that radio, but I don't like the idea of telling him that you're signed for that pistol."

"Oh, no, sir."

"And I don't see how we can survey it as a combat loss without some pretty serious risks of really bad trouble. It's like the joke about the Chinaman; too many people would have to know. Do you know anybody who has any kind of decent military pistol—not one of those sawed-off revolvers— that's not a government weapon, that he could be traded out of?"

"No, sir. Everyone I know is hanging on to their pistols, especially after this last go-round with the VC. What's he got to trade for one?"

"I think he might be able to get hold of a Thompson gun."

"That's a good weapon. Lemme see what I can do. Does he have any magazines for it?"

"He said four or five."

"Sir, that's even better."

"Good. Get that radio together, with the batteries, and we'll take it up there on the next supply chopper and at least get you back your pistol. But we've got to work on a replacement for it for Major Hamilton."

"Very good, sir. Will do."

The local field office of "Big Brother" at Phan Hoa, locally referred to as "the Embassy," is in a fair-size white stucco villa on the beach road between the MACV compound and the sector compound; it is surrounded by a high white wall and some barbed wire. This was Clark's next stop. By then it was getting toward evening. After the usual security rigmarole he was let in by Chip Crittenden, the number two man at the Embassy. Crittenden was dark-haired, slender, about thirty, and normally wore Vietnamese-style black cotton pajamas and a long drooping mustache; at times he gave the impression of having read a few too many spy thrillers and to have taken their contents too seriously. He ushered Clark in, and they adjourned to a back porch, each with a beer.

After they exchanged the usual courtesies and were settled, Crittenden inquired, "Is this just a social call, or are you promoting something as usual?"

"Chip, you have a suspicious mind. I suppose in your business, whatever it is, you have to. Really, I just came by to see how you all were getting along and if there was anything I could do to help you. This is excellent beer."

"Your solicitude overwhelms me. In other words, I have something you need and want to know what I want for it."

"Let's try not to be so crass about it, but, well, you know, one hand washes the other."

"Okay. What are you looking for this time?"

"Well, I was wondering how you were fixed for pistols and Thompson guns."

"You know we have these 9mm Browning pistols, but they're pretty closely accounted for. I could sign you out with one, but you'd have to bring it back, which probably isn't what you're looking for. For submachine guns, we mostly use Swedish "K" guns, but some of our Vietnamese still have the Thompsons. I could probably get one for you, but you'd have to sign for it also. The VN get all the captured weapons, which really aren't so many, and they don't like to turn them loose. They gave me that ChiCom pistol as an exception to policy, and unless something awfully good turns up, I'm taking that one home with me. If nothing else, if I gave it away or traded it, my counterpart would probably take offense."

Clark felt it unnecessary to inquire whether a Thompson gun came under the heading of "something awfully good" for these purposes, so he said, "I suppose there'd be objections to signing out one of your pistols to one of the subsector advisers."

"I'm afraid so. The agency takes the view that the army should provide its own weapons. Between you and me, more or less right in the same compound, I could probably get away with it, but for someone up-country, I'm sorry."

"Of course. You don't happen to know of anyone who'd be willing to trade some kind of reasonably good pistol for a Thompson gun, do you?"

"About half the civilians from up the street have been down here trying to scrounge weapons from us. But we don't have that many guns to hand out, they usually don't have anything to trade or offer other than piteous bleating noises about how frightened they are, and most of them I wouldn't trust with a weapon anyway. But I'll keep my eyes open. I assume that this Thompson gun is a captured weapon?"

"I think so."

"Hmmmm. . . . All the ex-VC Thompson guns I've seen have been in pretty nasty shape—pitted barrels, no shoulder stocks, pistol grips and fore ends in poor condition, the whole bit. Basically it's a damn good weapon, though; you shouldn't have any trouble finding a home for it."

"Anyway, I'll be grateful if you turn anything up. . . . Is there anything you need?"

"I was hoping you'd ask that. They are really very simple things. I need some plain old WD-1 commo wire; also, and this is more in the nice-to-have category, I would like to get steel helmets and, if possible, flak jackets for my perimeter guards. After everything that's happened, they might need them, and anyway I think that their morale needs a little pumping up. They have a pretty dull job, not much to do, but when you do need 'em, you need 'em real bad."

"You all didn't get hit the other night, did you?"

"You mean when they hit the PF training center? No."

"How many helmets and flak jackets do you need?"

"Twenty of each, if you can get 'em."

"Do you have any idea on sizes of jackets?"

"I didn't know they came in sizes, but I suppose a U.S. small would do for most of them, plus about three mediums for me and Jack and the boss. I assume that you still need tiger suits?"

"Of course. Right now I could use two Asiatic large and two U.S. medium. I have one more sergeant coming but I don't know his size."

"By the way, just what is the fascination with tiger suits?"

"Dandyism. Status symbol. CIDG and the Special Forces wear them on operations, so all the subsector people have to have them to wear on operations also. And they're a heavier material than the regular jungle fatigues, so they don't tear up so easy out in the brush. At least that's what they tell me."

"Also a nice souvenir to take home and tell war stories about."

"Oh, absolutely. I can probably do something for you on that commo wire. Helmets, I don't know; and flak jackets are going to be hard to get. Since this Tet business, everyone's been getting security-conscious as hell. I'll give it a try. . . . Isn't it about time we went down to supper?"

"I guess so. What are they having?"

"Ham steak, I think. Let's go find out. And thanks again for the beer and sympathy."

South of Phan Hoa Air Force Base, next to the army hospital there was a U.S. Army maintenance battalion. About midmorning on the day after his trip to Dong Hai on the supply chopper, Clark was in his jeep, headed for the shop office of this maintenance battalion. The main objects of his trip were to promote a starter and a fuel pump for one of the A&L Company's trucks, and to get a roll of commo wire for Crittenden, as well as whatever other useful items might be able to be had. Since the official mission of the maintenance battalion did not include support of the A&L Company (who theoretically drew repair parts through Vietnamese channels), Clark brought along three crossbows previously acquired from Dong Hai and a spurious VC flag made by the wife of one of the PF troops in Tuy Cau and furnished some time ago by Sergeant Osbert as payment for his tiger suit. He also brought along Sergeant Thurwell, who was going to pick up the radio and batteries for Hamilton and wanted to talk with his friends at the Air Police about various things.

The maintenance battalion area is noted for rather depressing-looking one-story wooden buildings and quite a lot of blowing sand. Clark got off at the shop office, and Thurwell departed with the jeep to pick up the radio. Clark was careful not to inquire where the radio was. His contact at the shop office was Chief Warrant Officer Smallwood, the shop officer, a big, stocky, gray man, who had been in the maintenance business, as a mechanic, motor sergeant, or maintenance warrant officer since World War II.

"Good morning, sir," Smallwood said. "Glad to see you. I thought you guys got overrun."

"They didn't even get inside the compound, thank heaven. It was noisy for a while, and I didn't get my beauty sleep, but what the hell. . . . How've you been?"

"Just pluggin' along, gettin' shorter every day. What do you need?"

Clark handed him a piece of paper with the descriptions and stock numbers of the parts he needed, then inquired, "Who would I talk to about getting about a mile of commo wire?"

Smallwood gave the piece of paper to his clerk, a

Pfc, and told him to get the items listed, then replied, "I'd talk to Mr. Thomas at Signal Supply; they've got lots of wire—really more than they need. Everybody uses radios."

The Pfc was out of earshot, so Clark went on. "Good, I'll go by there on my way out. Do you know of anyone who'd be interested in trading some kind of reasonably good pistol for a Thompson gun?"

"Hmmmm. . . . What's the deal?"

"One of my subsector advisers needs a pistol, or wants one, I should probably say, and he does have an ex-VC Thompson gun."

"Not around here. The old man keeps a pretty tight control on all weapons, including privately owned. I don't like to think of what he'd say if someone turned up with a privately owned Thompson gun. . . . Lemme see, Sergeant Nunn over in the artillery shop has a P-38 and he's been looking for a VC flag and some other things like that. Does that do you any good?"

"How about a VC flag, an NVA belt buckle, and a crossbow?"

"Lemme call him up; maybe he can come over and talk with you. His shop's just across the street."

Smallwood talked on the phone, the Pfc brought Clark his truck parts, and after several minutes, Sergeant Nunn, tall, balding, and with very large hands, arrived. The P-38 was only in fair condition, with no holster, only one magazine, and very little ammunition. After some discussion, Clark got it in exchange for the VC flag and two crossbows (which were much better than the average Phuoc Tre product).

Apparently, there was no market for NVA belt buckles and other items of enemy uniform. By the time they had settled all this, Sergeant Thurwell had returned with the jeep and the radio and Clark's crossbows, so the transaction was completed. Smallwood agreed to get the necessary paperwork for Sergeant Nunn taken care of at the company commander's office, and said nothing about getting something for the truck parts. Clark had done considerable shopping for him while on R&R in Hong Kong.

On the way back, Clark stopped by Signal Supply and talked Mr. Thomas, the warrant officer in charge, out of a one-mile reel of commo wire and gave him the last crossbow, more or less on account for future favors, checked on flak jackets and helmets, and sponged some M-16 ammunition and magazines from the Air Police, some of which he subsequently traded to the Vietnamese Sector S2 in exchange for two P-38 magazines that had been captured during the fighting in the city. Finally, he delivered the commo wire to Crittenden and collected two tiger suits and a good supply of 9mm ammunition for the P-38.

After lunch, he went up to the A&L Company, delivered the truck parts, had the P-38 cleaned up and reblued, and found out that helmets were also in short supply there.

The following Wednesday, both Clark and Thurwell rode up to Dong Hai on the supply chopper; they brought along the VRC-46 radio and all its components, including batteries, the P-38, and a radio mechanic to install the radio. Hamilton was delighted, especially since he got a substitute for his present pistol, including two extra magazines and a good supply of ammunition, and willingly parted with both the .45 and the Thompson gun and their accessories.

That evening, Clark and Thurwell were having coffee.

"Well, sir, that came out pretty well," Thurwell remarked. "What are you going to do with that Thompson gun?"

"I don't know. I didn't have to promise it to anyone. I think I'll keep it as a personal weapon for a while, anyway."

"Good God, sir, what did you give that sergeant for his P-38?"

"Two crossbows and one of Sergeant Osbert's VC flags."

"That's a pretty hard bargain, sir."

"You didn't see the shape that pistol was in. If I can trade the Thompson gun to someone over at Cung Hoa for a couple of bolt-action rifles, I'll let him have one of them at a cut rate just to make it up. It wouldn't do to have him sore at us."

"I think we should, sir. I'll talk to some of my boys over at Cung Hoa next time we're over there."

"If it's not an indiscreet question, what did you give for that radio?"

"Two SKSs, two of Sergeant Osbert's VC flags, and some NVA belts and stuff."

"How did you get all that?"

"Sir, why do you think I went out and helped with the body count this last time?"

XIV.

NEW FACES AND FAREWELLS

Sergeant Riordan was a large man with a round, florid face, small blue eyes, and a South Boston Irish brogue. He arrived at Dong Hai via the supply chopper about a week after the delivery of the new radio, as Sergeant Chambers's belated replacement. He had enlisted in 1948, had served most of his career in the Infantry, mostly overseas, including the Korean War, and had never married. He had made rank slowly and at times had difficulty in holding it, mainly because of a well-developed taste for beer and whiskey and, especially in his younger days, for bar fighting. Most of this had come to Hamilton from Sergeant Thurwell, who had served with Riordan in an earlier assignment, by way of Captain Clark.

Hamilton welcomed Riordan aboard, introduced him to the other members of the team and to Captain Lan and the other Vietnamese, and briefed him on the friendly and enemy situations, terrain and weather in the district, and the local ground rules. Sergeant Tinsley helped get Riordan installed in the bunk and lockers which had been used by Chambers, then took him to visit the RF and civilian dispensaries. For most of the next week Riordan accompanied Hamilton and Lan on their regular visits to Regional Force outposts, the RD Team, various hamlets, the refugee camp, and the various activities at Phuoc Tre. Riordan said very little on these trips, asked very few questions, and his conversation at table consisted mostly of reminiscences of various units he had served in, especially the 11th Infantry at Munich, and the superlative qualities of Bavarian beer and the Munich gasthauses. His consumption of American and Korean beer was more than Hamilton approved, but with less than a month to go before his own departure from Dong Hai, Hamilton decided not to make an issue of it. At least Riordan never got more than slightly high and was never unable to perform his duties.

Hamilton finally persuaded a reluctant Lan to put some of his PF troops to work digging a hole for a radio bunker for the advisory team. They did not have materials for putting a roof over this bunker and had only enough cement on hand for the floor and walls. If, by the time they had got that far, something hadn't turned up and Hamilton was still there, they could always make another run up to Vung Ngai for more cement and either heavy timbers or steel beams for the roof. Since he had not received an answer to his letter to Karla Bergman, he assumed that she had either been reassigned somewhere else or found a new lover. He felt no real desire to repeat the trip to Vung Ngai, and was reasonably sure that the task of completing the team bunker would be for his replacement. Now that the end was at hand, he felt more bored and weary than ever, and the time that remained seemed the more irksome now that so little of it stood between him and his departure.

Hamilton's replacement arrived less than a week before Hamilton's departure date, in the person of Major Andy Carlson. Like Hamilton, Carlson was an armor officer and a reservist on extended active duty. They had been passing acquaintances at Fort Hood. Carlson was of medium height, slender, dark-haired, and dark-eyed. He concealed considerable strength of character behind a scholarly and slightly abstract style and appearance.

On the morning of the day on which Carlson was to arrive at Dong Hai, Hamilton and Riordan in Hamilton's jeep, and Lan in his jeep with two of his people, were fired on while returning from a visit to Phuoc Tre. The action involved a squad of VC with two BARs; it was something more than a sniping incident but quite a lot less than a properly laid ambush. In the exchange of fire, Hamilton was nicked on the scalp. It was a minor injury, but a lot of blood got on his fatigue jacket.

Doc Tinsley bandaged Hamilton's head back at the subsector, and when the chopper delivering Major Carlson arrived, Hamilton was still wearing the bloodied jacket.

"Hello, Andy," he said when Carlson got off the

chopper. "Welcome aboard. It's nice to have a replacement."

"Holy shit, Charlie, what the hell happened to you?"

"Oh, nothing much. Had a little shoot-out down the road this morning. Nothing to worry about."

"Uh . . . how often does this happen?"

"I don't know. Lost count some time ago. . . . Come on inside and set down your bag and quit gaping like that."

Hamilton was thoroughly enjoying himself, but decided that the joke had gone far enough. Carlson was getting alarmed, so as soon as they were inside, Hamilton admitted, "Actually, it's the first time I've even been nicked the whole tour. I just had to start you off right."

"You sure did. I damn near got back on that chopper."

The day after Carlson arrived, he and Hamilton were seated on the porch of the team house quietly enjoying an after-dinner beer and the sunset. After a long silence, Carlson said, "Well, you've given me the official briefing, introduced me to my counterpart, and taken me around to the four corners of my future domain. Now tell me what the hell's really going on."

Hamilton took a quick glance around to make sure that no one was within earshot, and replied, "Really not a hell of a lot. It's pretty clear to everyone on both sides that the war is going to be won or lost somewhere other than in Dong Hai District. You can see that in the priorities we don't get. If they really felt this place was worth bothering with, there'd be some free-world troops up here, and they'd get us a civil deputy and not an old washout like Riordan to be the first sergeant. And if there were any prestige or glory to be had, you know there'd be a couple of regular officers up here to get it.

"What we do here is a holding action. Your little victories will all be of the negative kind: not getting overrun, keeping the casualties down, and so forth. The RFs and PFs and CIDG are all low-priority, low-cost improvised forces, made up of people the ARVN won't have and armed with the older series weapons. The PFs don't even have M-79s or steel helmets. With good leadership they fight pretty well, everything considered, but the real leadership hot-shots on the ARVN side aren't in the RF—they're mostly in the ARVN Airborne or somewhere where there's some glory and prestige—and the PF don't really have officers at all, just one of the boys who got stuck with the job.

"The VC know this, of course, but they also know that the political effect of overrunning a backwoods district like this for a day or so isn't worth the damage we'd do to them while they were running over us, or by the Koreans when they retook the place the next day. During the Tet offensive, they could have had all these back country districts for a fraction of what they expended in trying to get into Phan Hoa city and hold it. But they were going after the province chief, and it makes sense—if you take Phan Hoa, this place doesn't matter, and if you don't take Phan Hoa, this place doesn't matter very much either.''

''Is it really that bad? I always thought you were an optimist.''

''I am, but I also try to see things as they are. This type of job is hard on your mental health, and you're going to have to be watchful of the mental attitude and morale of the men on the team up here. There are some good points: Lan may be a difficult, unco-operative bastard, but he's tactically competent, if extremely cautious, and he's a fighter. Which is a hell of a lot better than your smiling yes-man who disappears in a hole somewhere when the first shot goes off. The palace guard platoon here and the RF mortar platoon are first-class. So is the whole setup down at Phuoc Tre: Truong Sans, CIDG, and Rod-man's eight-inch battery. Between Rodman's eight-inch and the Spooky, I've been got out of more than a couple of tight corners.

''Don't expect much sympathy or support from sector. Major Scammell, the S3 adviser, and Captain Clark, the A&L Company adviser, are reasonably straight and know what they're doing; they also seem to be on the side of the working stiffs out in the field. But the rest of the chain of command, from Saigon on down, doesn't seem to have grasped the fact that you, as the adviser, have no command authority at all over your counterpart. They invent all kinds of lovely schemes for improving the Vietnamese, some of which aren't bad ideas, then promulgate them through Amer-ican channels for execution without going to the bother of convincing the Saigon-level Vietnamese authorities to push them also. And everyone in the middle just puts the bee on his next-lower level of advisers until it comes to roost here, and it's a reflection on your leadership if you can't get Lan to do something that Colonel Nhieu may or may not be interested in having him do. Then they have the gall to put out all this crap about reinforcing the Vietnamese chain of command and Vietnamese leadership.

"Withrow's predecessor, Colonel Dace, had been a subsector adviser, so he understood the problem, and you could have a workable relationship, even if he was obnoxious. I don't want to prejudice you against the present management at sector, so I'll just say that you'll find working for them an interesting and challenging experience."

"Is it that bad? I won't rat on you if you tell me, and I would like to hear your conclusions on them."

"Well, okay. I evaluate Mr. Jack Leary as a thoroughgoing politician in the bad sense of the word, mostly interested in getting ahead and making himself look good. But he's been in Vietnam for a hell of a long time, speaks the language, and seems to understand at least part of the problem. He's also intelligent and will listen to you if you can ever get in to see him; that doesn't mean you shouldn't be very cautious in what you say to him.

"Old Mother Withrow and I don't get along at all. My version is that whatever his prior experience and imagination are, they have not given him anything like adequate insight on the problems of being a district adviser. You know, every battalion commander was once a company commander himself, and knows what his own company commanders are up against. This is Withrow's first exposure to combat, first tour in the Far East, and his first exposure to an advisory situation. His performance during Tet was not impressive.''

"I thought you said everything was pretty quiet up here during Tet.''

"It was. I got caught in Phan Hoa city on my way back from R&R when things started happening, and didn't get back up here until after the first phase of the whole thing was over with.''

"I see. . . . I take it that you really aren't broken-hearted at leaving this place.''

"Hardly. . . . Oh, well, as Sherman said, war is hell. It could be worse, though. We could be at sector.''

When the great day came, Hamilton said good-bye to Lan and Carlson and the members of the team except Tinsley, who was going on R&R, then Hamilton and Tinsley put their bags on the supply chopper and were on their way.

In the chopper, en route to Phan Hoa, Tinsley remarked to Hamilton, "Sir, you're lucky. You don't have to go back to that place.''

Hamilton suppressed the thought that being sent there had not been exactly a stroke of luck, and replied, "There are always worse places.''

"I suppose so, sir.''

Hamilton stayed two days at Phan Hoa, mostly occupied with going around and saying good-bye to various people from Mr. Leary and Colonel Nhieu on down, but including a small amount of administrative processing and a farewell swim in the South China Sea.

Colonel Withrow was absent at the Pacification Course in Saigon, so Hamilton was asked in to see Mr. Leary. After the usual preliminary courtesies, Leary observed, "Hamilton, I think you've done a very good job up there in Dong Hai, considering what you had to work with and against. I'd be interested if you have any suggestions or ideas on how the effort could be improved."

"With all due respect, I certainly do, sir. First of all, a couple of minor and specific things: It would be awfully nice if we could get a chaplain up there at least every six months, especially for the Catholics. I realize there's not many troops in any of the subsectors, and the chaplains probably have quite enough to do in places where there are higher concentrations of U.S. troops, but the whole time I've been here I have neither seen nor heard of the first chaplain visiting the first subsector team; I think that's a real reproach against the chaplains. Even the Red Cross girls get around with the pay team and the people who give immunizations. I mentioned this a couple of times to Colonel Dace, but nothing ever came of it.

"Second, it would be a big help to get a civil deputy up there at Dong Hai, someone who's familiar with the CORDS programs, and can deal a little better with the people on the CORDS side of the house here at province."

"Charlie, we've been working on that, but it's

extremely hard to get a qualified person who's willing to go up there. Dong Hai has a fairly grim reputation, not because of you, but, well, you know. . . . We've had the same problem with Cung Hoa. I wasn't aware of this problem with chaplains, but I see your point and I'll take it up with Withrow when he gets back. Since we don't own any chaplains, I don't think there's much that can be done, though."

"There's two other things, sir, if I may?"

"Of course. Go ahead."

"First, the PF: There's a lot that could be done to pump them up, to good effect. Mostly by way of propaganda and encouragement so it's not quite so clear that they're the absolute low man on the totem pole of the Vietnamese military. Like a distinctive insignia. And the platoon leaders and squad leaders should have some kind of regular insignia of rank and a little bit more of a pay differential over the troops."

"You don't know how far they've come," Leary pointed out. "When I first got here, they were called the Self-defense Force, and they were wearing black pajamas and shower shoes, and were armed with bolt-action rifles and shotguns. It was pretty bad."

"Sir, there's still a long way to go. These people are at a level of sophistication where symbols mean a lot."

"You know, Hamilton, there's not much I can do about this except pass it along to Colonel Nhieu and the people at Nha Trang."

"Sir, I know, and that applies even more to my last point, but I do think they make a very serious mistake in not making sure that all advisers—at least the people who are actually dealing with the Vietnamese, as against the staff and support people—are really fluent in Vietnamese before they get over here, even if it means a man spending a year in language school and a year in country and only having half as many advisers on the ground. I spent some time dealing with the French in French, and the difference in results between what you get when you compel a man to deal with you in what is to him a foreign language, especially in his own country, and what you get when you meet him on his own ground and in his own language is really amazing.''

"As you said, there's nothing I can do about that at this level. But I thought they sent at least some of the advisers to the Defense Language Institute to learn Vietnamese.''

"Most of them seem to end up on the higher staffs where they never see their nominal counterparts, who, in any event, generally speak very good English.''

"Is there anything they need up there that I *can* do something about?''

"I think they could use about fifty bags of cement and some heavy timbers or steel beams for a roof for the team bunker.''

"That I think I can do something about. . . . Anything else?''

"Sir, you know the rest of the story. I've been crying on your and Colonel Dace's shoulders for nine months.''

"Please. Just keeping us abreast of the situation. Hell, I know it's a damn unpleasant place up there, and I don't blame you a bit for getting a different job. As a civilian I can say this, but the only reason the army has all those jobs is they can be sent there and can't refuse to go. And nobody really expects you to do much on the CORDS side of the show. It's surprising as much gets done as does. . . . Let's go get a drink; it's five o'clock.''

Mr. Leary's quarters were sleek, air-conditioned, and very comfortable, and his whiskey was excellent. Hamilton wondered what it was all about. Shortly, Major Scammell and Hodgen and Clark and various others arrived, and it became clear that this, in effect, was a going-away party for Hamilton, involving most of the army officers and civil officials of the province-sector team. The usual courteous and laudatory things were said, Mr. Leary gave Hamilton the customary little wooden plaque with engraved brass plate, and everyone got busy with drinks and conversation. Eventually Hamilton found himself chatting with Jerry Schwartzman, the psychological warfare adviser. Jerry was a civilian, slender, dark-haired with horn-rimmed glasses; he was intelligent, analytical, and articulate. For these reasons Hamilton enjoyed arguing with him, even though their opinions on most subjects were not in agreement. Jerry was saying:

''Doesn't it ever bother you that the regime we're backing here really isn't the least bit democratic?''

''No, for two reasons,'' Hamilton said. ''One, I contend that the adoption of a constitution and the election last September of a parliament make this place at least as democratic as what goes on in North Vietnam or what would be the state of things if the other side won. And, two, I'm not at all sure that we have any real basis for elevating this notion of elective, parliamentary democracy to the status of Great Universal Truth. Most of mankind in most of history has lived under one or another form of stratified society where a single ruler or a very small group at the top made the decisions, and everybody else did what they were told to, usually with some type of an intermediate class to make sure that they did. This includes the present governments of the Soviet Union and China. Our own form of government, which, of course, seems best to us, is, after all, a product of rather specific cultural and economic conditions, and we may be just as arrogant as the Russians or the Chinese in insisting that our way is the only true path.''

"In that case, what is there to choose between Ho Chi Minh and Air Marshal Ky?''

"It's the same choice that the British made in 1939 between Hitler's Germany and Śmigły-Rydz's Poland, or the United States made in 1941 between Tojo and Chiang Kai-shek. As dictators go, Hitler and Tojo were probably quite a lot more efficient and progressive than Śmigły-Rydz or Chiang Kai-shek. The whole idea is that the attempt by one country to conquer another is an attack on the collective security of everyone and a breach of the peace, whatever the character of the victim. Murder is no less murder when the victim is a scoundrel.''

"But isn't Vietnam really all one country?'' Schwartzman challenged. "And why should we appoint ourselves a universal policeman of public morality?''

"Whether Vietnam is really 'all one country' depends on your definition and what you're trying to prove. They all speak more or less the same language, but so do we and the Canadians, and so do the Germans and the Austrians. But does this 'one country' notion any more justify North Vietnam trying to conquer the South with Russian and Chinese aid than it would an attempt by South Vietnam, with our aid, to conquer the North?''

"What you're saying is that this 'one country' argument cuts both ways, and that it supports Hanoi only if you further assume that they have a right to rule inherently so superior to the Saigon regime that it authorizes Hanoi to overthrow the present government here. But why did we get involved in this thing? Historically, it's never been part of our sphere of interest.''

"That was the same question that people asked when the Japs went into Manchuria in 1931, when Mussolini went into Ethiopia in 1936, and when Hitler put the arm on Austria and Czechoslovakia in 1938. The results of not becoming involved were expensive and unsatisfactory, especially for Great Britain and France, both of whom lost their empires and their status of what we would now call superpowers. Whence the doctrine of collective security.''

"Surely you don't really think that North Vietnam is any real military threat to the United States?''

"Of course not. But behind them is China, and if they are allowed to win, it will be a resounding triumph for Mao's doctrine of the prolonged war, the notion that an erosive guerrilla war is an effective means whereby a dedicated—I could use the word 'fanatical'—minority can seize power in an underdeveloped, agrarian, tropical country. This means the rest of Southeast Asia, India, Africa, and most of Latin America—in other words, about half the world. And that *is* a threat to the United States.''

"You're not saying we'd lose all those countries if we weren't here in Vietnam?''

"Certainly not immediately, but they all have rather fragile, vulnerable governments, in varying degrees and for various reasons, and we could have dangerous and expensive trouble a lot closer to home than here. Look at the trouble we've had with Cuba.''

"Weren't the VC originally a popular uprising against the Diem regime when he refused to hold elections in 1956?''

"In the absence of actual knowledge and facts, you can argue all night about the relative degrees to which the original outbreak of the VC was a popular uprising or a plot instigated from Hanoi. On the legal point, be it also remembered that the South Vietnamese government was definitely not a signatory of the Geneva Accords of 1954 which ended the Indochina War and provided for elections. The Diem regime was terminated, not by the VC, but by the ARVN generals, in 1963, which is quite some time ago. Two things are perfectly clear to me at this time, however: If the South Vietnamese people in general had really been on the side of the VC, they would have taken the opportunity provided by the Tet offensive to rise up and overthrow the government, and the war would be over now; but they didn't, and it isn't. And, if the Hanoi government withdrew its army and supply system from South Vietnam, Laos, and Cambodia—that is, within the frontiers they agreed to in 1954 and 1962—that would be the end of the trouble in all three places.''

"And in either event, you and I would be on our way back to the States to look for new jobs. You're leaving anyway; I suspect that your new job's a lot more your style than the subsector.''

"Now that it's all over with and I don't have to go back, I can say that it was an interesting and valuable experience. And, look, it has been fun knowing all you good people here at sector.''

"I'll miss having someone to argue with. Say hello to Saigon for me.''

"Thank you. I will. Look me up when you get to Saigon—you do have my address?—and meanwhile keep your head down.''

Schwartzman drifted away. Hamilton circulated and chatted with most everyone present, including Major Scammell, who paused long enough between war stories about the Airborne to thank Hamilton again for his activities on the first night of the Tet offensive, and Mr. Crittenden, who feigned great knowledge of MACCAT's real mission and tried to find out more about it than Hamilton was inclined to tell him.

By the time the party broke up, it was too late for supper at the MACV mess hall, but Hamilton was quite full of potato chips, peanuts, and other odds and ends that had been served at the party. Reflecting on his discussion with Schwartzman, he wondered why the man had taken the job if he really had such doubts about the war; or was he just trying the arguments on Hamilton to find out if he had done his homework?

The next morning Sergeant Thurwell drove Hamilton out to the air force base. The passenger terminal looked exactly the same; it even seemed that exactly the same people were waiting in lithic patience, each for a ride somewhere. Hamilton booked himself on a flight to Pleiku (he had to go there en route to Saigon, as the records for all the advisers in II Corps were kept there), bade farewell to Thurwell, and settled down to wait.

That morning he had received a letter from Karla Bergman, but had not had time or privacy in which to read it, until now. Among other things she wrote that, since Hamilton was being reassigned to Saigon, she was going to try to get sent there also: "Charlie, you've spoiled me. You make everyone else seem like a dirty old man or a fumbling teenager." Quite aside from CAT and all its works, with Liz and Karla both in the same town, life in Saigon was going to be interesting.

and M-113 armored personnel carriers, with a few "Commando" armored cars and old M-24 tanks. Normal uniform was "indig" fatigues (q.v.), Bata boots (q.v.), steel helmet (without cover), rucksack and U.S.-type web equipment. Soft caps included U.S.-type baseball caps and berets: magenta for Airborne (who also wore camouflage suits), brick-red for Rangers, green for VN Special Forces (LLDB), black for armored cavalry and the Saigon palace guard, and brown OD for the general line. The ARVN was composed almost entirely of ethnic Vietnamese.

Assault Rifle, AK-47. Best and basic individual weapon in NVA and VC Main Force units. Shoulder-fired, magazine-fed, air-cooled, semi- and fully automatic weapon firing the 7.62mm "intermediate" cartridge. Uses a heavy, curved, 30-round magazine. Cartridge is intermediate in power between the U.S. 5.56mm and the NATO 7.62mm. The AK-47 is compact, reliable and hard-hitting, but heavy (especially for Southeast Asians) and hard to control on full automatic. Standard weapon in the Cambodian and Chinese Communist Armies, most of the Warsaw Pact states (except Czechoslovakia, which has a comparable weapon), North Korea, Cuba and several Arab states. An improved version, the AKM, is the basic weapon in the Soviet Army. Recognition features of the AK-47 include a prominent front sight, short gas cylinder above the barrel, large curved magazine and wooden pistol grip. Cartridge is also used by the SKS carbine and the RPD light machine gun. AK-47s have been captured with markings indicating manufacture in the Soviet Union, China, North Korea and several Eastern European countries. Occasionally one turns up in Vietnam with a folding stock; in the countries of origin, this is mainly a tanker's and parachutist's weapon. AK-47s first appeared in Vietnam in the autumn of 1964.

B-52. Eight-jet heavy bomber, for years the backbone of the manned bomber fleet of the Strategic Air Command (SAC). Used in Vietnam for strikes against area targets such as troop concentrations and base areas. If the target was reasonably accurately located and had not moved, this was an extremely effective mode of attack, as the target had no warning of the attack and the aircraft's bombload (thirty tons, usually eighty-four 750 pound bombs) provided effective area saturation.

Bata boots. Common footgear for ARVN (except ARVN Airborne, who had U.S.-type leather boots), RF, PF, CIDG and South Korean troops in VN. Black canvas and rubber boot similar to a basketball shoe but higher on the leg and with a lug sole. Officers and other personnel who could get hold of them normally wore U.S.-type leather boots or canvas and leather jungle boots, mostly by way of a "status symbol" rather than from any active dislike of the Bata boots.

Battalion. Unit composed of three or four companies (or batteries) plus headquarters and supporting elements. U.S. and Korean infantry battalions were normally about 700 to 900 men, commanded by lieutenant colonels. ARVN battalions normally had about 500 men, if that, under a captain. Fire support included, for U.S. and Korean battalions, 4.2″ mortars; for the ARVN, 75mm recoilless rifles and 81mm mortars. VC and NVA battalions were ordinarily in the order of 250 to 400 men, with 81mm or 82mm mortars and 75mm recoilless rifles for support. Artillery battalions normally had three batteries of six (or four) guns each.

Battery. Basic Field Artillery unit. Normally six guns (four in the 8″ and 175mm units), about ninety men and commanded by a captain. The ARVN six-gun 105mm and 155mm batteries were commonly deployed as three separate platoons of two guns each at separate localities. A common U.S. practice was a mixed battery with two self-propelled 8″ Howitzers and two self-propelled 175mm guns, generally with a platoon of "dusters" (twin 40mm anti-aircraft guns on modified light-tank chassis) attached for local security. NVA and VC included everything from 75mm recoilless rifles and 81mm mortars under artillery, generally organized in batteries of six tubes.

Browning Automatic Rifle (BAR). Caliber .30, M1918A2. A basic standard U.S. infantry weapon in World War II and Korea; an earlier version was used in World War I. It is an air-cooled, fully automatic, 20-shot shoulder weapon with bipod, a hard-hitting, accurate, reliable and durable rifle, but also long (four feet) and heavy (20 pounds), especially for the Vietnamese, who used it essentially in a light machine-gun role. Phased out of U.S. forces about 1960. Used extensively in 1967 and

1968 by GVN forces down to PF platoons and RD teams, also by VC district and provincial level units. Uses same .30-06 cartridge as M-1 rifle and .30 caliber Browning machine guns. A similar weapon, the French *Fusil Mitrailleur* M-24/29, was also used by the VC in small numbers (the author once picked up a magazine for one of these weapons). Even less frequently encountered were British Bren guns, Czech BRNO light machine guns and various World War II vintage Japanese light machine guns in assorted calibers. Getting the right caliber of cartridges for these weapons must have been a real challenge to the VC supply people.

Browning Machine Guns. Caliber .30, M1919A4 and M1919A6. These were basic standard U.S. infantry weapons in World War II and Korea; minor variants were used as tank and aircraft weapons in both wars. Phased out about 1960 in U.S. forces (except the M-37 machine guns in M-48 series tanks). They are air-cooled, belt-fed, fully automatic weapons firing the same cartridge as the M-1 rifle and the BAR. They are reliable, durable, accurate and hard-hitting. Due to the requirement for headspace adjustment, training on these guns is more complex than on more recent weapons; also, since they fire from a closed bolt and do not have a quick-change barrel, they tend to heat up after prolonged firing. In 1967 and 1968 they were standard weapons with ARVN, RF and CIDG troops and with the Korean forces in-country. They were also used by the VC. The author saw no indication of the water-cooled version of this weapon in Vietnam.

The .50 caliber Browning machine gun, HB M2, was extensively used by the ARVN on tanks and other armored vehicles and by the VC as an anti-helicopter weapon.

The Russian SGM heavy machine gun in the 7.62mm Russian long cartridge, and its Chinese copy were standard in NVA and VC Main Force units. This is a much heavier weapon than the Browning, which it does not resemble mechanically, and commonly comes on a mount with two small wheels. Small numbers of the World War II German 7.92mm MG-34 have been taken from the VC. This is a bipod-mounted, belt-fed, air-cooled gun with a quick-change barrel, apparently from stocks captured by the Russians in World War II.

Carbines. Caliber .30, M-1 and M-2. The M-1 carbine was a very standard U.S. weapon in World War II. The original intent was to replace the pistol with a light, compact, semiautomatic shoulder weapon of moderate power. The M-2 carbine is a modification with selective semi- and fully automatic fire. Both versions occasionally appear with a paratroop-style folding stock; both take either a straight 15-round or a curved 30-round ''banana'' magazine. The banana magazine is generally associated with the M-2 version. In 1967 and 1968, the M-1 carbine was a standard weapon for PF troops, RD Teams, National Police, hamlet self-defense units and other low-priority outfits; the M-2 was a basic weapon for all elements of the ARVN, RF, CIDG and U.S. advisory personnel. The Koreans, who were mainly armed with M-16 rifles, also had a few M-2 carbines. By 1968 the ARVN, starting with the Airborne units, was re-equipped with M-16 rifles. Both versions of the carbine were also widely used by the VC. The carbine cartridge is not interchangeable with other U.S. .30 caliber cartridges. Generally, the carbine's light weight, compactness and low recoil (due to a light bullet and a fairly low muzzle velocity) make it an excellent weapon for the small-statured Southeast Asian soldier. The fairly light bullet and low velocity, however, mean that its range, penetration and stopping power are not comparable to, e.g., an M-1 rifle or AK-47.

Charlie. "VC" in the phonetic alphabet (q.v.) is "Victor Charlie"; thus "Charlie" was a common term for the VC. "Clyde" was Charlie's big brother from up north, otherwise known as the NVA.

Chieu Hoi. Vietnamese for "open arms." Name of a rather successful program aimed at persuading VC and NVA soldiers and adherents to rally to the government side, and to provide training, rehabilitation, etc., for individuals who did come over. More successful with the VC than with the NVA, mainly because an NVA who defects thereby cuts himself off forever from his family in North Vietnam. Ralliers under this program are called *Hoi Chanh.* Many Hoi Chanh were employed as "Kit Carson Scouts" with U.S. units.

Civilian Irregular Defense Group (CIDG). Full-time "paramilitary" troops raised by and under control of U.S. and VN Special Forces. Not considered to be part of the regular GVN military establishment or juridically military personnel. Mostly composed of Montagnards, Nungs, Cambodians and other "ethnics." Leaders did not have legal military rank and wore grade insignia different from the ARVN and RF. Common organizations were Mobile Strike Force (MSF or "Mike Force") battalions, which could be deployed anywhere, and Camp Strike Force (CSF) companies and Camp Reconnaissance Platoons (CRP), more or less permanently based at the various Special Forces camps along the Western border of South Vietnam and in the Central Highlands. CSF companies normally had about 120 men, one 60mm mortar, two 57mm recoilless rifles, two .30 caliber machine guns, and nine BARs. Individual weapons were mainly M-2 carbines, with a scattering of M-16 rifles and M-79 grenade launchers. Camps normally had two or three 81mm or 4.2″ mortars and/or a pair of 105mm Howitzers. Normal CIDG uniform was the black and green "tiger suit" with matching round hat, Bata boots (q.v.), rucksack and U.S.-type web equipment. CIDG were paid and equipped by the U.S., acting through the U.S. Special Forces "A" Team at each camp. Legal command was exercised by the VN Special Forces (LLDB) team at each camp. Common mission was border surveillance and maintenance of the GVN presence in sparsely inhabited areas of the Central Highlands. By 1968, some CIDG units in the eastern foothills of the Central Highlands were being converted to Regional Force (q.v.); later other units were converted into ARVN Rangers.

Claymore. A type of mine consisting of a curved block of explosive with a large number of steel pellets embedded in the convex side. It is set up aboveground, with the convex side toward the enemy; when it goes off, it blows a lethal spray of pellets in the direction of the enemy. Normally command-detonated, but may also be set up to be fired by trip wire or other booby-trap. It is a highly effective weapon, commonly used for ambushes, in front of night defensive positions and more permanent perimeters.

Company. Infantry unit commonly composed of three platoons, headquarters and support elements. U.S. and Korean rifle companies were about 150 to 180 men (at least on paper). ARVN, RF, CIDG, NVA, VC Main Force and provincial force companies were all about 100 to 130 men; some provincial force and most VC district force companies varied down to as low as 30 men. Company level support weapons included mortars (81mm for U.S. and Koreans, generally 60mm for the Vietnamese on both sides), recoilless rifles (106mm for U.S., 57mm for ARVN and CIDG) and, especially with the NVA and VC Main Force and provincial force units, machine guns. U.S. and Korean companies were normally commanded by captains, Vietnamese companies by lieutenants.

Compound. An enclosure, commonly walled or fortified, for some official or business function. District/subsector compounds normally included the subsector headquarters, offices for the civil administration of the District, a team house or other lodgings for the U.S. advisory element, the District Chief's quarters, and accommodations for a defensive garrison. At Province/Sector and higher levels, the Vietnamese and U.S. advisory elements usually occupied separate compounds.

Concertina Wire. A type of barbed wire made of very hard spring steel. It comes in coils which are installed by being pulled out concertina-fashion (hence the name) making a cylindrical barrier, rather than being uncoiled and attached to picket stakes as with ordinary barbed wire. This makes it very quick and easy to install. The hard steel wire is very difficult to cut with ordinary wire-cutters and makes it a formidable obstacle even to tracked vehicles.

Corps Tactical Zone (CTZ). For military purposes, the Republic of Vietnam was divided into four CTZs, numbered I through IV from North to South. I Corps included the northern five provinces abut-ting on the so-called Demilitarized Zone (DMZ) and Laos. Major U.S. units were III Marine Am-phibious Force (III MAF) and XXIV U.S. Army Corps. II Corps included the Central Highlands and the adjacent coast. Corps headquarters were inland at Pleiku. Headquarters of the major U.S. command, I Field Force Vietnam (I FFV), the U.S. civil effort in II Corps, and of the 5th Special Forces Group were all at Nha Trang on the coast. III Corps included the "upper delta" surrounding and north of Saigon. The city itself and immediate environs constituted a separate command called the "Capital Military District" (CMD). Major U.S.

command in III Corps was II Field Force Vietnam (II FFV) at Long Binh, about 15 miles northeast of Saigon. This was also the location of Headquarters U.S. Army, Vietnam (USARV) which headed up all the U.S. Army forces in-country, other than the advisers and the Special Forces, who belonged directly to MACV. IV Corps, with headquarters at Can Tho, was the great, flat, swampy, fertile Mekong Delta. In 1967 and 1968, the U.S. 9th Infantry Division was the main U.S. unit here. In 1970, the CTZs were redesignated Military Regions, but, like Sixth Avenue/Avenue of the Americas, the older designations died out very slowly.

Dai-uy. Vietnamese for Captain. Other officer ranks as follows:

Chung-uy:	Aspirant (equivalent to 3d lieutenant)
Tieu-uy:	2d Lieutenant
Trung-uy:	1st Lieutenant
Tieu-ta:	Major
Trung-ta:	Lieutenant colonel
Dai-ta:	Colonel

Dai-uy was the normal rank for District Chiefs and battalion commanders in 1967 and 1968.

DEROS. Abbreviation for "Date of Estimated Return from Overseas," i.e., the expected date of an individual's return to the United States (also referred to as "the real world," or "the world"). Normal tour was one year from day of departure from the States to day of return to the States. Any reduction in this was a "drop."

Duster. Common term for the M-42 self-propelled twin 40mm automatic cannon based on the M-41 light tank chassis. Commonly used as an escort vehicle with motor convoys. Not to be confused with dustoff (q.v.).

Dustoff. Standard call-sign for medical evacuation (Medevac) helicopters; by extension used as a common term for any helicopter medical evacuation, sometimes even as a verb.

FAC. Abbreviation for "Forward Air Controller." A specially trained air force officer with the primary job of directing tactical air strikes in close proximity to friendly ground troops. FACs can operate either on the ground with the supported force, or in a light aircraft or helicopter equipped with radios communicating with the supported force and the strike aircraft, and with smoke rockets to mark targets. In 1967 and 1968 in Vietnam, FACs normally flew in O-1As (air force version of the L-19 "Birddog") painted gray. Other common activities for FACs included calling and adjusting artillery fire, general visual observation, liaison, and relay for reconnaissance teams on the ground.

FO. Abbreviation for Forward Observer. This is the officer or NCO who calls in, observes, and adjusts artillery and mortar fire. They operate either on the ground with the supported unit, or ride in some type of aircraft or helicopter. In 1967 and 1968, the common FO aircraft was the L-19 "Birddog."

GVN. Abbreviation for Government of Vietnam, i.e., the government of the Republic of Vietnam (RVN) in Saigon.

Grenade Launcher. 40mm, M-79. Standard weapon in U.S., Korean, ARVN, RF, and CIDG units (not issued to PF troops and RD Teams in 1967–1968). Looks a little like a deformed single-shot shotgun with a one-and-one-half-inch bore and an 18-inch barrel. Cartridge looks like a grossly oversized pistol round and fires a grenade about the size of a lemon. Replaces the rifle-mounted grenade launcher to cover the gap between the maximum range of a hand grenade and the minimum range of a mortar. Very handy, effective, and popular weapon. Also used by the VC and NVA when they could get launchers and ammunition.

Indigenous ("Indig") Fatigues. Common uniform worn by ARVN, RF, PF, and South Korean troops in VN. Also worn by CIDG when "tiger suits" not available. Olive-green shirt and trousers similar in cut to standard U.S. fatigues, but made of a light-weight poplin material; shirts had the usual two pockets, trousers had only two large, flapped pockets on the thighs.

IV. Short for "intravenous," i.e., the intravenous injection of blood plasma, Ringer's lactate or other blood expander, commonly used as part of the field treatment of casualties.

L-19. Light, two-seat observation aircraft, also known as the O-1A or "Birddog"; derived from the Cessna 180. Used by the army for VRs (q.v.) and for observation and adjustment of artillery fire. Used by the air force's forward air controllers (FACs) (q.v.).

LLDB. Abbreviation for Luc Luong Dac Biet, the Vietnamese Special Forces. At each Special Forces camp, an LLDB team exercised legal command over the CIDG (q.v.) troops and provided representation of the interests of the Saigon government.

Liberation. Euphemism for conquest and enslavement.

MACV. U.S. Military Assistance Command, Vietnam. Highest in-country U.S. Headquarters. Directed the activities of the U.S. forces through U.S. Army Vietnam (USARV), III Marine Amphibious Force (III MAF), 7th Air Force and Commander U.S. Naval Forces Vietnam (ComNavForV). The military advisory effort and the Special Forces were directly under MACV. The advisory effort was commonly referred to as the MACV side of the house, as contrasted to the U.S. units and to the civil side of the advisory effort.

NVA. North Vietnamese Army. The regular force of the Hanoi government. Essentially a foot-mobile light infantry force organized on conventional lines in battalions, regiments, and divisions. Basic weapons include AK-47s, SKSs, RPD machine guns, RPG-2, RPG-7, 57mm and 75mm recoilless rifles, 60mm, 81mm, 82mm and 120mm mortars, and in some areas field artillery to 122mm, artillery rockets to 140mm, and anti-aircraft weapons up to 37mm. In North Vietnam and Laos they also had heavier equipment, including heavier anti-aircraft guns, SAMs and tanks. Uniforms in-country varied, but a common one consisted of round hat, shirt and trousers in a greenish, ocherous brown shade, ''Ho Chi Minh'' sandals (made from old truck tires) or Bata boots (q.v.), rucksack, and weapon. Regular NVA units first appeared in South

Vietnam in the summer of 1964; they were preceded and accompanied by an influx of North Vietnamese cadres and fillers for nominally VC units. In 1967 and 1968 most nominally VC Main Force units were composed in substantial part of NVA troops. Substantial NVA forces were also maintained in Laos and Cambodia in violation of several treaties and international accords.

Phonetic Alphabet. Used for spelling out words in radio-telephone procedure. Old (World War II and Korean War) and new (NATO) phonetic alphabets as follows:

	Old	*New*		*Old*	*New*
A	Able	Alfa	N	Nan	November
B	Baker	Bravo	O	Oboe	Oscar
C	Charlie	Charlie	P	Peter	Papa
D	Dog	Delta	Q	Queen	Quebec
E	Easy	Echo	R	Roger	Romeo
F	Fox	Foxtrot	S	Sugar	Sierra
G	George	Golf	T	Tare	Tango
H	How	Hotel	U	Uncle	Uniform
I	Item	India	V	Victor	Victor
J	Jig	Juliett	W	William	Whiskey
K	King	Kilo	X	X-Ray	X-Ray
L	Love	Lima	Y	Yoke	Yankee
M	Mike	Mike	Z	Zebra	Zulu

Someone once made the comment that when something as straightforward as an "Able Roger" became an "Alfa Romeo," we're getting pretty fancy.

Platoon. Infantry unit normally composed of three rifle squads plus a fire support element. RF, PF, and CIDG platoons were commanded by NCOs and consisted only of three squads (25 to 35 men). U.S. and Korean platoons usually included one or two machine guns and were commanded by lieutenants (40 to 45 men). VC Main Force and NVA platoons sometimes included RPD machine guns and RPG-2s or RPG-7s.

Popular Force. (PF) (VN: Nghia Quan, NQ). Formerly (under the pre-1963 Diem regime) Self Defense Force. Full-time "paramilitary" troops in each District. Under command of district chief/subsector commander. Under terms of enlistment, could not be assigned outside of district where raised. Leaders did not have military rank; platoon and squad leaders were "equivalent" to NCOs but did not wear grade insignia. Common organization was a platoon (25 to 35 men, three BARs, M-1 carbines, a few M-2 carbines and M-1 rifles, no M-79 grenade launchers). Each province had a PF training center where newly raised platoons were trained and existing units received periodic refresher training. PF composed mainly of ethnic Vietnamese who were too young or too old or with some physical disability (commonly bad legs or blind in one eye) which prevented their serving in the ARVN or the RF. Normal uniform consisted of "indig" fatigues (q.v.), Bata boots (q.v.), rucksack and U.S.-type web equipment. Headgear was either the U.S.-type baseball cap or various styles of jungle hats, most commonly a green canvas version of the cowboy hat. At this period the PF did not have steel helmets. Occasional units wore neck scarves of various colors. Up to about 1965, PF wore black pajamas and were armed with bolt-action rifles, Thompson submachine guns and shotguns. Common mission was hamlet security. Some platoons remained permanently in place; others were periodically rotated within the district.

Radios. The PRC-25 was the standard back-pack "walkie-talkie," battery powered and rather short in range. PRC-46 was the then basic tank and vehicle mounted set, a much longer-range transmitter. Both were FM voice radios with no sort of on-line security device. The M-292 antenna was the standard command-post antenna, which considerably improved the range of any compatible radio that was attached to it. A PRC-25 hooked up to an M-292 antenna would get about 40 miles on a good day.

RD Team. "Revolutionary Development (RD)" was one of the heavy buzz-words. It was really a rather well-thought-out scheme of rural civic action. The RD Team consisted of about 60 people; their job was to go into their assigned hamlet and help the people with better wells and farming, a new school or public-health clinic, and so on. The RD Team also had some military training and was armed about on the scale of an infantry platoon. Normal uniform was black pajamas, olive-green "Steve Canyon" hat and Bata boots (q.v.).

RPD Machine Gun. Standard light machine gun in NVA and VC Main Force units. Also used in Cambodia, Communist China, Cuba, North Korea and several Warsaw Pact and Arab countries. Formerly a standard Soviet weapon; replaced by the RPK, a derivative of the AK-47 (q.v.). Shoulder-fired, bipod-mounted, air-cooled, fully automatic. Fires the same 7.62mm "intermediate" cartridge as the AK-47 and SKS, in a non-disintegrating metal-link belt carried in a drum on the left side of the weapon. Other identifying features include a prominent wooden handguard and odd-shaped shoulder stock. It is a light, handy, reasonably hard-hitting weapon, but suffers from an unduly complex feed mechanism.

RPG-2 and *RPG-7*. Anti-tank Grenade Launchers. Also known respectively as the B-40 and B-41. Basic squad and platoon level anti-tank and anti-bunker weapons in NVA and VC Main Force units. One or the other or both are also used by all the other Communist countries, several Arab countries and Cambodia. Each consists of a tubular launcher open at both ends with a pistol grip and firing mechanism in the center. The bore of the tube is about one-and-one-half inches. The round consists of a propelling charge and a bomb-shaped grenade about three-and-one-quarter inches in diameter. The propelling charge and the tail of the grenade are loaded into the front of the tube. The grenade has folding fins and relies on the hollow-charge principle against armor. The RPG-7 differs from the RPG-2 mainly in having an optical sight, a rocket-boosted projectile, and an improved design of warhead.

R&R. Abbreviation for "rest and recreation." This was a vacation of five days and four nights, not

chargeable as leave. In principle, each U.
viceman in Vietnam was entitled to one during h.
tour. R&R centers included Tokyo, Taipei, Hong
Kong, Manila, Australia, Singapore, Kuala Lum-
pur, Penang, Bangkok and Hawaii. Married personnel commonly went to Hawaii and met their
wives; others went to the other places. Transportation for the service member (but not for the wives)
was furnished by the government.

Regiment. Unit composed of three or four battalions,
plus headquarters and support elements. Only current
U.S. Army regiments are Armored Cavalry Regiments (three Armored Cavalry Squadrons etc., about
3000 men commanded by a colonel). In the
1967–1968 period, U.S. Marine Corps and Korean
infantry regiments each had three rather strong
battalions, and were commanded by colonels; the
ARVN infantry regiments each had four small battalions and were commanded by lieutenant colonels or majors. The VC Main Force and NVA
regiments each had three small infantry battalions
and an artillery battalion armed with heavy (i.e.,
82mm and 120mm) mortars and recoilless rifles.
The equivalent U.S. infantry command was a Brigade, which, however, had varied numbers of battalions and could include armor, artillery and other
elements as well.

Regional Force. (RF) (VN: Dia Phung Quan, DPQ).
Formerly (under the pre-1963 Diem Regime)
Civil Guard. Full time "paramilitary" troops in
each province. Under command of province chief;
under terms of enlistment, could not be assigned
outside of province where raised. Officers and

NCOs had military rank and insignia. Common organization was a company (100 to 135 men, heavy weapons usually one 60mm mortar, two .30 caliber machine guns, seven to nine BARs; individual weapons were M-1 and M-2 carbines, M-1 rifles and M-79 grenade launchers; vehicles, one or two one-ton trucks; troops had steel helmets). Each province had an RF "Administration and Logistics" (A&L) Company to support provincial RF units. Other typical RF units were headquarters, medical and mortar platoons at subsectors. Normal uniform consisted of "indig" fatigues (q.v.), Bata boots (q.v.), helmet, rucksack, and U.S.-type web equipment. Authorized insignia included a hexagonal yellow shoulder patch with a black "classical trophy" device. This same device, in silver-colored metal, was also worn on a dark-blue beret. Neither the shoulder patch nor the beret were commonly worn. Occasional units wore neck-scarves, commonly bright red cotton or mottled green parachute cloth. Common headgear when helmet not worn was the U.S.-type baseball cap or various styles of jungle hats. Companies were normally assigned security missions under operational control of subsector commanders, and were rotated about every three months.

Rifles, bolt-action. By 1967, bolt-action rifles had disappeared from the equipment of even the lowest-priority government forces in Vietnam. They were still used in small numbers by VC civil cadre and village/hamlet guerrillas. There were three common types, all five-shot, World War II models:

French MAS-36s in 7.5mm caliber. Apparently weapons taken from French or French-supported units in the 1946–1954 war. This weapon has a two-piece stock and a skewer-type bayonet carried in a tube under the barrel.

German and Czech 7.92mm Mausers. This is the standard World War II Kar-98k or the Czech variant, either captured by the Soviets in that war or made in Czechoslovakia after the war. The Chinese Nationalists produced very large numbers of a copy of this rifle, the so-called "Gimo" Mauser, of which the Chinese Communists must have acquired a great quantity in the civil war of 1945–1949, but none of the Mausers seen by the author in-country were of this type, and he has heard of no instance of Gimo Mausers being taken from the VC. Curious.

Russian 7.62mm K-44 carbine. This is a short-barreled version of the M-1891 Moisin Nagant Rifle, firing the Russian 7.62mm long cartridge (sold in the U.S.A. as ".30 caliber Russian"). It features a skewer-type bayonet which folds along the right side of the barrel. There is also a long barreled version of this weapon with a telescope sight for sniping. Both long and short versions were produced and supplied to the VC by the Russians and the Chinese.

Rifles, caliber .30, M-1, and 7.62mm, M-14. The M-1 was the basic U.S. rifle in World War II and Korea. It is an eight-shot, clip-fed, semiautomatic weapon. It is very reliable, durable, accurate, and hard-hitting. The cartridge is sold commercially as

.30-06. It is also unduly long and heavy for the Southeast Asian soldier, and was mainly used in 1967 and 1968 as a grenade rifle by units, such as the PF, who did not have M-79 grenade launchers, and by the Saigon palace guard. The M-14 is essentially an improved replacement for the M-1. It features a tappet gas system akin to the carbine's, a 20-round detachable magazine, and selective semi- and fully automatic fire. The 7.62mm cartridge (which is also used in the M-60 and M-73 machine guns and by most of the NATO countries) is one-half-inch shorter but has the same ballistics as the cartridge for the M-1. It takes a big man to hold down an M-14 on full automatic. This weapon, which replaced the M-1 in the U.S. Army about 1960, was never issued in any quantity to the South Vietnamese forces. In 1967 and 1968, it was in the hands of most of the U.S. logistic and support units, and a few advisory personnel had them also. The U.S. .30 carbine, U.S. .30-06, NATO 7.62mm and the three types of Russian/ Chinese 7.62mm cartridges (long, "intermediate," and pistol) are not interchangeable with each other in either direction. In all six cases, the bore and bullet diameters are the same, but the cartridge case dimensions are all quite different. The VC used a few M-1s and hardly any M-14s.

Rifle, 5.56mm, M-16. Originally appeared as the Armalite AR-15, a development by private industry in the early 1960s; espoused first by the Special Forces and the U.S. Air Force, and later by the U.S. Army and Marine Corps. It is a light, compact and very effective semi- and fully automatic weapon. Normally used a 20-round magazine; some 30-round magazines were available. Cartridge is sold commercially as the .223 caliber. By 1967 it was the standard individual weapon in U.S. and Korean combat units, and some ARVN units (e.g., the Airborne). Beginning in 1968, M-16s progressively replaced the M-2 carbines and other World War II vintage individual weapons in all South Vietnamese units, including CIDG and PF. There is also a short-barreled version with a telescoping stock called the CAR-15. In 1967, very few M-16s were in the hands of up-country Vietnamese units, advisers, or the VC. Generally its light weight, compactness, and low recoil make the M-16 a worthy replacement for the M-2 as the basic weapon for the Southeast Asian soldier, but its light weight bullet and low muzzle energy do open the M-16 to criticism in matters of range, penetration, and stopping power.

Ring Knocker. A graduate of the United States Military Academy (USMA) at West Point, New York; so-called because they all wear prominent class rings. USMA graduates constitute about one fourth of the career-officer corps of the Army, and tend to regard themselves as a professional elite.

Roger. Radio pro-word meaning "I understand and/or agree." Not to be confused with "Wilco" which means "I understand, agree, and will comply."

Rules of Engagement. (1) Measures taken to snatch defeat from the jaws of victory, thereby sparing the politicians and the State Department the task of throwing away whatever may have been gained by success in battle; (2) Measures taken to prolong hostilities, increase friendly and civilian casualties, and prevent achievement of national objectives.

SKS Carbine. A standard individual weapon in NVA and VC Main Force units. Also used in Cambodia, Communist China, Cuba, North Korea, and several Warsaw Pact and Arab countries. Formerly a standard Soviet weapon; replaced by the AK-47. Shoulder-fired, air-cooled, semiautomatic weapon firing the 7.62mm "intermediate" cartridge also used in the AK-47 and RPD machine gun. Fixed, 10-shot magazine loaded by a strip-in charger. Recognition features include prominent front sight, gas cylinder above the barrel, and projecting triangular fixed magazine. Some versions have permanently attached bayonets folding under the barrel. Has been produced in the Soviet Union and Communist China. Main drawbacks are length (compared to the AK-47) and lack of fully automatic feature. First appeared in-country autumn of 1964.

SOP. Standard Operating Procedure. Can refer either to the procedure itself or to the document describing and directing it.

Sapper. As used by the VC and NVA, these were highly trained assault engineer troops, whose normal method of attack was to infiltrate by stealth, then attack with grenades and satchel charges. After the failure of the conventional offensives of 1968 (Tet, "little Tet" in May, and the August rerun), the enemy turned more and more to this form of operation.

Short. As used in-country, referred exclusively to length of time remaining before an individual's return to the States.

Squad. Smallest basic infantry unit, normally composed of eight to twelve men commanded by a corporal or sergeant. ARVN, CIDG and RF squads were normally armed with individual weapons (generally M-2 carbines in 1967; in 1968 and thereafter, M-16 rifles) plus one M-79 grenade launcher and a BAR. PF squads substituted an M-1 rifle with grenade launcher for the M-79, and had a proportion of M-1 carbines. U.S. and Korean squads normally had two M-79s each, the balance being armed with M-16 rifles. VC and NVA squads varied in armament, but were usually limited to individual weapons.

Tet. Short for Tet Nguyen Dan, the old-style Chinese lunar new year. Traditionally observed in China, Korea, and Japan (under different names), as well as in Vietnam. Normally falls in the last part of January or the first part of February. In Vietnam this is a three-day festival devoted to reverence of one's ancestors and parents and visiting family and friends. The VC and NVA offensive which violated the customary lunar new year truce in 1968 gave very great offense, not so much as an act of truce-breaking, but as a sacrilege in the eyes of most Vietnamese, including a great many not theretofore committed to the government side.

Thompson Submachine Gun. Caliber .45, M1A1. World War II military version of the "Chicago violin." This was the simplified, straight-blowback

version. It is an extremely durable, reliable, accurate (for a submachine gun), and hard-hitting weapon;
it is also beastly heavy to carry and quite expensive to manufacture. Between 1965 and 1967 they
were almost entirely phased out of the equipment
of GVN forces. In 1967 it was still a fairly standard weapon with provincial and lower level VC
units.

Tiger Suit. A style of camouflage suit, predominantly black and green irregular horizontal stripes,
made of fairly heavy material. In 1964 and 1965 it
was primarily worn by South Vietnamese Marines;
by 1967 its use had extended to most of the CIDG
troops. It was also worn by U.S. advisers when
accompanying these troops in the field.

VR. Abbreviation for "visual reconnaissance," as
distinct from photographic, electronic, and "technical" reconnaissance. In the 1967–1968 period it
was the common practice for all areas to be covered daily, or as near it as possible, by visual
reconnaissance. This was normally flown by Army
L-19s (also known as O-1s or "Birddogs"), a
light, two-seat, fixed-wing aircraft. Observers were
commonly officers on the sector advisory staffs, or
District Senior Advisers. The idea was that by
becoming very familiar with the area, any change
indicating enemy activity would be immediately
apparent.

Viet Cong (VC). Abbreviated version of Vietnamese
for "Vietnamese Communist." Common generic
for all South Vietnamese insurgents, i.e., everyone
on the other side except the NVA (q.v.). The VC

civil organization with its maze of cadres, fronts, and committees, constituting a clandestine "shadow government," was commonly referred to as the VC infrastructure. The military side of the VC ranged from hamlet and village guerrilla squads and platoons, through district companies and provincial "local force" battalions, to the regimental and divisional formations composing the VC "Main Force." As on the GVN side, the division between military and civil structures, especially at the district and lower levels, was obscure and for practical purposes nonexistent. At all levels the mission of the infrastructure was to control the people, influence their thinking and extract from them the wherewithal (mostly in the form of rice, information and recruits) to support the military side. VC province and district boundaries and names sometimes varied substantially from those established by the GVN. Armament varied considerably: Civil cadres (when armed) and the hamlet and village guerrillas normally had bolt-action rifles (commonly German or Czech Mausers or French MAS-36s) or M-1 carbines. District and provincial forces seemed to favor M-2 carbines, Thompson submachine guns, BARs, Browning machine guns and RPG-2s, supported by 60mm and 82mm mortars, and 57mm and 75mm recoilless rifles. The Main Force were by this period generally armed on the same basis as the NVA, i.e., with SKSs, AK-47s, RPG-7s, RPD machine guns supported by mortars, recoilless rifles and artillery rockets.

ABOUT THE AUTHOR

Alexander McColl is the only person you're likely to meet who is both a graduate of Harvard Law School and the MACSOG jump school at Long Thanh in what used to be the Republic of Vietnam; and a lot of other things in between: scholar, lawyer, paratrooper, intelligence agent, graduate of the U.S. Army War College and veteran of thirty months in Vietnam, most of it in activities that are still highly classified. But it included eight months of holding down the Dong Xuan subsector, a remote, low-priority, low-security area where the "senior headquarters" was the 95th NVA Regiment. While at Dong Xuan he instigated and took part in the only night counterattack ever conducted by the Vietnamese Popular Force. Later there were secret missions to unlovely places like the A Shau Valley.

He is now a reserve colonel in the U.S. Army Special Forces (Green Berets), managing partner of an investment firm, Secretary-Treasurer of Parachute Medical Rescue Service, President of the Institute for Regional and International Studies, and Director of Special Projects for *Soldier of Fortune* Magazine. This last has involved numerous trips to Central America supervising SOF training teams, including five parachute jumps in two different countries and enough hostile contact at least to justify eating quiche whenever he feels like it (which isn't often). Bilingual in English and French (plus a bit of Spanish), single, his sports and hobbies include sport parachuting, hiking, deep-water sailing and military history.

This is his first full-length novel; he has published numerous articles in *Soldier of Fortune*, *Military Review*, *Infantry*, etc., on history, military operations, and international affairs.

SOLDIER
of FORTUNE
MAGAZINE PRESENTS:

BESTSELLING BOOKS FROM TOR